SERGEI'S ANGEL

HELEN BRIGHT

VINCI
BOOKS

Vinci Books

vinci-books.com

Published by Vinci Books Ltd in 2026

1

The publisher and the author have made every effort to obtain permissions for any third party material used in this book and to comply with copyright law. Any queries in this respect should be brought to the attention of the publisher and any omissions will be corrected in future editions.

A CIP catalogue record for this book is available from the British Library.

Paperback ISBN: 9781036707712

The EU GPSR authorised representative is Logos Europe, 9 rue Nicolas Poussion, 17000 La Rochelle, France

contact@logoseurope.eu

By Helen Bright

The Night Movers Vampire Series

Bitten and Bound

Blood & Secrets

Gregor's Reason

Sergei's Angel

Chapter One

Sergei

Snow fell silently from thick grey clouds while we waited for the undertakers to carry the coffin into the old village church. A young woman stepped out of a black funeral car, and an odd sensation struck me. I studied her closely, watching snowflakes settle on her halo of golden hair blowing in the cold winter breeze.

As befitting a funeral, she wore black. Her azure-blue eyes glistened with tears, and the surrounding skin was red and puffy. She gripped the hand of a small boy who appeared dazed and maybe a little scared as he studied all the people making their way into the church. Once again, an odd feeling came over me when I watched them take their seats. It was a feeling I couldn't decipher but felt fiercely nonetheless.

I was at this funeral at Maggie Saunders' insistence. She'd said that because the recently deceased Beryl Fraser had worked for Night Movers for so long—before her retirement three weeks ago—at least one of the owners should attend.

It appeared I'd drawn the short straw because I was standing here on this cold winter's day at the funeral of a woman I had only met twice.

Beryl Fraser had sought me out after she'd made up a mixture of oils and cleaning products that removed blue dye from my hands. Yuri and I had a bit of a mishap with Daisy during a day out, and we all ended up with blue dye staining our skin. Keeley had asked the woman if she knew how to remove it.

Beryl had been a cleaner at Night Movers for twenty years, so she knew plenty about removing dirt and stains.

Keeley told her not to tell me she had a way to remove it, but Beryl found me and gave me a bottle of something she'd made up herself. It removed the stain after leaving it on my hands for ten minutes, although I do not know what it was.

I thanked her with an enormous bouquet of seasonal blooms I made up myself. I was filling in for Chloe at her flower shop at the time, and the only other occasion I'd conversed with Beryl was when she came to thank me.

I sent Chloe to Russia with a drunken Gregor to get them together after they'd had a falling out. Less than a week later, they were Bonded, and three weeks after that, Chloe found out she was pregnant. So my interference proved positive in more ways than one.

I am happy for my friend, and I look forward to having another child around for me to love and be an uncle to. But since they found out, Gregor has become extremely overprotective, which is getting the typically independent Chloe down.

I'm staying at her flat until the cottage I'm having built

on Night Movers' land is ready to move into. It's situated next door to Nik and Gina, although I'm not sure if that's a good idea now. The build is being held up temporarily by the wintery weather.

Since my move to Chloe's flat, I've spent little time with Nik and Gina—other than when we are at work. Instead, I visit with Josh, Keeley and Daisy, and, surprisingly, Alex and Julia.

Their baby, Rory, is so pleasant. I pop by whenever possible, and it's great to see him as often as I do. It enables me to witness every new development he makes, no matter how small.

Rory is just over four months old and can push himself up on his hands and roll over from his belly to his back. Alex and I have videos of this on our phones and will often argue over which is the best. But half an hour with the baby every couple of days is not enough to fill up my week, so I spend more and more time with the humans in this small Yorkshire village.

I'd taken on a partnership in Night Movers during the summer and have worked some of Joshua York's evening shifts for him on a four-on, three-off night shift pattern.

He's recently Bonded with his love, Keeley, and wanted to spend more time with her and her daughter, Daisy— whom he's adopting—but the night shifts he worked didn't allow for much of that. I was happy to take on a partnership because I considered everyone to be a great friend and, in Nik and Gina's case, family.

But months have passed since I made that decision, and as time has moved on, I've been much less comfortable with the situation than I was previously.

Most of my immortal friends are busy being a couple

and have little time to spare—wedding planning and babies taking precedence over their social life.

I used to rely on Nik and Gina to keep me company on my days and nights off, but after some revelations I made when Keeley was attacked, Nik—someone who I always thought of as a brother—had become distant and seemed to resent my close friendship with Gina.

I have always loved Gina. Many years ago, I thought she might have been it for me. But Nik had met her first, and I would never come between them.

Over the years, I realised while my love for Gina was strong, it was not, and had never been, as powerful as the love between true soulmates destined to Bond. I think Nik understands this, but his vampire side probably still sees me as a threat.

Yuri is over from Russia with Dmitry, one of Gregor's human guards. We've been out drinking together, but I feel that something is not right between the two friends, although they hide it well whenever Gregor's around.

I've seen how Yuri looks at Mel, the bar manager of the Red Lion—the pub he owns in the village. But the last time I was with them, I noticed Dmitry share the same look with her. From experience, I don't think that will go down so well.

Because of all this, I have been integrating more with the humans of this village, and I thoroughly enjoy their company. I've made good friends here, and if it were not for that and my position within Night Movers, I would have gone back to Russia.

I have trusted staff to manage my business dealings in my home country, but I feel I should do more to oversee the business that my grandfather created.

Chapter Two

Sergei

After the funeral service, the mourners walked along a flagstone path from the church to the graveside. The young woman crouched in front of the tearful boy, offering words of comfort before taking him in her arms while he cried.

The child was scared and grief-stricken, and my heart ached to see his tears. I turned to Maggie, who was sobbing at the sight of the little boy's distress.

Taking her in my arms, I stepped aside with her to let the other mourners pass.

I asked why there were no other family members to support the young woman and child, whom I assumed to be Beryl's grandchildren.

Maggie told me that Beryl's husband had passed away just after their grandson, Matthew, was born. She said that Beryl had raised Matthew and his sister, Holly, after their mother committed suicide when Matthew was a baby.

Beryl's friend Moira took a weeping Holly and Matthew

into her embrace when they lowered the coffin into the ground.

It took everything I had not to walk over and carry them away from here. It felt wrong that there were no other living relatives around to help.

Their father, maybe? Maggie informed me that their mother "*had been a bit flighty in her youth*" and had taken off to some protestor camp. She came back heavily pregnant with Holly two years later.

Maggie said Matthew's father was rumoured to be a married man from Lincolnshire, and as far as she was aware, he'd had little to do with the child.

Their plight disturbed me. I felt I could relate to them somewhat.

Nik and I were orphaned when we were babies. Our parents had been killed by the vampire hunters—a religious group who sought out and killed immortals and their families. Our mothers, who were cousins, had left us with a relative named Petre—a priest who ran an orphanage some miles from where they lived in Romania.

Our fathers had joined the immortal army and had met our mothers over 294 years ago. But the vampires had been betrayed by one of their own, and the hunters' numbers were much more than anyone had expected, backed at the time by Rome itself.

We stayed in the orphanage with Petre until our grandfathers came to take us away years later when the hunters had finally been defeated.

The orphanage had been a way to hide us in plain sight, and I never forgot my roots—despite my reasons for being there. But as good a man as Father Petre was, I missed having a family to care for me.

Nik and I were as close as brothers and always had each other's back. Until now, it seems.

Maggie and I were told a funeral buffet was being held in the local community hall. We went along so we could speak to Holly and offer our condolences.

She moved around the room, thanking everyone who'd attended. Moira sat with the little boy, who now seemed more settled. Maggie said that Holly must only be eighteen or nineteen; no age at all to take on the sole responsibility of bringing up her seven-year-old brother.

Before Holly got to speak with people on our side of the room, she filled up a plate of food and took it to her brother, ensuring he had everything he needed. Unable to take my eyes off the beautiful angel in black, I watched as she went back to the table and wrapped more food in a napkin, which she placed in her handbag. She glanced around, ensuring no one was watching, before doing the same again.

This was her grandmother's funeral, most likely paid for by her or from funds put away by her grandmother for this very occasion. So she wasn't stealing food, as I often had to do in the orphanage when hungry.

When that memory hit me, my gut clenched. Holly was hungry and was taking food for her and her brother for later. My suspicions were confirmed when she came over to thank Maggie and me for attending.

Maggie embraced Holly and then turned to me.

"Holly, this is Sergei Petrov. He's one of the new partners at Night Movers. He's also the one who sent your grandmother that huge bouquet of flowers that she was so thrilled about."

Holly turned to me and smiled. It was genuine and was the first I had seen on her pretty face all day.

"Thank you, Mr Petrov. My gran loved them. They filled two of her favourite vases and lasted for weeks. It was very sweet of you."

"Not at all, my dear Holly. I was grateful to her for helping remove the blue from my hands," I told her, and she looked at me, confused.

"Don't ask," voiced Maggie. "You would never believe how his hands came to be blue even if he told you."

"Oh, okay," Holly replied, a little puzzled but still smiling.

"Maggie, I wanted to ask you something," she added before taking a deep breath. "Do you have any vacancies at Night Movers? I did my business administration course at college, so I'd be happy to take on an office role or perhaps even my gran's old cleaning job. I need something in the daytime when Matthew's at school."

"I'm sorry, Holly, we don't have anything in the office in the daytime, and we filled your gran's old job the day after she retired. Doesn't the hotel you were working at have any places nearby that you could transfer to?"

"No, it wasn't part of a group or chain, which meant I had to hand in my notice so I could look after Matthew. I've been without work since she passed away."

"What about your boyfriend? Paul, wasn't it? Is he still at the hotel? I thought he would have been here with you."

"Paul and I split up before Gran died," Holly said, looking down at her feet. She took a deep breath, then looked back up at us.

"If any daytime jobs come up at Night Movers, or if you hear of anyone else hiring locally, will you let me know?" she asked.

Maggie nodded and told her she would before hugging her once again.

"It was nice to meet you, Mr Petrov. Maybe next time it will be under better circumstances," Holly said as she held out her hand to shake mine.

As soon as I placed my hand in hers, I felt a deep yet familiar connection. My heart skipped a beat, and my mouth went dry. If Holly's gasp was anything to go by, she, too, felt the same as I.

I knew I had to see her again. In fact, I didn't want to let her out of my sight. I quickly thought of a way for this to happen, one that would benefit her, too.

"Holly, did you say you were familiar with business administration?" I asked.

"Yes. I did a two-year college course on the subject when I left school, and I've been working in a hotel up in the Lake District for the last five months—on reception and in the back office. Why?"

"Because I need a PA with experience in business administration to help manage some aspects of my business dealings in Russia. It's paperwork mostly."

"I'm sorry, Mr Petrov, but I don't speak Russian," she said with a sigh. I heard her words as soon as she uttered them, but I found myself staring at her full, pink lips as she spoke, so I didn't immediately reply.

"Sergei," prompted Maggie.

"What? Oh yes, Russian. Well, all my staff speak English and can also communicate any paperwork and emails in English. I need someone who's competent and reliable and can work during the day because I do the evening shifts at Night Movers. I will understand if you need to take some time to grieve, and I'll hold the job open for you until you feel you are ready—if you are interested?"

"Yes, of course I'm interested, and I can start immediately. It's Friday now, so I have Matthew off until school on Monday, but if you want me to work the weekend, I can ask if Aunt Moira will watch him tomorrow."

"No, Holly. You need to take this weekend for you and your brother—to come to terms with what has been a very distressing time for you both. It would be unfair to ask you to work," I told her.

"Actually, Mr Petrov, I need an income as soon as possible. So if I could start tomorrow, that would be great for me," she replied with hope in her eyes.

"Okay, but only if you are sure," I reiterated. "I'm currently living in the flat above Chloe's Flowers and Gifts in Barrowfield Village. I will expect you around eleven o'clock, and you can bring your brother. We'll find something to entertain him while I go through what I need you to do."

"Thank you, Mr Petrov," Holly said as she went on her tiptoes and threw her arms around my neck.

I closed my eyes while breathing in her scent, savouring the exquisite fragrance while hugging her back.

"You are more than welcome, Holly," I told her in a deep, throaty voice, much lower than my usual tone.

I felt her shudder before she loosened her arms and tried to step away from me. I held her a little longer before letting her go, and after brushing her golden hair out of her stunning blue eyes, I said, "Until tomorrow, Holly."

Then I left the hall without looking back.

Chapter Three

Holly

Matthew and I arrived at Mr Petrov's flat half an hour early. We were just glad to get out of the house, truth be told. The central heating had broken down last week, and because of the ridiculously high call-out fee, I couldn't afford to get a repairman out—never mind paying for parts and labour to get it fixed. Even though there was still a smattering of snow on the ground, the sun was emerging, and it seemed less cold out here than in the house.

I'd received the last of my pay from my old job the previous week, and that was fast running out. Luckily, Gran had an insurance policy that would cover the funeral bill, but there would be little to nothing left over for anything else.

She'd spent her redundancy pay on having the roof replaced and buying a new oven and washing machine. If it wasn't for Mr Petrov from Night Movers offering me this PA work, I'm not sure how Matty and I would survive.

I'd put a few sandwiches and other items from the buffet table away so we could have supper last night, and we were going to have peanut butter on toast when we got back home later. I felt guilty that I couldn't afford something more nutritionally balanced for Matthew, but at least I knew he'd enjoy it.

We approached the row of shops that Mr Petrov's flat was above, walking around the back to the steps that led up to his home. Before Matty and I could climb them, I heard a deep, masculine voice call out my name.

I turned to see Mr Petrov come out of what must be the back of the flower shop, with a large bouquet of flowers in his hand.

He'd dressed casually in dark blue jeans and a black sweater. His dark brown, almost black hair seemed longer than it did yesterday, having a slight curl in places. Long black lashes that would make any woman envious framed his dark brown mischievous eyes. Mr Petrov was most certainly handsome, and being over six feet tall with a muscular build, was clearly all man. Yet the glint in his eyes spoke of a boyish charm.

The smile he gave Matty and me showed he was genuinely pleased to see us, dissolving some of my nervousness.

"Good morning, Holly and Matthew," he said as he strode towards us.

"Good morning, Mr Petrov," I replied, offering him my hand to shake. Instead, he turned it over and kissed the back of it. I hissed in a breath when his warm lips touched my cold skin, blushing at the feelings he created from such a simple gesture.

"Holly, you are freezing," he stated. He grabbed Matty's hand, too, and said something in what I assumed to be

Russian while hurrying us along to the steps of his flat. He opened the door at the top of the steps and led us inside.

The flat was warm and welcoming, if not a little feminine, but he quickly explained he was renting the flat temporarily until his cottage was built. He handed me the bouquet of flowers and said, "Welcome to your first day at work, my dear Holly," before crouching down in front of Matty and helping him remove his coat. I thanked him for the flowers, and he gave me a dazzling smile, showing his perfectly straight, white teeth and full lips. The man was utterly gorgeous. No wonder my gran was so taken with him when he gave her those flowers.

"I have an X-box if you would like to play some games, Matthew, or I am sure I could find you a movie to watch that I can download. Tell me, what are your favourite movies and cartoons?" Mr Petrov asked, seeming totally at ease talking to children. I wondered if he had any of his own.

Matty chimed in with his all-time favourite cartoon—for the moment—which is *The Knights of Dellot*. He unzipped his backpack and took out the stickers and cards he'd been collecting over the last six weeks. The sticker book was looking tatty, and I think the cover might be coming loose. But Mr Petrov seemed genuinely interested in what Matty was telling him about all the different knights and each of their individual powers. After switching on the huge TV, he searched through the channels to find the cartoon, which would be on in around fifteen minutes.

I placed the beautiful bouquet of pink and white carnations and lilies on the round wooden dining table, then removed my coat before placing it on the back of a chair.

A small grey cat came into the room and wound its way through my legs, meowing continuously.

"Boris, say hello to Holly and Matthew," said Mr Petrov with a smile. He tapped his hand on the sofa and gestured for the cat to come to him. Then he picked him up and set him next to Matty, saying that Boris liked having the area behind his ear rubbed while he sat and watched TV.

Once Matty was settled, Mr Petrov came over to the table and asked what we wanted to drink. I said tea and Matty chose hot chocolate, and I watched, unsure, when he went into his kitchen.

I worried that, being his PA, I should have been the one to make the drinks, so I got up and followed him in.

"Mr Petrov, surely it's the role of a PA to make and supply drinks and such?" I questioned, while he turned and took three mugs out of a cupboard.

"First of all," he replied as he came to stand in front of me, "you must call me Sergei. And second, it is no hardship to make a beautiful woman and her wonderful little brother a drink. Now tell me, lovely Holly, how do you take your tea?"

Five minutes later, we sat at the table while Matty watched his cartoon. Sergei placed a contract in front of me, detailing my primary duties as his PA. When I got to the next page, however, I almost screamed out in shock.

"TWO THOUSAND POUNDS! You are offering to pay me two thousand pounds per week? Are you sure? Is this an error?"

"Is that not enough? We can negotiate pay and bonus if you wish. Nothing is set in stone, Holly," Sergei answered, a worried look appearing on his face.

"That is far too much to pay someone who has no experience as a PA," I told him. "Are you sure you wouldn't rather advertise for someone who can speak Russian?"

"I have told you before, it is not necessary for you to speak Russian. I'd much rather have someone who can deal with the administrative side of things, as I find it so—how you say—*tedious*. I need someone who lives locally because I don't have time to travel far with my shifts at Night Movers.

"I also want someone I trust will do their very best, Holly, and I think you'll be perfect for the role. So, if you are happy to take the job, could you fill in the relevant areas on the paperwork provided, then I can show you some of the things you will be dealing with day to day?"

His eyes seemed to plead with me. Like he desperately wanted me to take the job. I bit my lower lip nervously and looked through the rest of the contract. I was only required to work thirty hours per week, which would be flexible to accommodate childcare. I'd be paid extra for any additional work I did in my own time. He'd supply me with the relevant materials needed to perform my duties and I'd be compensated for any further costs incurred. I'd have thirty days' annual holiday…and the rest was pretty standard stuff. I took the pen Sergei offered and signed and dated in the relevant areas, as well as adding my contact details, address, my bank account details, and national insurance number as requested.

I looked up to find Sergei smiling at me. I smiled back, both nervous and excited at the prospect of a new career. He took the paperwork, folded it in half and placed it in his pocket, saying, "I will make a copy for you tonight when I get into work. I need to get my own copier. Perhaps you could show me where I could purchase one from?"

"Of course. There's an electrical store near Barnsley we could go to," I told him.

"Perfect. I can drive us there later. Now, let me show you what I need you to start with."

Sergei went through two boxes of paperwork, some of which was a little disorganised.

He explained that as well as the Petrov family business in Russia, which is split into two separate divisions, he's also a partner in a similar business to Night Movers in Moscow. He owns three vineyards in France, and of course, a partnership in Night Movers here in Yorkshire. As well as all that, Sergei supports several charities for orphaned children, including orphanages in Romania and Russia. The orphanage in Romania was currently undergoing substantial improvements—paid for in full by profits from Petrov Energy. He was keen to see if the improvements were going according to plan and said he'd be flying out the week before Christmas to check for himself how everything was progressing.

Sergei asked if Matty and I would be available to accompany him. I told him that neither of us had passports, having never left the country before. He said he'd help sort that out for us and suggested that we go to the post office to get the forms as soon as we'd finished our lunch.

I found him intriguing. He had all those business dealings going on throughout Europe and beyond, yet he bore no airs and graces. He seemed content enough to live in a flat above a flower shop in this small Yorkshire village.

Most of the writing on the paperwork was in Russian, but the figures shown were more than impressive. I asked if he wanted to reconsider getting someone else in for this position because I honestly didn't have the experience to be the PA he so obviously needed.

"Holly, all things can be learned, and everyone has to start somewhere. I'll work closely with you over the next few weeks so that you know what I need. All I ask in return is that you are honest with me and let me know if I go too fast, or if you don't understand something I say. Never feel you cannot tell me to slow down or repeat myself. I would hate to learn that you are too uncomfortable in my presence to tell me you need help. And that goes for anything else. If you ever need my help, Holly, you have to let me know."

He steepled his hands and looked at me in all serious-ness as he said this, his heavy Russian accent suddenly becoming less so in a bid to make me understand more clearly what he meant.

"Okay," I confirmed with a nod. He smiled.

"Good. Now that is settled, we will go out for our lunch and get to know each other a little better. But first, I wish to know more about *The Knights of Dellot.*"

Sergei left me at the table and went to sit beside Matty and the cat on the sofa. He asked Matty questions about the various characters and wanted to know which one was his favourite and why.

I tried to concentrate on what I was doing, but I found myself watching Matty. It was the first time since Gran died he'd had any enthusiasm for anything, and it had taken a stranger to bring that out of him.

At the end of the cartoon, Sergei and my brother were chatting like old friends, each saying which superpower they would prefer. Sergei said he thought that being able to fly would be a great superpower, while Matty thought running extra fast would be great because he would never be late for school again.

When Sergei told Matty to put on his coat so we could go out for lunch, my little brother looked at me for guidance. I had barely enough money to spare in my purse to buy a loaf of bread and milk, and I needed to save it to help pay for his school dinners next week.

Sergei caught the look that Matty gave me, and embarrassingly, I think he understood all too well the words that weren't spoken out loud.

"It would be an honour to treat you both to lunch today. I wish to get to know you better, and I get lonely when I have to eat by myself every day. It will be nice to have some company," he said.

"You can come to our house for supper," Matty invited as he took Sergei's hand. "We're having peanut butter on toast, and it's my favourite."

"My favourite too," declared Sergei. "I must work tonight, so I can't. But maybe another time when I'm not working, I can come and have supper with you and Holly?"

"That would be okay, wouldn't it, Holly?" Matty asked before leaning towards Sergei. "Holly might let me stay up late if you come to see us, but not on a school night."

"Okay," replied Sergei. "I won't make it a school night."

Chapter Four

Sergei

I took Holly and Matthew out for a three-course lunch at a popular pub chain in Rothley that had a play area for children. Before we got there, I called in at the post office and general store for passport forms and a few packs of The Knights of Dellot stickers Matty had shown me earlier.

I hadn't missed the look that passed between Holly and her brother when I'd asked if they'd like to go for lunch. As if I would ever have let them pay! Before we'd left the flat, I discreetly transferred an advance of Holly's first week's wage into her bank account, then keyed her contact details into my phone.

The pub lunch was delicious, and Matty enjoyed having unlimited ice cream with various toppings for dessert. After his third bowl, Holly said that was enough. She told him if he had any more, he would be ill later. Although Matty protested valiantly, she wouldn't back down, so when Holly left to go to the bathroom, I promised Matty I'd bring them back again next weekend.

The boy was desperate to go to the indoor play area as he'd spotted one of his friends from school in there. So I ordered Holly and myself two coffees while Matty went to play.

Holly looked around anxiously when she returned to the table, so I quickly pointed out Matty's whereabouts. With a relieved look on her face, she sat down and thanked me for the coffee she'd just noticed. She poured extra cream into her cup and added half a pack of sugar before stirring absentmindedly. She was quiet and seemed unable to meet my gaze.

"Are you all right, Holly?" I asked, taking her hand in mine when she put down the spoon. Her small, soft hand felt good in mine, so I didn't let go.

Still not meeting my gaze, she sighed heavily before saying, "I feel guilty."

"Why? What would you have to feel guilty about?"

"Because…my grandma died two weeks ago, and we only buried her yesterday. Yet here we are, enjoying ourselves. That can't be right."

Her eyes filled with tears, so I got out of my chair and sat in the one next to her that Matty had vacated. She sobbed silently as I pulled her to my side and held her against me.

"I am so sorry, Holly. I should not have insisted we come here. And I should not have accepted your offer to start work today. Clearly, you need time to grieve, so I will take you both home, and you can contact me when you feel ready to work again."

"No, no, Sergei, please. You don't understand. I need to work. I…"

"Holly, you will still have a job with me. That will not change, I assure you. And if you check your bank, you will find your first week's wage already in your account."

Holly looked like she was about to protest, so I placed a finger against her lips to silence her. For a moment, I forgot what I was about to say as I stared at the sight. Then I took my finger from her lips and brushed the tears away from her cheeks with the back of my hand.

"I want to help you, Holly, and I think you might need help financially. The date I pay you your wage has no relevance to me. I could not rest if I did not do this. It is not in my nature to watch women and children suffer. I saw that often enough in my childhood. So, please, accept this small gesture and grant me another beautiful smile.

"Being here with you and Matty has made my day, and I feel blessed to have had your company. I confess I knew very little of your grandmother, but if she was anything like mine, I will assume she would have been happy that you and Matty came here and have eaten well today. My grandmother never let me leave the table until I had eaten all my vegetables and had second helpings. Even when I was an adult, she would still insist on this."

Holly smiled and nodded. I took her hand in mine again and kissed the back of it. She looked up at me and took a deep breath. Her azure-blue eyes were still glassy with tears, and her full lips parted slightly.

I wanted to kiss her—more than I have ever wanted anything in my life—but right now, it would be wrong to do so. Thankfully, a waitress came by and distracted me by asking if we needed another coffee.

We hadn't drunk the ones we had, so I politely told her no, then asked for the bill.

Chapter Five

Holly

When we finally prised Matty away from his friend in the play area, we headed back to Sergei's car. He drove a midnight-blue Lexus SUV with black leather seats and wood trim. It was pure luxury, yet the open bag of sour jelly sweets on the dash and the empty bottle of cola in the cup holder showed the vehicle wasn't purchased as a status symbol.

When we pulled up at the traffic lights, I thought the car had stalled, but Sergei explained it was a hybrid vehicle. That meant it also ran on electricity from the hybrid battery, which uses zero CO_2. Both Matty and I found this fascinating, and I remarked that he was doing his bit to save the planet—to which Matty added, "Just like The Knights of Dellot."

We were supposed to be shopping for a printer/copier, but after my tears at the pub, Sergei decided we should go back to his flat to pick up the flowers he bought me, then he'd take us home.

Matty immediately became quiet. All the happiness and energy left him completely when he knew we'd be home soon, and my heart broke for him. I told Sergei I'd be fine to go shopping for the printer, but he insisted on taking us back to our house.

When we arrived, I turned to thank him once again for my beautiful flowers, and for treating Matty and me to lunch. Also, for the advance on my wage. I needed that more than he could ever know, and I'd be eternally grateful for it.

He came around to help Matty out of the car and noticed his slow movements and sullen expression.

"What is wrong, Matty?" he asked as he crouched down so that he was eye level with him.

"I didn't want to come home," he admitted.

"Well, my young friend, your sister became very upset today, and I know the last few days have been hard for you both, so I thought it would be better if you came home and got some rest."

"But *I* don't need to get some rest," Matty whined.

"Your sister does, though. She needs someone to look after her today and give her lots of hugs."

"Should I phone Auntie Moira?" Matty asked.

"Why? Can't *you* give her lots of hugs?"

"I can, but sometimes that makes her cry, and then I cry, then she cries more because I'm crying. I don't like it when she cries. When her boyfriend made her cry, me and Grandma got mad, and I wanted to punch him. But now she cries because she's sad about Grandma, and there's no one for me to punch."

Sergei glanced at me with an eyebrow raised, then he looked back at Matty and asked, "What do you think that one of The Knights of Dellot would do if they saw their sister crying?"

Matty screwed up his face, deep in thought. "Well, I think they would hug and protect her from what was making her sad. And if it was her boyfriend that made her sad, the knight Davian could use his super-punch on him, or Caspian could stomp his foot and cause the earth to crack so he would fall into a giant hole never to be seen again, or—"

"What if she was sad because she missed someone who hadn't done her any harm? What would they do then? I think they would hug her and hold her hand and tell her how much they love her, don't you?"

"I suppose so."

"So, while you may not have a super-punch or be able to stomp a crack in the earth, you can be just like the knights when it comes to taking care of their sisters—with hugs."

Matty nodded, and Sergei smiled.

"Good. Now, I have something for you both to do."

Sergei stood and opened the car door. He took some forms out of the glove compartment and handed them to me.

"These are the passport forms for you to fill in. You'll need to have photographs taken and have them signed by someone professional who knows you, like a doctor or a teacher. As soon as you've done that, we can send them off to the passport office. I will pay the fee. After all, it is I who requested you have them. And when you've made sure that your sister is okay, Matty, you can see if you need any of these stickers in your book," he said, passing them to my wide-eyed brother.

"Seven packs of stickers!" Matty exclaimed loudly. "Holly, look, Sergei has given me seven packs of stickers. I wonder if I'll get the king this time. Or Torsten."

Matty threw his arms around Sergei's legs and hugged him.

"Thank you, Sergei. If you get yourself a sticker book, we could share some stickers or do swaps like we do at school. I can't do a lot of swaps because I don't get many stickers, but some of the older kids at my school get loads, so they can do lots of swaps."

"You know what, Matty? I think that's a great idea. I will get a sticker book and do swaps with you. Of course, I'll need to learn much more about these knights. Perhaps next Saturday when Holly comes to my flat, she could bring you, too, and we could watch the cartoon again."

"I can work tomorrow, Sergei," I told him. "Aunt Moira invited us for Sunday dinner, but I don't feel up to going. I can drop Matty off and come to you after that."

"Aww, Holly, can't I go to Sergei's with you?" Matty asked.

I shook my head. "Jamie will be at Aunt Moira's, Matty. I wonder what he'll say when he sees your new stickers?"

"He might want to do some swaps. I'll see if I can get you some of the good ones, Sergei. Jamie had three stickers of Caspian, and they're *really* hard to get. He gave me my Caspian one," Matty said, taking out his sticker book and showing him the elusive knight.

"Well, that's settled, then. I'll drop Matty off at Aunt Moira's just before eleven, and then I'll go straight to your flat. It's not far from Aunt Moira's, so it shouldn't take me long."

"If you call and let me know when you are ready, I will pick you up," Sergei said. Taking my hand in his, he tugged me closer. Leaning down a little, he tucked my hair behind my ear and said in a very serious voice, "If anyone ever makes you cry again, *angel moy*, you are to tell me. Is that understood?"

I was a little taken aback by that statement, but I nodded in agreement. It seemed to appease him because he smiled and kissed my cheek. Before he stepped away from me, I felt his nose and mouth touch my neck as he inhaled. Instead of finding that slightly odd, I went weak at the knees, like a schoolgirl with a swoon-worthy crush.

"Until tomorrow, Holly," he said while climbing into his Lexus. Lowering the window, he shouted to Matty, "Don't forget, look after your sister like you would if you were the bravest Knight of Dellot."

Sergei waited until I'd opened the door and we were both inside before driving away.

Chapter Six

Sergei

I stomped around my flat for hours, my mind conjuring up scenarios in which Holly's ex-boyfriend had made her cry. Then I thought up several ways to hurt him. Odd, really, as I'd never even seen his face, but I already knew I hated him. I discussed it with my cat, Boris, and from the way he meowed and flexed his claws, I knew he agreed we should find and hurt this person who dared make my angel cry.

Before leaving for my shift at Night Movers, I called to see Pam and Chloe in the shop below my flat. As expected, Gregor was already there, helping bring in the flower buckets and displays from outside the shop.

"Hello, Sergei. Did Holly like her flowers?" Pam asked before kissing me on the cheek as she passed by me.

"Yes, she did. She was surprised to receive them, I think."

"Perhaps she hasn't been treated to flowers very much," added Chloe. She walked past Gregor with a huff.

From the way Chloe scowled at Gregor, I could tell they'd been arguing again. There was tension in the air, and when I looked from Gregor to Pam, she rolled her eyes.

Since Chloe became pregnant, Gregor's need to protect her had gone into overdrive. I understand his worry about her carrying heavy items and climbing up ladders to reach the high cupboards. But when Gregor suggested she cut down on her working hours, Chloe was far from happy.

She's not even three months pregnant yet, so how he'll be when she gets further into her pregnancy is anyone's guess.

"Sergei, tell my w—tell Chloe that lifting the boxes out of the candle supplier's van was too much for someone in her condition. And where were you, anyway? Surely you would have seen the van pull up. You should have been the one to carry the boxes in," Gregor grumbled.

Gregor thought I wasn't aware that he and Chloe were already married. The number of times he nearly made the slip of referring to her as his wife was comical. Nevertheless, they are all set for a spring wedding ceremony at his palace chapel in St Petersburg.

However, I knew he'd married Chloe within days of Bonding with her, at a private ceremony in the same chapel we were supposed to witness them wed in. Yuri had been there, although it wasn't he who informed me of their marriage. I've known Gregor for centuries, so I knew he'd want Chloe to be his in every way as soon as possible.

Gregor always got his way, yet not with Chloe. She is feisty, steadfast in what she believes in, and determined to remain as independent as possible. They say opposites attract, which was more than evident in Gregor and Chloe's case. I could see that my long-time friend adored his woman. He admired in her the same independent streak that also frayed his last nerve.

I did not get involved in all their bickering; it would serve no purpose. But I did not like Gregor's opinion that just because I lived above Chloe's shop, I should be at her beck and call to fetch and carry whenever Gregor thought it was necessary. Chloe did not like this either, and I watched silently as she marched up to Gregor and poked him in the chest.

"Firstly, Gregor, you do not own this shop. I do. Therefore, you get no say in the running of it. As such, you wouldn't know that there were only nine medium-sized candles per box, so they weren't heavy at all. Secondly, it's not Sergei's job to check on deliveries. He only lends a hand here when I ask him or when he wants to; the same goes for Yuri and Dmitry. And thirdly, do you honestly think I'd put our baby at risk by doing something that could harm this pregnancy? Honestly, Gregor, you haven't just seriously pissed me off today; you've upset me, too. So if you know what's good for you, you'll keep out of my way until I calm down."

"Chloe, I—"

"Just leave, Gregor. I can't deal with you right now," Chloe yelled angrily.

Gregor looked like he was about to turn away, but instead, he bent slightly and picked Chloe up, draping her over his shoulder.

I held the door open and watched him carry her to his SUV. Chloe was yelling out all the different ways she would make him pay while repeatedly beating at his back and ass. Gregor replied, "Yes, my love. I know I will suffer for this later, but I cannot leave you upset. It's not good for you in your condition. And quite frankly, your temper tantrum has me harder than steel, so I will take you home where we can both ease our frustrations."

"If you think for one minute that I will sleep with—"

With my vampire hearing, I heard Gregor tell Chloe in an almost whisper, "The cellar refit is complete, my darling. They left an hour ago."

"Oh," replied Chloe as she finally stopped beating at him.

Gregor placed Chloe next to the passenger door of his car.

"I'm still angry with you, Gregor," she whispered as he lowered his mouth to hers and kissed her softly.

The kiss became heated, so I stepped back inside the shop and closed the door as quietly as possible before locking it.

"Don't tell me," Pam said as she opened the cash register and took out the money drawer. "I bet they were swallowing each other's tongues when they got to the car."

"How did you guess?" I laughed, following her into the back room.

"It's the same thing week in, week out with those two. Gregor tries to lay down the law, Chloe gets all indignant with him, and then comes the battle to get the upper hand. Before you know it, they're practically having sex in the car. Well, maybe that's exaggerating it a bit, but whatever it is, it's not healthy. One day soon, there'll be an argument that will be hard to come back from."

"That won't happen, Pam. I've told you before, when we Bond, it is for life."

I told Pamela many weeks ago about my immortality and need for blood. Telling a human is not something we do lightly, but she's been a great friend to me, and I genuinely adore her.

I got to know her while working in the flower shop after helping Gregor unwittingly kidnap Chloe, which involved sending them both to Russia.

Pamela—or Pam, depending on my mood—often spends time with me socially. More so since my other friends became too busy with wedding planning and children. I also spend time with Old Joe and Ken Fearn, the baker, and a few others from the darts team at the Red Lion. Yet Pamela is the only one I have trusted to keep my secret. She's annoyed that Chloe didn't trust her enough to tell her about Gregor because, through his association with me, she's figured out that he is immortal, too.

Being in her mid-fifties and living in this village since she was a child meant Pam had her suspicions about the rest of the Night Movers' staff. Although, I only smile at her when she asks. Most of the village thinks that Alex, Josh, and Nik took over the running of the business from their fathers. I have no idea how they managed to pull that off.

"Will you speak to Gregor about it, Sergei? He might listen to you."

"I doubt Gregor will listen to relationship advice from me. After all, he's the one who's Bonded to the love of his life. I am still single."

"Not for long, though, Sergei. I saw the way you and Holly were looking at each other."

"But she is so young," I pointed out. "And she's grieving over the loss of her grandmother. It wouldn't be right to begin anything with her now, even if I wanted to. Although, I admit to having feelings for her."

"No matter what Holly's birth certificate says, that girl isn't young. She's seen too much sadness in her life to keep the naivety that comes with youth," Pam said.

"How do you mean?"

"Holly's mum was always a bit of a rebel. She would throw her support into a cause and obsess over it. Anything that grabbed her imagination at the time. She had a drug problem as a teenager, but she got some help and seemed to be doing well. Caroline was Beryl's only child, and her parents spoiled her despite having very little money. Beryl's husband fell from a ladder when putting a TV aerial on the roof; he never worked after that.

"I always thought Caroline had mental health problems, but nothing was ever said about it, so maybe I was reading too much into her behaviour. It's just that something didn't seem right to me, you know? Anyway, Caroline went off to some protestor camp down south and returned two years later, ready to give birth.

"She stayed around until Holly was nearly a year old before she took off again somewhere, leaving her with Beryl. I think Holly would have been about to start school when she came back again. She seemed to have turned her life around and even worked here with us for a few years. Joyce—who owned the shop back then—was a friend of Beryl's, so she gave Caroline the job as a favour. She left here to work for a double-glazing company, answering the telephones. I think that's how she met Matthew's father. They had contractors working all over the country, and the guy she started seeing was from Lincolnshire. She rented a house in Doncaster, and eventually, Holly went to stay with her. When Caroline became pregnant with Matthew, she discovered the guy she'd been seeing was married, and he didn't want her or the baby.

"Joyce and I had a conversation about it; we worried that Caroline wouldn't cope, but she seemed to be doing great and surprised all of us. Then Jock, Beryl's husband, got cancer. He died ten weeks after being diagnosed. Caroline lost it, but because Beryl was so utterly devastated, she could barely take care of herself, never mind a young family. I will never forget the day we got the news that the woman on the radio we'd heard about all morning was Caroline," Pamela said, shaking her head, the sheen of tears appearing in her eyes.

"What do you mean? What was on the radio, Pamela?"

"There'd been a news report that a woman had been killed by a train at a level crossing. We later found out that Caroline had driven herself, Holly, and little Matthew to the middle of the crossing and waited for the train to hit. Luckily, Holly got herself and baby Matthew to safety. But what that young girl must have gone through at the time and afterwards is unimaginable. I think she would have only been around eleven years old. I remember a man on the news saying Holly wanted to go back and get her mum out of the car, but someone who'd been out walking their dog had stopped her. If he hadn't, Holly would have been killed, too."

When Pamela stopped speaking, I took her hands in mine. She felt cold to the touch. Reliving a memory so devastating will do that to you. My poor Holly would have that memory every day. My heart broke for her.

"Joyce and Moira, Beryl's other close friend, helped as much as possible. I went round and sat with Holly and Matthew while they helped Beryl with the funeral arrangements. Holly was great with Matthew. She would dress, feed and change him like a little mother, and it occurred to me she must have been doing it for some time. If Caroline had been living closer, maybe we would've seen how badly she was coping. But no one knew. Not even Joyce or Moira.

"In the end, having Holly and Matthew to care for gave Beryl a reason to carry on. She'd taken care of them ever since, but Holly has always been like a mother to Matthew. I think that's why Beryl was so glad she went to work in that hotel in the Lake District. She wanted her granddaughter to have the chance to be young and carefree for once. But that's never going to happen now. She'll have to be a mother to Matthew because the poor boy has no one else."

"I am sorry to have made you think of these terrible memories, Pamela, but I am glad to have learned a little about Holly's past. I wished to help her and offered her a job as my PA. I guessed she might need help financially. And I do need a PA, as you have told me many times," I said while squeezing her fingers playfully. "But there's also something else I feel when I'm near her; something that would have confused me a few years ago because I thought I'd found someone who held my heart."

"You mean Gina?"

I nodded and sighed heavily. I'd told Pamela about the love I thought I'd felt for Gina, and about telling Nik about it. I was drunk at the time and needed to talk to someone. Usually, Gina would have been the one I told everything to, but for obvious reasons, I couldn't tell her that.

"Sergei, from what you told me, you'd already realised that Gina wasn't it for you. I know you love her, but there are different types of love, and while each involves the heart, not all involve the soul. When you have a love that comes from the heart and soul, there is no mistaking that."

I nodded in agreement. "I see that more clearly now, and I recognise my feelings for what they were. But I am confused as to why I couldn't see that before."

"Love can be confusing, Sergei. It can make us behave in ways we would never dream of normally."

"Like absinthe?"

"Yes," she said with a smile. "It can make us feel great

and mighty, or small and meek. We can feel sexy and confident, anxious or sad. What I think you had for Gina was like a crush. Like a schoolboy would have."

I laughed at that. "I am hardly a schoolboy, Pamela. I haven't been one for centuries."

"No, but you are young at heart. You still find joy and humour when many are too serious. You know, I think you and Holly will make a good match. She needs someone like you. Someone who will love and protect her yet will also bring fun and laughter into her life. You will be good for Matthew, too. The boy needs a father figure."

"You think I would make a good father? There will be many who would disagree. Especially after the blue horse incident," I reminded her.

"Then those people are fools. Don't doubt yourself, Sergei. You are a good man, and I love you dearly."

"Pamela, you are a great friend to me. I think I will keep you." I leaned over and kissed her on the cheek. In truth, it was a distraction, so she couldn't see the tears in my eyes. My human friend believed in me and had given me hope that a happy future may await me after all.

Chapter Seven

Sergei

I had an idea that Holly wouldn't call me for a lift. Yet I had been ready and waiting to pick her and Matthew up, despite only having four hours' sleep.

My last few shifts at Night Movers had been chaotic. Alex had flown out to Lanzarote on holiday with his family last week and was due back on Tuesday. On Thursday, Josh and Keeley had taken Daisy along to see Sandra, Keeley's friend who had just had a baby. She lives near Knightsbridge in London, so I'm sure there'll be shopping involved. They were due back later, so Josh will probably come into work to help out tonight. Sundays are always busy because of the supermarket deliveries.

Nik would have been here to share the burden, but Gina's aunt had fallen and broken her hip on Thursday night, so they'd flown out to be with her and oversee her care. She lives near Newry in Northern Ireland and has no other family living nearby, so I imagine Nik and Gina will be there for some time.

Although it meant Maggie and I had been working flat out over the last few days, at least I hadn't had to deal with the continuing awkwardness that had been developing between Nik and me.

I told him what I felt for Gina now was a love that existed purely through friendship—like the love I felt for him. But I knew he didn't believe me. He never said anything, but it was there in his actions and was written all over his face. He hid it well from Gina, but Freya had sensed something was wrong, and Maggie saw it too.

I hope time will heal whatever resentment he feels towards me. It would be a monumental task to get used to a life without the close friendship and brotherhood I share with Nik.

When I heard the doorbell ring, my spirits soared. She was here. My angel had arrived. I allowed a moment to compose myself and steady my heartbeat before I opened the door.

"Hello," was all she said before my steady composure fled, and my heartbeat erupted into rapturous, joyful applause.

I drank in the sight of her to quench the thirst in my dry mouth. My fingers gripped the edge of the door while I took in her appearance. She wore her shoulder-length, wavy blonde hair down today, and she'd applied a little mascara and pale green eye shadow that made her pretty blue eyes stand out even more. She had on knee-length, black leather boots that reached a knee-length black pencil skirt. The same black parka jacket she had worn yesterday was zipped up to her chin to keep out the cold. I stepped aside and invited her in, then closed my eyes and concentrated on her scent as she moved past me into the hallway.

After closing the door, I took her coat, making sure I casually brushed against her as I hung it up. *Careful, Sergei; you don't want her to think you are a pervert.* Thoughts of a "sexual harassment in the workplace" charge brought me back to earth.

"Are you all right, Sergei? You seem a little distracted today," she said, a concerned look on her pretty face.

"Of course, my dear. I'm just a little tired, that's all. We have been busy these last few nights, and I had very little sleep when I got back."

"I'm sorry. I should have come later in the afternoon. What time did you get home?" she asked.

"About six twenty this morning."

"So you've had less than five hours' sleep! You must be exhausted. I should leave you to rest. You ought to have said something yesterday, Sergei. I feel so bad about making you get up."

"Nonsense, Holly, I feel fine. Josh is back tonight, so I'm only on until he takes over at midnight. If I'd slept any later, I wouldn't have slept tonight, so it is all good. Now come, let me get you a hot drink to warm you up from the cold."

"No, let me make the drinks. I watched you yesterday, so I know where everything is."

"Lead the way," I said with a sweep of my hand, gesturing towards the kitchen.

Truthfully, it gave me a warm feeling to see Holly pottering about my kitchen. I asked how her brother was after all the ice cream he'd devoured yesterday. Holly laughed and told me he'd enjoyed it so much he'd asked to go back on his birthday—which was in March—so he had a long wait.

I didn't tell her I'd already promised the boy I would take him there again. Holly, too. Perhaps Matty didn't think I would keep my promise? If so, he was wrong. I would never let him down.

I told her that I had wanted the refillable ice cream option too, but I didn't think adults could have it. Holly laughed again and admitted she'd chosen from the *"grown-up"* dessert menu because she didn't want to appear immature in front of me. Still, she would have loved the unlimited ice cream option with chocolate buttons and raspberry juice. She licked her lips and made a smacking sound with them, which gave my cock an unwelcome wake-up call. *Fuck!*

I turned away from her quickly and concentrated on what I wanted to speak to her about. Something that had been on my mind since I heard Matty mention it yesterday: the boyfriend who'd made her cry. Who was he? Did she still have feelings for him? And what did he do that made her cry and made Matty, and now me, want to beat the living daylights out of him?

I carried our drinks to the table where I'd already spread out the paperwork that needed filing in date order. Then I opened my laptop and showed her how to use the P.E.13 programme my company, Petrov Energy, uses.

I found this programme, which my friend Viktor co-created, simplified every aspect of accessing, updating and tracking all the data that my upper management team and I needed. We could access the programme in conference mode for our fortnightly business meetings.

Growth in the gas pipeline expansion side of the business has slowed somewhat, but we've been focussing on renewable energy for the past ten years. During the previous two years, we've seen enough growth and profit to enable us to expand this side of the company.

I often wonder what my grandfather would think of the successful business he created. I think he would be proud that his company was becoming a world leader in energy that will save the planet for future generations.

Holly wrote notes and created diagrams with all the information she'd need to access and work her way around P.E.13. She'd stop me and have me explain something to her now and again, but it wasn't often.

Showing her how to operate my company programs allowed me to sit close to her. I appreciated every time my arm *"accidentally"* brushed against hers, pressing shoulder to shoulder as we looked through various ways to change the spreadsheets.

Holly was so young—still in her teens—yet it was I who had the behaviour of a lovestruck teenager. My heart beat wildly in my chest, and when she sighed heavily, the breathy sound went straight to my cock. I had not been so affected by a female in a long time, but I had to remember her age and the fact that she was grieving. Any lust I felt had to be tempered and kept at bay.

Considering my many years of immortality, that should have been an effortless task. I had done it so often with Gina and found it easy. Evidently, it would not be as simple to manage around Holly. My cock refused to stop its rapid growth, and I had to alter my position discretely before its confinement in my jeans became painful. Luckily, the table hid my dilemma.

"Do you want to pick up a new printer today?" she asked as she turned to look at me. Her pretty blue eyes were mesmerising, and her full lips beckoned my own. She licked them nervously, and I watched her throat move as she swallowed.

"I want to kiss you, Holly," I heard myself say.

"What? Why?"

"Because you're beautiful." I turned to face her, put a hand on the back of her neck and brought her towards me. "Because you are sweet," I continued, inhaling her scent as I drew her closer. "Because I want you to be mine," I whispered before my lips found hers.

My lips moved softly against hers, gently coaxing them apart for my tongue to gain entry. I traced the seam and felt her shudder, then groan before she kissed me back. My angel kissed with a passion I hadn't expected, and I had to end the kiss before I lost control and took more than would be right. When I pulled away from her, she opened her eyes and lifted a shaking hand towards her kiss-swollen lips. Her fingers touched her mouth, and she closed her eyes again.

"What are you thinking, *angel moy*?" I whispered. I could scent her arousal, yet that didn't necessarily mean she wanted—or needed—my advances.

"I don't really know what to think," she said. "It was… unexpected."

"What if I told you I wanted to kiss you again?"

"I…I don't… Sergei, what do you want from me?"

I could see the confusion in her eyes; the line between her brows made it more obvious.

"I want only what you are willing to give right now. I have all the time in the world for the rest, *angel moy*."

"I thought you wanted me to be your PA?"

"I do. But that doesn't mean you couldn't be more than that."

She shrank back at my answer.

"I didn't see anywhere in the contract that said I'd be required to sleep with you, Mr Petrov."

"*Shit, now you have done it, Sergei,*" I said to myself, following a harsh mental slap.

I took a deep breath and prepared to bare my soul.

"I'm sorry that my words have caused you to think poorly of me, and I know that my timing is not the best—given your circumstances. However, I need you to know I did not expect something like this to happen—that I would develop feelings for you so quickly. I am attracted to you; I will not deny that. After all, you are a very beautiful woman. But I also find that being in your company gives me great pleasure. You are caring, intelligent and…everything I've been looking for, for a very long time."

"You think I'm beautiful?" she whispered.

"I do."

"And you think you're developing feelings for me?"

"I know I'm developing feelings for you."

"But how can that be? You hardly know me."

"I see you are of the belief that only time can create deep and meaningful feelings in a relationship. In my world, that is not always the case, *angel moy.*"

"Well, I know that's not the case in my world, especially after…." Holly closed her eyes and took a deep breath. "You keep calling me angel moy. What does that mean?"

"It means my angel. You look like an angel to me—with your beautiful golden hair and pretty blue eyes. So sweet, so innocent. The guiding light to my darkness."

She shook her head and laughed cynically.

"If I were an angel, my wings would be black. God must hate me to allow so much sadness to be sent my way. Everyone I've ever loved has either died or hurt me. All except Matty. He's my world."

"As he should be, *angel moy*. He's a wonderful little boy. Now, tell me about the boyfriend that made you cry. I assume he was the one you just said hurt you. Do you still have feelings for him?"

"No. Not anymore. I *was* hurt and angry at the time, but he didn't break my heart. My grandmother dying broke my heart. Catching my boyfriend screwing the head receptionist at the hotel made me feel worthless. Like I was nothing.

"We'd been boyfriend and girlfriend since we were fifteen. I followed him to the hotel in the Lakes because he said he couldn't be without me. I wanted to stay here with Gran and Matty, but he talked me around. He said he wanted to get engaged, but everything seemed to change when we got up there.

I wasn't happy being away from home, and that caused arguments. There were always biscuits and other goodies in the offices and reception, and I put on weight. He didn't like that and told me so all the time.

"He'd mention other things about my appearance, too. Paul often remarked that the other receptionists looked more groomed and professional. They always wore full make-up and had fancy hairstyles, even when they were on at six in the morning. I've never worn much make-up, and my hair generally does its own thing after a few hours, no matter what products I use. So I could never look as good as them.

"He'd been comparing me to Rachael, the head receptionist. She was pretty, a bit condescending, but otherwise a nice person—or so I thought. I went to find him one day. He was supposed to be off for a couple of hours, and I'd swapped shifts with another girl to spend some time with him. Paul wasn't in our room, so I went looking for him. I caught him having sex with Rachael in one of the kitchen's stock cupboards. She was still perfectly made up without a hair out of place, by the way. He had the affront to tell me it wasn't what it looked like. Can you believe it? I went straight to our room, packed my stuff, got a taxi to the station, and came home."

"I'm sorry that happened to you. He is crazy. He had a true beauty in his midst, yet he wanted a painted one instead. Utter fool," I told her.

"Rachael was beautiful, painted or not. She turned all the guys' heads in that hotel and had slept with most of them. That was the reason I wasn't there the day Gran died. When I told her what had happened, she advised me to get an appointment at the hospital to check for STDs, just in case. I should have gone the first week, but I'd been trying to work up the courage. I felt ashamed, even though it wasn't me who'd done anything wrong. So that's where I was when Gran died. Getting checked for sexually transmitted diseases while my gran had a cardiac arrest in the back garden."

I was so angry and upset over the trauma and pain that Holly had experienced, and I had to turn my face away so that she didn't see my eyes flash red.

Holly stood up so quickly that the chair fell over. She tried to run out of the room, but I caught her arm and pulled her back to me.

"Where are you going, Holly?"

"I have to leave. I need to be somewhere."

"No, you don't. I won't let you leave like this, even if you have to go. Come sit with me, Holly. Tell me what made you get up and run."

She stood completely still and stared down at the floor.

"Holly, please, I want to know. I think you need to get

this off your chest. I am a good listener, and I would never breathe a word of what you tell me to anyone."

"So, I'm back to Holly now. Not *'your angel'* anymore."

"Ah, so you are directing your anger at me. Go ahead, *angel moy.* If that's what you need to help you heal, then do it. Scream, shout, lash out, take what you need. Let me help you get to a better place."

"You can't," she said while choking back tears. "I can't...."

She placed her hands in front of her face and cried. Huge shudders heaved her upper body as I picked her up and carried her to the sofa. I set her on my knee and cradled her against me. It took about ten minutes for her to calm down, but I didn't care. I'd have sat there the whole day with her if she'd needed it. My T-shirt was wet from her tears, and she blew her nose with a tissue she had tucked away in her sleeve.

"I'm sorry," she said, her voice still broken with sobs.

"You have nothing to be sorry for, my love. Not to me, nor to your grandmother for not being there when she died. You could have done very little for her even if you were there. Despite all the best medical intervention, sometimes it's just not enough."

"I know that. It's not really about Gran. Well, it is a little."

"Who is it about? Not your boyfriend, I hope. He doesn't deserve your tears."

"No, it's not him. It's Matty. He's the one who needed me more that day. He was the one to find her, you see. She'd popped out into the garden to get Grandad's old toolbox. The fuse had gone on the lamp in the living room, so Matty said she went to get a screwdriver for the plug. He was doing his homework. He had some maths and spellings to do, so he didn't notice how long she'd been gone. When he finished, he went outside to see where she was…and that's when he found her body.

"She'd split the back of her head open as she hit the concrete paving slab when she fell. The post-mortem showed that the head injury had nothing to do with her death; she was probably gone before she hit the path. Her heart had just stopped. But to him, a seven-year-old boy, he just saw his gran dead on the ground. Her lips were blue, there was blood around her head, and her eyes were open as if staring at the sky. Matty said he was shouting and shaking her, but he couldn't get her to move, so he ran inside and rang for the ambulance. The woman on the phone asked him if Gran was talking and if he could check her breathing. Matty kept saying, *'she's not breathing because she's dead.'* The woman told him to put a blanket around Gran to keep her warm until the ambulance arrived, so he did. Then he dropped the phone and ran to Aunt Moira's, which is a ten-minute walk from our house. I didn't know anything about it until I rang home to tell Gran that all the tests were negative. Aunt Moira was crying so hard she couldn't tell me what had happened.

"A policeman took the phone from her and explained that I needed to get home. I kept asking him what had happened as I got on the bus and sat down, but he wouldn't tell me. I asked if Matty was all right—if he was hurt. The policeman said, *'Yes. Your brother is all right.'* That's when I knew Gran was dead. They didn't have to tell me. Sometimes a lack of words can tell you much more of what you need to know.

"It was hard coming to terms with the fact that she was gone. But I had the funeral to plan, and the police were involved with all their extra checks because she'd died at home. Aunt Moira helped. Gina—Gran's friend from Night Movers—helped with stuff, too, as did Mr Singh from the shop. She was still working part-time for him, even though she'd retired from Night Movers. But none of them could help with what really mattered."

"And what was that?" I asked while stroking my thumb across her tear-stained cheek.

"Matty. He didn't want to come home, and to be honest, I didn't want to be there either. We stayed at Aunt Moira's place that first night. Matty kept shaking, and the police officer who came to speak to him said he was in shock and wanted to take him to the hospital to be checked out. Matty wouldn't go, so the doctor made a special home visit at the officer's request.

"He clung to me desperately, and I held him all night. Matty was exhausted, but he kept crying out in his sleep, and during the night, he wet the bed. He hadn't done that since he was three years old. Even though Aunt Moira said it didn't matter, Matty was so upset.

"Aunt Moira lives in a small two-bedroomed bungalow. Matty and I couldn't stay cramped up in that single bed another night, so we went back home. But Matty didn't want to be there. He was terrified. Apart from telling us what happened on that first night, he refuses to talk about it. Ever since then, he's wet the bed every night. He wakes up crying and shaking, and it takes forever to calm him down.

"Since the boiler broke, we've been sleeping downstairs in the front room because I can keep it warm with the gas fire. It means I can be there for him as soon as he starts crying. But by that time, he's already wet the bed.

"I've put the shower curtain on his mattress under his sheets, but it takes forever to get them dry. I boil the kettle a few times so that there's enough hot water for him to get clean, but the bathroom's cold because there's no central heating or hot water due to the broken boiler. And all the cold seems to do is wake us up more. I've taken him to see the doctor, and he's referring him to someone to talk about it, but I don't know how long that will take."

After kissing her forehead, I held Holly a little tighter. I think she needed it, and I know I did. I remembered Matty's face from yesterday. He hadn't wanted to return home, but I made them do so because I knew Holly had been upset. I sent them back to a cold house in the middle of winter—one they both didn't want to be in. Well, there was something I could do about that, at least.

"Holly, how long has your boiler been broken?"

"About a week."

"So you've been living in a cold house with no hot water for the past week?"

"Well, yes. We've had a couple of showers at Aunt Moira's, and I boil the kettle for hot water to wash the pots or to get a strip wash at home. And the washing machine only has the cold water tap as it heats the rest. Gran bought it with her redundancy money. If it hadn't been for the cost of the new roof, I could have had the boiler fixed. Because of the advance in wages that you gave me, I can now afford the call-out fee. They're coming out to look at the boiler tomorrow, so hopefully, we can get the heating back on when he fixes it."

"Well, until then, you can stay with me. I refuse to let you go back to a cold house," I told her.

"No, we can't. Thank you for offering, Sergei, but we can't stay here. Not overnight, anyway."

"If it's because of what happened earlier, about what I said after I kissed you, you needn't worry. I would never take advantage of you in that way. Please believe that, Holly."

"It's not that. Well, it's not *just* that. Like I've said, Matty keeps wetting the bed. We can't—"

I held up my hand to stop her from speaking.

"I am not a man who would refuse a woman and child in need because the child may wet the bed. I don't care if he does that; it's one of those things. Something he will overcome when he comes to terms with what happened to your grandmother. You can bring the shower curtain, or we can pick up something more suitable while the shops are still open. Either way, I refuse to let you spend another night in a house where there is no heating in winter. I'm out at work during the night, so you can stay in my bed, and Matty can sleep in the spare bedroom. You can both take a bath or shower whenever you want, and I will stock up with food if you tell me what you like."

"Sergei, I only met you two days ago, yet you've invited my brother and me to stay in your home. Can't you see that seems strange?"

"To whom? It seems perfectly acceptable to me. Please, Holly, stay here. At least until you get your boiler fixed. Do it for Matty. The change could do him good. He may open up more in a place without memories."

She bit her bottom lip and looked down at her hands, wringing them tightly. Then she looked back up at me and smiled nervously.

"Okay, we'll stay. Just until the boiler's fixed. You've been kind enough as it is with everything you've done for us. I wouldn't want to impose any more than necessary."

"I would never consider an act of kindness an imposition, and I'll enjoy the company, as will Boris. He gets fed up with just the two of us. Boris always prefers it when I have visitors."

Holly smiled at that.

"Where is Boris, by the way?"

"He's curled up on the chair in my bedroom. He got out last night when I was going to work. I think he has the hots for the cat that lives five doors down, though he has a rival for her affections. There is a large black cat who tries to court the female, and I fear that he and Boris will get into a fight over her."

"Maybe you should have him neutered?"

I gasped and instinctively placed my free hand over my balls, which made Holly laugh. The sound was sweet and calmed my emotions somewhat.

"*Angel moy*, it is not a subject a man wishes to discuss, ever, yet you are the second female to do so. My good friend Gina also suggested I do this to my poor Boris. But I cannot bring myself to do it. I fear it would be a betrayal he would never forgive."

She laughed again and shook her head.

"He'll forget about it once he's recovered. It's a common operation that vets do every day. He'll be fine."

"I can assure you, Holly, if someone were to remove my balls, I could *never, ever* forget it."

Either my words, my dour expression, or the sharp swing of emotions set Holly off into a fit of giggling that also made me laugh. Well, eventually, it did. After all, talk of removing any part of what makes you a man takes some time to recover from.

When she finally stopped laughing, she placed a hand on my cheek and said, "Thank you, Sergei."

"What for, my love?"

"For listening. For offering Matty and me a place to stay. And for making me laugh."

I turned my head a little, kissed the hand she still held against my cheek, and placed my palm over it.

"I will always do those things, Holly, and anything else you need."

She looked deep into my eyes and nodded.

"I know you will, Sergei. Somehow I…I just know that to be true."

"Will you kiss me, Holly?" I asked, placing the ball firmly in her court this time. Her eyes grew wide, and for a few seconds, I thought I had made a terrible mistake. But then she leaned towards me until her lips were just a breath away from mine.

I kept as still as I could until our lips met, and even then, I let her control the kiss. However, when she pressed her lips against mine more firmly, and then placed her hands at the back of my neck, all bets were off. I helped her move from being cradled on my lap to straddling me, lifting her skirt up around her waist to aid the position. The heat of her sex covered my jean-clad erection, and I relished the feeling of her breasts as they pressed against my chest.

Our tongues lapped against one another, and Holly's exquisite taste flooded my mouth. We both groaned as Holly rocked her lower half against me. The scent of her arousal filled the air, and that was my undoing.

I quickly flipped us over, so she lay underneath me on the large sofa cushions. After adjusting the near painful position of my cock inside the restricting denim, I pressed it against her core and kissed her again. She was wearing tights under her skirt, but I didn't think they would last as I rocked against her. She wrapped her arms over my back and kissed me with a passion I was happy to match.

Taking both her hands in one of mine, I pinned them above her head. If she carried on touching me, I would lose all control, and that wasn't something my angel could deal with right now.

I slipped my other hand underneath her ass and pressed her mound more firmly against my erection. Her mouth broke away from mine as she cried out in pleasure.

"Sergei, please, I can't. I…"

"Yes, you can, my love. Just let go."

Before I'd finished speaking, Holly threw her head back and gasped out her release. I kept myself still as she rocked against me, taking what she needed from my body. Then I kissed her again, soft and slow, bringing her down steadily from her climax-induced high. I wanted so desperately to kiss and lick that throbbing pulse in her neck, but if I did that, I knew the urge to bite her and taste her blood would surely take over.

I knew it then, although I think I'd known from the moment I first laid eyes on Holly that she was mine. My always and forever love.

She was my angel, but she had no idea that she belonged to a vampire. I just needed her to give us a chance, and I also had to be careful. Despite what Pamela had said, Holly was barely nineteen. There was so much of life she had yet to see and do. It would be an honour to be by her side during those new discoveries. Sharing them as a couple, with Matty too, of course.

Chapter Eight

Holly

I couldn't believe what had just happened. I was panting hard, the most exquisite feelings still racing through my body; Sergei planting whisper-soft kisses on my forehead, eyelids and chin.

I needed to get out from underneath him, compose myself, straighten up my clothes…but I didn't. I stayed right where I was, relishing the feel of the after-effects of my first ever orgasm. And with my clothes on, too. In fact, at no point during what had just happened did Sergei touch me directly on my…you know. Or my breasts.

I'd thought something was wrong with me. Paul and I had been having sex since I turned sixteen, and not once had I had an orgasm. Don't get me wrong, I enjoyed what we did and thought that once or twice it would happen for me. But then Paul would come, and I, well, I didn't. I tried to talk to him about it once, but he got angry. He said it wasn't his fault that I was too prudish to enjoy it fully, and he refused when I asked if we could try a vibrator. Now I was lying here sated after having what I considered a fabulous orgasm, with my tights on.

I giggled at the absurdity. The giggle turned into a belly laugh, one that I couldn't seem to stop, and the look of sheer confusion on Sergei's face wasn't helping.

"What is so funny, Holly?"

"I…" Trying to get the words out made me howl with laughter, and luckily, Sergei didn't seem annoyed.

"Let me in on the joke, my love. It seems unfair not to share something that is causing so much mirth," he mused while nuzzling my ear.

The lazy kisses he trailed down my neck helped calm the laughter, and when he finally looked into my eyes, I blurted out, "That's never happened to me before."

Sergei once again looked confused as he stared down at me.

"What has never happened to you before? Explain your words, *angel moy*."

I could feel myself blushing profusely as embarrassment filled me.

"I've never had…you know. And with my clothes on, too," I told him, avoiding eye contact.

Sergei lifted my chin to make me look at him.

"Are you saying you are a virgin?" he asked, his eyebrows raised.

"No, I've had sex—just not one of those."

I saw the moment he figured out what I meant because surprise, then what appeared to be disgust, clouded his features.

"So your boyfriend neglected you in this way, then sought out another female? It makes me extremely angry that you were treated so poorly. He is a selfish and despicable human, and if I ever meet him, he will regret the day he ever laid eyes on you."

Sergei seemed to growl before moving position and distancing himself from me, breathing harshly.

I sat up quickly, the sudden movement making me dizzy.

"I'm well rid of him, Sergei, I know that. He was my first, and I had nothing to compare him to. I'd thought it was me, you know. Like I had a problem. Because I never could…on my own, I mean. God, this is so embarrassing. Why am I telling you all this?"

I stood and adjusted my skirt before turning away from him, but his arms wrapped around me from behind as he said in a throaty voice, "I want to know everything about you, *angel moy*, so I'm glad you are sharing this with me. Rest assured, I am a very generous lover, and your needs will *always* be met above my own, sexually and otherwise."

"Is that what you are now? My lover?"

"If you will have me, Holly, I want to be everything for you," he said as he turned me to face him, his arms still wrapped around me.

"So you want to be my boyfriend or something?"

"For now, yes, I want to be your boyfriend. Are you okay with that?"

"I suppose. It's just a bit sudden, that's all. And I'm not sure what you see in me," I told him honestly.

"I see my future, Holly. And it makes me happy."

After both of us trying yet failing to carry on with more paperwork, we decided to break for lunch.

Sergei made a phone call to his friend Gregor, asking where to go for an intimate lunch date. Then we got in his

Lexus and drove to an Italian restaurant in Rothley that I've always wanted to go to but could never afford.

Truth be told, I was glad to be out in public with him; being alone in his flat was way too tempting. I wanted to kiss him again, and I felt we needed to distance ourselves from that. I'd only met him three days ago, and now he was my boyfriend. Which was laughable, really, because apart from his grin and the twinkle in his eyes, there's nothing boyish about him.

He's tall and muscular, although not overly so. But the difference between being held by him and held by my ex-boyfriend was vast, and something I was desperate to feel again.

All the way to the restaurant, Sergei rubbed the back of his fingers against the outside of my thigh and took my hand in his whenever he was able. He held my hand again when they guided us to our table, and then he pulled out my chair for me, kissing my cheek when I sat down.

I tried to concentrate on reading the menu, but I found myself watching him instead, blushing when he noticed and smiled at me.

I ordered carbonara, as did Sergei, and they brought us olives and garlic bread while we waited for it to arrive. Sergei's friend had recommended a particular wine for us to have with our chosen dish, and I was thoroughly enjoying it.

I rarely drank alcohol, but I didn't want to appear unfamiliar with having the odd glass of wine with a meal. Sergei told me he wasn't normally a wine drinker. He said his drink of choice was vodka, although Old Joe told him that vodka was a woman's drink and had been trying to get him to have a beer instead.

When he asked me what my favourite tipple was, it felt silly to say I normally only had lemonade or a Coke, so I told him brandy. Gran used to give me brandy in hot water for period pain or bellyache, but it was only ever the cheap stuff from Mr Singh's. I wouldn't know a fine brandy unless they labelled it as such—even after working in a hotel.

During our meal, which was even more delicious than I'd expected, I asked him about his childhood and where he grew up. It shocked me to learn that he'd lived in an orphanage in Romania until he was fifteen.

He told me that his father had been a soldier and had met his mother when fighting in Romania. Sadly, both his parents had died during the conflict while Sergei was still a baby, so they'd placed him in an orphanage. I asked him why it had taken so long for his grandfather to find him, but he'd been more than a little evasive and told me there'd been extenuating circumstances.

I could understand his evasiveness. I was the same with events from my past that I didn't want to retell. But Sergei became animated when he told me about his home in St Petersburg and the apartment he kept in a hotel in Moscow. He said that once we'd visited the orphanage, we could fly out to St Petersburg with Matty and see the sights—weather permitting.

I asked him about his grandparents and how long they'd been gone. He told me about his grandfather's movie obsession and how he'd loved to dance the night away with his grandmother. They'd both been fond of animals, and his grandmother often rescued and rehabilitated wildlife—hedgehogs and birds in particular. Sergei said he'd never met anyone who had a bad word to say about the fun-loving couple, and he'd been blessed to have them in his life. He told me they'd been killed in an explosion when some type of rocket grenade hit their car nearly fifteen years ago. They'd been visiting a Petrov Energy site in a supposed safe zone just outside of Chechnya when their convoy was attacked.

I told him how sorry I was that they'd passed away, and in such terrible circumstances. I also said how difficult it must have been for him—losing them so soon after he'd got to know them. He must have only been in his early twenties when they died. Sergei smiled and said he'd known them for many more years than I imagined and still felt they were with him now, if only in spirit.

It looked like he was about to carry on telling me about his life, but he seemed to think better of it as his eyes scanned the restaurant, then came back to rest on me.

Sensing his restlessness, I declined the offer of dessert, suggesting we make our way to mine to collect some clothes before calling to pick up Matty from Aunt Moira's. Sergei agreed, and once the bill was paid, we made our way back to Barrowfield.

Once again, Sergei held my hand wherever possible. I enjoyed the feeling and missed it when he took it away to aid his driving. He was about to place his hand in mine again, but a vehicle came speeding towards us at a crossroads outside the village.

"Ty che, blyad?" Sergei yelled as he swerved his Lexus out of the way. It was a close call that had me gripping the door handle and breathing heavily.

"Are you all right, Holly?" he asked when we came to a stop at the side of the road.

"Yes, I'm fine. Bloody Darren Crossley! He'll end up killing someone one of these days."

I looked out of the window behind me, but the speeding car had long since gone.

"You know that idiot?" Sergei questioned.

"He went to my school, but he's about four years older

than me. He causes so much trouble in this village with his vandalism and thieving. Now he's got that car, and he and his cronies are tearing through the village like they're on a racetrack. He's probably high, too."

"Hasn't anyone reported him to the police?"

"They don't seem to do anything. If someone reports him, either one of his gang or his family will say he didn't do it, and he was with them the whole time. We haven't got CCTV in Barrowfield, so no video evidence to dispute any alibi they provide him with."

It made me so angry that he could get away with what he did. It was a waste of time calling the police, but what else could people do?

Neither of us spoke during the rest of our journey. We were both pretty shaken due to the near miss.

Within seconds of us pulling up outside the gate, Sergei was helping me out of the vehicle. He had a thing about opening doors for me and could move pretty quickly to do so.

"You don't have to come in with me, Sergei. I'll grab a few things for tonight and get the rest tomorrow when the repairman comes. Anyway, it's probably warmer out here today than in there."

"I will come and help you. If it is as cold as you say, then the sooner we are in and out of there, the better."

The determination in his handsome face told me there was no point arguing with him. So I shrugged my shoulders, took the key out of my bag, and made my way to the front door.

As always, the cold stillness inside the hallway hit me hard. I hadn't been aware before the boiler broke how icy cold it could get inside an unheated property. Gran used to tell me stories about life without central heating and having to use an outside toilet, but I could never really imagine how hard life must have been. I turned to Sergei to apologise for the cold and found him glaring daggers at me.

"Sergei, what's wrong?"

He slammed the door behind him and pushed me up against the wall, pinning my arms by my sides. A frisson of fear ran through me when I looked up at his face.

"You let me bring you back here yesterday—to a home where you can see your breath in front of your face. Never again will you keep secrets from me, *angel moy*. I will not have it. I want to know everything there is to know from now on. I need to ensure that you are safe and well." His expression changed from stern to regret, and he shook his head. "Matty did not want to come back here. I could have taken you both back to my flat and kept you warm. I should have—"

"Let go of me, Sergei," I commanded, trying to sound less worried than I was.

"No. Not until you promise never to keep secrets from me again."

"What the hell? I only met you a few days ago; who are you to demand things from me?"

"I am yours, Holly. As you are mine. We agreed on this."

"This is madness. You were being so sweet, and now this…" I pushed my arms against his solid grip, showing him I took objection to his manhandling. Instead of him letting me go, he moved closer, pressing against me.

"Do not fear me, *angel moy*, but do not underestimate my need to keep you safe and well. You and Matty could have caught a chill living like this. You do not feel sick, do you?"

He let go of one of my hands and placed his palm against my forehead. I knocked it away and tried once more to shove him off me. I couldn't move him one inch. It was like pushing against a brick wall.

"I could not bear to lose you, *angel moy*. Not when I have only just found you. Not ever, in fact. That car was driving straight at us. It could have hit us head-on. Now here, it is so cold. You and your brother could have become sick or worse. I need to know that you are safe and well. If that is so, then I will relax; just now, I cannot."

His expressive brown eyes and desperate look seemed to reinforce the words he'd just spoken. As bizarre as it sounded for those words to come from someone who I'd only recently met, I knew he meant every one of them.

I cupped his face with my free hand, and he closed his eyes. The tension left him as he took a deep breath. I wanted to kiss him. My breathing quickened, and I wet my lips in anticipation of them meeting his. But instead of our lips coming together in a passionate kiss, it was his forehead that rested against my own as he sighed and whispered, "*YA ne znal, chto budet chuvstvovat' sebya, kak eto.*"

Chapter Nine

Sergei

YA ne znal, chto budet chuvstvovat' sebya, kak eto—I didn't know it would feel like this. I whispered those Russian words while pressing against her. But it wasn't the exquisite feeling of her body touching mine I was talking about. No. It was the emotional bond that was forming. The moment that car nearly hit us, I panicked—feeling an overwhelming need to keep this woman safe from harm. Then, when I walked into this hallway and saw my breath in front of my face like fog, worry and doubt took over in my head. Worry that something would take my angel away from me, and doubt that she would accept my protection willingly.

I knew I'd scared her when I gripped her arms and held her against the wall, and that didn't sit well with me. I would never physically hurt my Holly, but for a short time, she feared me. Then something changed within her. I heard the hitch in her breath and saw her eyes fix on my mouth. When she licked her lips, my feelings changed completely. I wanted to be inside her body in every way possible, needed to claim her as mine by Bonding so I could sense when she needed me without words. I hungered for the taste of her blood and the heat between her thighs.

My vision clouded with a red haze as my vampire side emerged, so I stepped away from Holly and suggested we get her and Matty's things together and head back to my warm flat.

Holly led me through a small kitchen and then opened the door to a large room with a dining table at one end and a sofa, TV and coffee table at the other end. There were also two single mattresses with bedding on the carpeted floor. The room was pleasantly warm because Holly had left the gas fire on low to dry a pair of Matty's pyjamas and a sheet. They were draped over a clothes airer in front of the fire.

"Sorry about the beds and everything, but it was too cold to stay upstairs."

"Do not apologise for doing your best to cope with a difficult situation, Holly. But regarding the mattresses, I can put them back upstairs while I am here. You won't be needing them down here again."

"Hopefully not, anyway. As long as the repairman can fix the boiler."

I said nothing, thinking Holly might take exception if I told her they'd be living with me from now on. I couldn't force her to stay with me. Well, technically, that is a lie. I could use mind control to keep her with me. But that would be unethical, and I wanted Holly to be with me of her own free will. It is frowned upon in our circles to use mind control on the one you are destined to Bond with—unless it's to keep them safe or save them from unnecessary suffering. I hope I never have to do that. My angel has experienced enough suffering in her life.

We took off our jackets and footwear and set to work. Holly gathered up and folded the bedding before taking it upstairs. I followed behind with each of the mattresses, one after the other.

Matty's room was tiny and could only fit a bed and drawers in. The walls were pale blue, a stark contrast to the vibrant, green-coloured Knights of Dellot bedding. I suggested to Holly that we take his duvet and pillowcase with the knights on so he'd have something familiar with him. Holly agreed but declined to take any of the toys he had in his room. She said he rarely played with them since he became obsessed with his sticker book.

Holly's room was a pale duck egg blue and had matching curtains, bedding, and fluffy cushions. Once again, her room was quite small, although it housed a large white wardrobe and a chest of drawers. I glanced around her room while she straightened her duvet and added a white throw across the bottom.

She had quite a few photo frames on the walls, some with photographs of her grandmother and Matty; others were photographs of Holly and her school friends. I knew from the CV she supplied me with yesterday that she went to the secondary school in Rothley. The navy-blue blazer and school uniform suited her, and the radiant smile she wore in each photograph made me smile, too. I wanted to see that same smile on my angel's face every day, forever.

"That one was taken a week before we left school. The tall girl with brown hair is Gemma, and the one next to me is Marie. They've been my best friends since nursery school, and I miss them so much. Gemma's at Leeds University, and Marie's studying in York. Neither of them could make

Gran's funeral because of their exams, but they'll be home next weekend and will come to church to light a candle and lay flowers for her then."

Some of the multiple frames had gaps where photographs should have been, so I asked her about them.

"I took all the photographs of my ex-boyfriend out of them. I don't want any reminders."

"I can understand that," I told her, watching her expression to see if it revealed any emotion that would let me know if she still had feelings for him. But she either felt unbothered by the break-up or schooled her features well.

I heard the footsteps of someone descending the path outside before the doorbell rang. Holly went to the window and almost groaned the words, "Speak of the Devil."

"Who is it?" I asked as she shook her head.

"It's him, Paul, my ex. He must have the weekend off because he came to the house last night. Matty and I were watching TV in the dark, so we pretended we weren't in, and he went away."

The doorbell rang again, followed by a loud knocking on the window.

"Holly, I know you're in there. I just want to talk. Open the door, please."

The pathetic excuse for a man was on his knees, shouting through the letterbox, grovelling for my woman's attention. Would she give it?

"Why won't he go away? I've told him repeatedly that I'll never forgive what he did. Why can't he accept that?" Holly grumbled.

"I will make sure he accepts it," I muttered, making my way through the bedroom door, fists clenched at the ready. I wanted to do this man harm. He had hurt my angel, so it was only right that he suffered at my hands.

"No, wait, Sergei, please. Don't fight with him."

"Why not? Do you still want him?"

"No, of course not. But you don't have to go swinging your fists around on my behalf, and I don't want a commotion for all the neighbours to see."

"You do not wish to see him, Holly, and I do not want him near you. What do you suggest?" My tone showed my anger and possibly the jealousy racing through my system.

"Sergei, I don't have feelings for him. I'd have never agreed to be with you if I had."

Damn! This woman could read me so well. Before I could voice my need to see this man hurt, Holly began removing her sweater.

"I have an idea how to get rid of him. Will you help me and promise not to hit him while I put my plan into action?"

She removed the black skirt and tights she wore while I nodded in a daze. I heard her words, but their meaning took longer to penetrate my brain as I watched her undress. I stood there mute while Holly grabbed the white throw off the bottom of her bed and wrapped it around herself.

"Take your sweater off, Sergei, and follow me down after a minute or so. You could ask me to come back to bed or something along those lines. Let him know I've moved on. Then hopefully, he'll take the hint."

I watched as she slipped the bra straps off her shoulders and tucked them into the throw, making it appear as though she wore nothing underneath. She ruffled her hair to make it look messy and then made her way downstairs.

I removed my sweater as requested and listened as she opened the door.

"Holly, I've missed you. Can I come in? We need to talk."

"What about?" Holly asked with an air of indifference.

"Us, our relationship. Where we go from here. You wouldn't answer my calls or texts, and I wanted to check you were okay after everything that's happened," he told her, a hint of desperation in his voice.

"There is no *us*, Paul; we have no relationship. And please don't worry, my boyfriend's been so supportive. He's helping me through this difficult time."

"What? *I'm* your boyfriend, Holly! We've been together too long for you to throw it all away, so you can cut the crap. I know you only said that to make me jealous."

Arrogant bastard. I fought through my need to bury my fist in his face and instead took off my jeans and socks. Fuck! It was too cold in this house to be walking around in our underwear. I descended the stairs, and Holly opened the door a little wider for him to see.

"Who the fuck is that?" yelled the lanky, blond fool.

"This is Sergei, my boyfriend," replied Holly as she turned to look at me. Her mouth fell open when she took in my near-naked appearance. I wore black jersey boxer shorts and nothing else. Walking up to her, I gave her a quick, loud kiss on the lips before spinning her around, her back to my front.

"I thought you were going to get rid of the visitor and come back to bed, *angel moy*," I remarked while kissing down her neck and shoulders.

I looked up to see him take a step back before finally taking in Holly's dishevelled, *just jumped out of bed,* appearance.

"No," he said, taking another step back and becoming paler by the minute.

"As you can see, I'm busy at the moment," Holly informed him in a quiet, breathy voice.

I carried on kissing along her neck and shoulders, running a hand down the front of her body, stopping as it reached the top of where her mound lay hidden. Holly shivered, and I knew it wasn't only from the biting cold.

Her ex was staring at us, and in particular, at where my hand was resting.

"What the fuck, Holly? How could you do this? We were supposed to be getting engaged. Were you seeing this guy all along? Or is this a way to get back at me?" he shouted, glaring at her angrily.

"I suggest you leave right now and never bother my angel again," I told him, trying to remain calm for Holly's sake.

"Your angel? Are you for fucking real? We've been split up less than a month, and she's already shagging someone else. That makes her a whore, not an angel."

In less than two seconds, I was in front of him with a hand around his neck, lifting him up in the air. I was taller than him, much broader, and more muscular. I could have just intimidated the insolent fool with a few well-chosen threats, but his words had riled my vampire side, and it wanted—no—needed to see him hurt.

"How dare you call my woman a whore? You will suffer for your behaviour and lack of respect."

I wanted to bare my fangs and let my eyes take on their crimson rim, but I hadn't told Holly about my vampire side yet, and I didn't want to risk exposure.

She grabbed the hand I had wrapped around his throat and yelled my name, begging me to let him go. So I did. He dropped to the ground in a crumpled heap, struggling to get his breath. Holly sank down beside him, checking him over. Why? He didn't deserve her attention.

I grabbed his arm and pulled him into a standing position.

Looking him in the eyes, I told him, "You will leave now and forget about what happened here today. You understand Holly has moved on and has found someone to spend the rest of her life with. Someone who will love and respect her forever. You know she is more than deserving of this, and you are happy for her. Now go. And do not bother my Holly again."

His heart rate became steady as the mind control made him forget I'd almost choked the life out of him.

I let go of his arm, and after two more steadying breaths, he turned and walked up the path.

"Paul," Holly called out. He spun around and smiled at her.

"Bye, Holly," was all he said before continuing his journey up the road.

I turned to Holly and touched her shoulder. She shrank away from me and said, "Don't."

Holly stepped past me into the house and ran upstairs. Shaking my head, I closed the front door and locked it before following her.

I was confused—unsure why she would care about the well-being of someone who had cheated on her. Maybe that was a human trait? Compassion and tolerance even in the face of betrayal? I found that unacceptable, but if it was something that my Holly valued…

No! I could not change who I was in that respect. Sergei Petrov does not have the patience and social conscience to deal with men like that.

Chapter Ten

Holly

I hid out in the bathroom for a few minutes while I gathered my thoughts. What the hell had just happened down there?

One minute Sergei was touching me and kissing my neck and shoulders, making me throb in some very intimate places—the next, he had Paul by the neck, his feet kicking furiously in mid-air. Paul's face had gone from bright red to shades of burgundy the longer he was deprived of oxygen.

Sergei's strength was frightening. Paul was almost as tall as him, though not as built, yet Sergei had lifted Paul off the ground as if he weighed less than a bag of sugar.

Was Sergei a weightlifter in his spare time?

He certainly had muscle. When he walked downstairs in nothing but his boxers, he'd taken my breath away. He had the kind of body you see on an Olympic swimmer, with muscular arms and shoulders and real-life actual abs. It was like looking at the cover of one of Aunt Moira's romance novels. Only this guy and his abs were here, in my home, probably in my bedroom right now. Which would have been perfect if he hadn't just nearly strangled my ex.

What was I going to say to him? I wasn't sure someone who could turn so violent so quickly was safe for Matty and me to be around.

Sergei had shown me nothing but kindness in the last few days, and yet...I don't know. Something was off about the whole situation. The way he insisted I was his and he was mine. Even outside in front of Paul, Sergei said I had someone who was going to love and respect me forever.

Meaning him.

A man I'd only met three days ago!

"Deep breath, Holly. Go out there and be brave. Tell him it's best that you and Matty stay here," I told myself. But all that bravery fled when I opened the bathroom door and saw him and his abs in the doorway to my bedroom. His arm and shoulder muscles flexed as he gripped the top of the doorframe.

"You fear me, *angel moy?* My reaction to your ex-boyfriend calling you a whore did not sit well with you, and you are upset. Am I right?"

"Yes, I was frightened," I admitted.

Sergei nodded, then asked, "Were you being truthful when you told me you had no love for him?"

"What? Of course I was being truthful."

"But you wanted to offer him comfort when I let him go."

"I wanted to make sure he wasn't dying," I argued.

"I hardly touched him," he protested.

"Sergei, you were starving him of oxygen. He could go to the police; they could charge you with grievous bodily harm or something."

"He won't be visiting the police; I can guarantee you that," he said with a smirk.

"How the hell do you know? He could have phoned them. They could be here soon to take you away."

"I told him not to do that, and he seemed happy when he left, did he not?"

"He…he could have been putting it on to save face and get away," I replied, but the images I was replaying in my mind were confusing. I'd watched Paul's angry, scared demeanour change with Sergei's words, which were delivered like an order or command. The entire scene played over and over as if on a loop, and with each replay, it still made very little sense.

I looked up to find Sergei in front of me. He backed me up against the cold wall and slipped his hand through the hair at the back of my head. His brown eyes were so expressive and told of a softness that the current hard set of his jawline contradicted.

"Holly, he called you a whore. It is a derogatory term that sickens me. It is so often used by men against women who are doing nothing wrong. Would it have mattered if you had split up with him and had sex with someone the day after? No! Even if you have sex with different men every week, it's still nobody's business but yours, and you should not be judged by him especially. There should be no such label placed upon a woman who does the same as most single men would—given the opportunity. And yet, more often than not, men, and also some narrow-minded women, feel it is their right and duty to exert their bigoted morals and attitudes this way. I hate the word and the reason it is used. Of all words, it is one that most of all highlights the inequality in how men and women are treated.

"I will always defend you, Holly. You and Matty. Whether I do that because of petty name-calling or physical danger, the outcome will be the same. No one gets to hurt what is mine, and you and Matty are mine. Mine to defend, mine to care for, mine to love."

I opened my mouth to object, but he silenced me with a kiss. I didn't struggle against him. It would've been pointless, I knew that much. And besides, I wanted this kiss. I welcomed the hardness of his body when he pressed against me. The cold wall had been a shock to my skin when it touched my back and shoulders, but with every second of his kiss, my body heated further, negating the coldness of the surface.

The way his tongue moved against my own and his free hand skimmed up the inside of my thigh only stirred the irrational need I was developing for this man.

I shouldn't feel like this. So wanton and needy, desperate for anything he could give as long as I experienced the same exquisite feelings I did earlier. I just didn't care.

When he reached the top of my thigh and began tracing the front of my now damp knickers, I hitched in a breath and broke the kiss. Pulling away from me slightly, he held my gaze while working his way inside my underwear, running his fingers up the hot cleft, putting pressure against my clit. I moaned and closed my eyes, so he tugged on my hair, making me open them again.

Sergei slid his fingers down to my entrance and pushed two inside. Instinctively, I opened my legs a little wider to aid his efforts. I was rewarded with a slight nod of his head and the barest hint of a smile. He curved his fingers at the same time as his thumb breached my slit and found my clit. The dual stimulation made me cry out and rock into his hand, finding a rhythm that created the deepest pleasure within my core and throughout my body. My hardened nipples chafed against the lace of my bra and more wetness left me, coating his fingers as he moved them inside me;

creating sounds that would be embarrassing if I could feel anything other than pure, unadulterated bliss.

He used more pressure on my clit, then licked his lips and I felt it. The orgasm building with a rapid, pulsing wave that crested at my sex and flowed to every part of my body in a heated rush. I may have screamed, my fingers digging into his back so hard I'd probably drawn blood. And all this time, his eyes never left mine. It was intense and overwhelming, yet I wanted more.

Sergei slowed the movement of his fingers inside me yet increased the pressure of his thumb rubbing against my clit, and I rocked against him again. Just when my body began heading for another orgasm, he pulled his hand away completely.

"No!" I cried out, panting hard.

Sergei pressed his lips against my ear and whispered, "Sshh," then he placed both hands underneath my bottom and lifted me. I wrapped my legs around his waist and he carried me to my bed.

After standing me at the side of my bed, he pulled back the duvet, removed the throw that was still tucked around me, then made quick work of stripping me of my underwear. My body gave an involuntary shiver, which made him frown. Without saying anything, he lifted me up and laid me down on the bed. The sheets were cold, as was everything else in this house, but the anticipation of what was to come next made me ignore it. However, when Sergei removed his boxers and fisted his huge, weeping erection in his hand, I started to protest.

Before I could utter a full word, Sergei placed a finger against my lips and once again whispered, "*Sshh.*"

But I was nervous. I'd only ever seen a man who was that well-endowed in a porn film Paul had made me watch.

Paul convinced me that the size had been a camera trick; seeing Sergei's huge length and thick girth made me re-think that.

It slapped against his belly button when he climbed in bed beside me, and I scooted away from it, as far as my single bed would allow. Instead of trying to reassure me, Sergei pulled me towards him and kissed me once again. He rolled me onto my back and lay above me, rocking his erection against my clit. After a few seconds, he tore his mouth away from mine, and this time it was he who was panting. It thrilled me to learn that this was affecting Sergei as much as it was me.

He kissed a path down my neck, around my collarbone and down to my chest, licking and sucking on the full globes but avoiding my nipples. I became more brazen and fisted my hands in his hair, trying to force his mouth towards the needy nubs, but he wouldn't be swayed from his oral assault.

When I finally gave up trying to move him where I needed him, he let out a hoarse chuckle, then fixed his mouth over my left nipple and sucked hard. I cried out and tried to rock my core against him, desperate to come once again. He went from one nipple to the other, sucking and biting, bringing me to the edge again before sliding further down my body.

Sergei kissed me from hip bone to hip bone as he parted my thighs. The heavy throb in my sex and knowledge of what was to come made my legs tremble. Sergei placed his hands on the insides of my thighs, stilling the movement. He used his thumbs to part my sex and thrust his tongue inside repeatedly. I cried out in high-pitched gasps and gripped his hair tightly, keeping his head in place. He moved his tongue to my clit and began licking and sucking at the sensitive bud. I rocked against his face, crying out, "*yes, yes, yes,*" over and over again until he fixed his lips around my throbbing clit, flicking it repeatedly with his tongue. The hard, rapid flicks sent me spiralling into a powerful orgasm, and for a moment, I lost all sense of awareness.

Everything seemed to hit me at once when I finally came down from what seemed like heaven. The icy chill in the room, the feeling of utter bliss that reached every nerve ending, and Sergei placing gentle kisses all the way up my body.

I could taste myself on him when he kissed my mouth, and it only added to the need that was building within me. I wanted him inside me. I didn't care how big he was anymore, and I didn't even care if it hurt me—I just needed to feel him moving within my body. The whole experience had been a near-silent one apart from my moans and screams, which only added to the eroticism of the encounter.

Sergei looked me in the eye once again as he placed his cock at my opening and pushed inside. I maintained eye contact, even though I wanted to throw my head back and shout his name. The feeling of his huge length filling me for the first time is something I will never forget. Stretched and impossibly full, the little bite of pain only added to the plea-sure. Sergei bottomed out inside me, making a breathless groaning noise, and I swear it was the sexiest sound I'd ever heard.

He took my mouth in a kiss so thrilling it caused more wetness to gather around his cock. Then he moved inside me, gently at first, but when I raised my hips to meet his thrust head-on, all that changed.

The rhythm of our coupling was like a perfectly timed drumbeat, hitting just the right spot with the right amount of pressure that almost had me coming. It was like Sergei knew this somehow and changed the tempo slightly, pressing against me more firmly and for a second longer each time he filled me. The orgasm hit me hard, shooting through my core, taking over my mind, body and soul. I cried out Sergei's name over and over, and his movements became harder and faster as he chased his own release. Wrapping my legs high around his waist, I pulled him down for a kiss. When he came, he threw his head back and yelled something in Russian. I wasn't sure what the words meant, but when he looked down at me, I could see the adoration in his eyes, and at that moment, I felt more loved and cherished than I ever had in all the years I'd spent with Paul.

A sudden thought occurred to me, and I panicked.

"Sergei, we didn't use protection. Oh God, I can't believe I let this happen. After all the worry I went through before, I never thought I'd be this stupid."

I was horrified. I placed my hands on his chest to push him away, but he wouldn't be moved.

"You have nothing to worry about, *angel moy*. I carry no diseases, and I cannot get you pregnant. Not yet anyway. Trust me when I say your health and safety are of great concern to me. I would never put you at risk of anything that could harm you. I will spend my life making you feel happy, loved and protected, both you and Matty. Now relax, my love, and let me become lost in your kiss once again."

I had so many questions about what he'd just said, but when his lips met mine, I forgot what I wanted to ask.

We kissed for what seemed like forever, and I could feel Sergei's length pulsing inside me as it maintained its solidity.

I needed to get up and use the bathroom. I could already feel the evidence of our combined release on the sheets below me, and I needed to pee. But Sergei's kisses were drugging, and when he rocked inside me slowly, I was lost to anything and everything that wasn't him and me.

He made love to me gently, caressing every inch of me he could reach without faltering his movements. I don't know if it was because I was so sensitive down there after everything we'd done or if it was the skill of the man above me that made my orgasm happen so quickly, but within less than a minute, I was gasping out his name. His teeth grazed my neck when he came, and he groaned loudly against my pulse point.

When our breathing had steadied, he whispered in my ear, "Thank you, my beautiful angel."

His voice sounded strange like he had something in his mouth. When I tried to turn his face to see him, he wouldn't let me.

"What's wrong?" I asked with concern.

After a few deep breaths, Sergei looked down at me and smiled.

"Nothing is wrong, my love, but I fear that if we do not get up now, I will keep you in this bed until tomorrow. We should pick up your brother and get you settled in my flat before I leave for work. As much as I would love to stay with you both tonight, we are unusually short-staffed, and Sunday is a busy night in the warehouse. We need to make sure that the order invoices are correct before they get picked up, and there is only Maggie and me to do that tonight."

Sergei laughed, and I looked up at him, confused.

"Why are you laughing?"

"I was trying to think of ways to overcome my need to take you again, and talking about work has done the trick," he said while pulling out of my body and then getting out of bed.

Sergei stood there in all his naked glory. His cock still looked semi-hard to me. Or was it just that big even when soft? My eyes trailed upwards, taking in the rest of him. Those bloody abs were a turn-on even after all we'd just done. The way they tapered down to a V-shape between his hip bones made me want to trace my tongue all over him.

"Holly, we can talk about work all afternoon, but if you keep looking at me like that, I can't promise I'll keep Little Sergei asleep for long." He chuckled at my groan as I pulled my duvet up over my head in embarrassment.

"Come on, *angel moy*, do not be shy. You can look at any part of me whenever you want. I am yours, after all."

He pulled back the duvet and handed me the throw I'd worn earlier. I wrapped it around my body and made my way to the bathroom, with Sergei following behind.

"Where are you going?" I asked.

"I assume this is the bathroom?"

"Well, yes, but *I* need to go first," I told him while dashing inside and closing the door.

I sat down to pee and winced at the burning pain that way too much activity down there had caused. I needed to soak in a hot bath, but that would have to wait until I got to Sergei's. No way was I risking anything other than a quick wipe around with the cold water here.

Sergei was waiting outside the bathroom door, wearing his sweater and nothing else. We didn't say anything as he passed by me when I came out, and he didn't even close the door behind him.

I heard Sergei switch on the taps as I got to my bedroom. He was humming a catchy jingle from a local radio ad, totally at ease. Opening my drawers, I took out clean underwear, deciding to forgo the skirt and tights for the warmth of jogging bottoms and a fleece sweatshirt. I was about to put on my socks when I heard Sergei yell, "Fuck, shit, cold, fuck, argh!"

I dashed into the bathroom to find him with a towel wrapped around his hips.

"I did not mean to startle you, Holly, but I forgot there's no hot water, and I gave myself quite a shock. Now I can safely state that Little Sergei is well hidden and will not want to come out to play again for some time," he said with a shiver.

I laughed so hard and couldn't seem to stop. He didn't make it any easier for me when he opened the towel and said, "Little Sergei, the woman we have chosen to spend our life with is making fun of us; she is not the angel we thought she was."

He shook his head and walked back to the bedroom, tutting and offering comforting words to Little Sergei as he went. After wiping the tears from my eyes, I went back to the bedroom to find him fully dressed and stripping the sheets from my bed.

"These will need a wash, so I thought we could take them to my flat to do them. There's a dryer, too, so we can bring anything you have of Matty's that hasn't yet dried— and any other things you would like to wash."

"Thank you, Sergei. That's very thoughtful of you."

I took down a holdall from the top of my wardrobe and placed the bedding inside, along with towels and a few items of clothing from the laundry basket in the bathroom.

After gathering nightclothes and Matty's school uniform, I bundled some clean clothes together for myself and followed Sergei downstairs. Standing in front of the gas fire in the front room helped chase the chill away for a couple of minutes before I turned it off and headed for the kitchen.

"What are you doing?" Sergei asked.

"Collecting something for supper," I told him as I got out the peanut butter, bread, and the last few pieces of fruit.

"I have food in my flat, Holly, and we can stop off at the shop for anything we don't have. I want you to treat my flat as your home from now on. What's mine is yours. Although you can take the peanut butter. I thought about buying some after you mentioned it yesterday." He patted me on the shoulder and popped the peanut butter inside his jacket pocket.

I took one last look around my gran's hallway before turning to lock the door. Her padded rain jacket was hanging on the last coat hook, and I gathered it in my arms and hugged it. It smelled of Gran, her perfume, and the strawberry bonbons she always carried in her pockets.

"Holly, it is turning even colder now the evening is drawing in. We should collect Matty while it's still light out."

Sergei put an arm around me and guided me to the door. As it closed behind me and I placed the key in the lock, a strange feeling came over me—almost like I was saying goodbye to this home and my life here. I swallowed past the lump in my throat and continued to lock the door. With tears in my eyes, I took Sergei's hand and let him lead me to his Lexus.

It was only a short drive to Aunt Moira's. Even though we added five minutes onto the journey when Sergei called at the local shop, my eyes were still red and puffy. I worried Matty would notice I'd been crying again, so I took out a clean tissue and wiped my eyes before blowing my nose. I asked Sergei to wait a few minutes before we got out so I could compose myself.

"Come here, *angel moy*," he commanded, unclipping my seat belt and tugging my upper body across to him.

I thought he'd continue to wipe my eyes and make me presentable. Instead, his lips began a slow, gentle caress from my mouth to my throat, hovering over my pulse point. When his lips met mine again, the kiss became heated, making my heart race and my sex throb. I couldn't believe how turned on I was from kissing alone, but my body responded to Sergei just from looking at him, so it should be no surprise that I'd want him again so soon.

"I need to be inside you again, my love," Sergei whispered between kisses. "Tell me you feel the way I feel right now."

"I do. But this can't be right, Sergei. It's not even been thirty minutes yet."

Sergei chuckled against my throat. "Oh, my love, this is only the beginning. When you are fully mine, the need we feel will only intensify. And I cannot wait for that day to come."

He pulled away from me suddenly and looked over my shoulder.

"It appears we have an audience, *angel moy*," Sergei said with a smirk and a little wave to whoever was looking.

I turned to see Matty and Jamie—Aunt Moira's grandson—swinging on the gate while they peered inside the Lexus.

"Oh shit, did they see all that? What am I going to say to him?" I hadn't thought about what I'd tell Matty. This was still new to me, after all.

"You can tell him the truth: that I am your boyfriend."

"But he knows I've only just met you. He thinks you're just my boss. I don't want to confuse him."

"Holly, sometimes children see and understand more truths than we give them credit for. He will see that I care for you very much. Trust me on this. And don't worry, seeing your kiss-swollen lips and that enamoured look in your eyes is much better than him seeing your tears."

He grinned at me and winked. Is that why he'd started kissing me? Did he do it to take away the sad, tear-filled look I'd had earlier?

We got out of the vehicle to a barrage of lip-smacking kissing sounds from Jamie. Although Matty laughed along with him, I could see he was desperate to ask questions. I was about to say something when Sergei beat me to it.

"Hello, Matty, and hello to who I assume must be Jamie," Sergei said, nodding towards them.

"Matty, your sister told me about the heating breaking down at your home, so I said you could both stay at my flat until it is fixed. She has agreed to be my girlfriend, so I thought we could celebrate and order pizza before I go to work. I also bought more Knights of Dellot stickers I thought you could help me with," he told them, taking out five packs of stickers and handing them to Matty.

"Here are some stickers for you, too, Jamie. Perhaps we will find some good ones in those packs for your books. Mr Singh has more books coming in tomorrow, and I have ordered one of those. So do not forget about swaps, you two."

After a loud chorus of *"OH WOW"* and *"THANKS"* from both Matty and Jamie, they ran inside to open up the little packets to check if they had whatever missing knights they needed.

Once we entered Aunt Moira's kitchen, Sergei became the centre of attention. Aunt Moira had a soft spot for him and was already putting cupcakes and flapjacks into a Tupperware container for us to take to his flat. Her daughter, Janine, couldn't take her eyes off him, and when he gave her that sexy grin, I swear I saw steam rising from her.

As far as they were aware, Sergei was just my boss—until Jamie yelled, "Look, I got the knight Luthor in the stickers that Holly's boyfriend got me. Luthor can spin up a whirlwind and make everything blow away."

Aunt Moira hugged Sergei, then me, and welcomed him into the family. I said she was getting ahead of herself because we'd only just got together, but she shushed me and said we made a lovely couple.

Janine pulled me in for a hug and whispered, "Lucky bitch. He's as sexy as sin. I would do him in a heartbeat." She laughed at my blush as she pulled away, then winked at me.

Sergei refused a cup of tea, telling Aunt Moira that we had to get back because he was working tonight, and he wanted to make sure that Matty and I were settled in his flat before he left.

We said our goodbyes and gathered Matty's things together, collecting pizza on our journey to Sergei's flat.

Chapter Eleven

Sergei

After giving Holly and Matty a quick tour of the flat, we sat at the dining table and ate our pizza. They'd opted to share a large pepperoni pizza while I had ordered a meat feast. I was getting to be an expert on the local takeaway options, as I rarely liked to cook for myself, but that would have to change. I had a family to take care of now. With that thought, an unstoppable grin spread across my face, prompting Holly to ask what was so funny. She quickly wiped her face, thinking my grin was because she was wearing her food, which made Matty and me laugh. Holly got up to check in the mirror, causing us to laugh even harder.

I had also ordered a large garlic bread—this pizza shop did one of the best I'd ever tasted. It was a good job that the vampire legends of old were untrue, as I love to eat garlic. Onions, too. I placed two large slices of garlic bread on

Holly's plate because I didn't want to be the only one with garlic breath tonight.

After we had eaten, I put Matty's favourite cartoon on for him, then Holly and I went to make up the bed in the spare bedroom. She'd brought the shower curtain to put under the bottom sheet, and I saw how uncomfortable it must have been for him these past few weeks. I told her we would go out tomorrow and buy something more suitable.

When we entered my bedroom to change my bedding, I took her in my arms and showered her face with garlic-flavoured kisses, which she didn't complain about. After kissing my angel into a state of high arousal, I pulled away. Her brother was down the hallway, so I knew I couldn't take this any further tonight, even though I wanted her so desperately again.

I went to a built-in cupboard and took out linen that had belonged to Chloe's aunt. It had a lilac floral pattern and was extremely feminine. Holly raised her eyebrows and stifled a grin, so I told her I was using everything that Chloe had left behind. Other than a TV and new towels, I had yet to shop for household items.

Once the cottage I was having built on Night Movers' land was completed, I would have to go shopping for all new things, but I wasn't looking forward to it. Holly offered to help, so I smiled and thanked her. I was glad she was on board with shopping for the cottage. After all, it would be her and Matty's home, too; she just didn't know that yet.

After we'd made the bed, Holly thanked me again for letting her and Matty stay. She said she couldn't wait to get a hot bath and climb into bed later. Picturing her lying naked in that hot bath wasn't doing the now semi-erect Little Sergei any favours, and as I had to leave soon, I tried to put thoughts of a nude, wet Holly out of my mind.

Holly let out a yawn, then apologised.

"Do not apologise for being tired, *angel moy*. You've had a busy day, and I particularly enjoyed our joint activity earlier."

"Sergei," she admonished.

I laughed at her blush and pulled her in for a hug. "Do you have regrets about what we did, Holly?"

"No. Although I feel a bit…" Holly sighed and looked down at the floor.

"Hey," I said, lifting her chin up so I could look into her eyes. "Tell me exactly how you feel, Holly. Do not be afraid to say something you do not think I would like to hear."

"Well, it's just… I haven't done this sort of thing before. Casual sex isn't really my thing."

"Holly, we are in a relationship. It is not casual sex if you are in a relationship. And I would never call what we did just casual. Spectacular maybe, but never casual."

"But that relationship just started today, Sergei," she protested.

"Not for me, Holly. You were mine from the moment I first saw you. I wanted to give you time—time I knew you needed because of everything that had just happened in your life. But I cannot fight the pull to be near you, to touch you, and to kiss you. I will try harder to slow things down if that's what you want, although I cannot guarantee that will happen. There have been so many times today when I've watched you concentrate on something and bite your lower lip—I wanted to bite it too, then kiss away the sting. When you give me one of your beautiful smiles, my heart beats double time in my chest. And when I touch you, even my fingers against yours, it is like an electrical power surge coursing through my body. I have never felt this way about anyone, Holly, in all my years. So I know that what we have is very special."

"You have a silver tongue, Sergei."

"Do you not believe me, *angel moy*? I will never lie to you. There is much you have to learn about me yet, but when you ask me a question, I will answer you truthfully."

"Okay, then I will do the same. You asked me a question earlier. The answer is no; I don't regret what we did. And I can't wait to do it again." Holly blushed and was about to look away, then seemed to think better of it and looked me in the eye instead.

I smiled at her, and she smiled right back at me. Grabbing her around the waist, I pulled her towards me. She squealed, then giggled when I nuzzled my face into her neck, inhaling her delicious scent.

"I must go now, my darling, but I would give anything to stay with you tonight. I need to call into the Red Lion to see someone before I go to work. You probably know Joe Potts from the village. I play cards with him at the pub. The man is ninety-four and has no family nearby, so I like to make sure he is okay."

Holly nodded. "My gran used to do a bit of shopping for him. He's a sweet old man, and his dog is getting on in years, too. I remember when she was a puppy. My grandad took me with him and Old Joe to collect her. She was so cute and fluffy, and I wanted to keep her for myself."

So, my Holly likes dogs. I'll buy her one once our cottage is ready. Of course, I would have to choose carefully so that I did not upset Boris.

"I will call you later to check on you and Matty, and if you need me for anything beforehand, just let me know. I will text you all my contact details before I leave; you can add them to your phone."

Once we'd left the bedroom, I texted Holly all the numbers she would need to get in touch with me. When I said goodbye to Matty, he jumped up from the sofa and hugged me tightly, thanking me once again for his stickers. I hugged him back, overwhelmed by the love I felt for this little boy and his beautiful sister.

Holly walked me to the door and gifted me with the sweetest kiss before I left. Halfway down the steps, I turned back to look at her. How lucky was I to have found such a wonderful woman to share my life with?

Chapter Twelve

Sergei

It was after five in the evening when I walked into the Red Lion. I noticed Yuri behind the bar, and when I walked towards him, I heard someone shout, "He'll be having a beer, Yuri, not one of them fancy drinks."

I turned to see Old Joe lifting his beer glass and winking at Yuri. Yuri smirked and poured me a half-pint of beer. I took a sip of the cool ale and wished I'd refused the drink. I much preferred vodka over this stuff or any other alcohol. But Old Joe was of the opinion that you only had whisky or brandy if you were coming down with a cold. Vodka, he said, was a woman's drink.

I called in to see him and Meg at the Red Lion before my shift at Night Movers four nights per week. He sits at the same place in the pub for an hour or two every evening, drinking a pint of beer that he shares with Meg. Joe says it keeps them both healthy, and as he's ninety-four and Meg is fifteen, who am I to argue?

He's here for the company, not for the alcohol, that is plain to see. His wife passed away twenty years ago, and his son and his family live in Kent, which is the other end of the country. So other than the friends he has at the pub and in the village, he has no one. I find that upsetting, but understand that for a human, Joe has lived a long, full life, and most of his friends have long since passed. Still, it makes me sad to think of him on his own at such a great human age.

I bent down to fuss over Meg before taking my seat at the side of Joe. Meg is a wheat-coloured, wire-haired lurcher who doesn't seem her age at all—until you look in her eyes, that is. It's clear to see that Meg is going blind in her old age, and deaf, too. Although Joe will often joke that she can hear the rustle of a crisp packet on the other side of the room. She's crossed between a Bedlington terrier and a Greyhound and stands around knee high, but just now, she lay on a fluffy pink dog bed Yuri had bought her. He adores Meg, which isn't surprising. He used to own a dog just like her about thirty years ago.

"Sit thi sen darn, young-un," Joe said in his broad York-shire accent, pushing out a chair for me.

"Thanks, Joe." It always made me chuckle when he called me young-un. I was his age over 150 years ago. Yet even though I had the longevity, Joe had known true love, had a family, and fought in wars. He truly had lived a full life. But now I had Holly and Matty in mine. My own family to love and cherish. For all I had done in my life so far, I knew that being part of a family with them would be my greatest achievement.

I took my seat and carried on stroking Meg, who'd placed her head on my knee. The smug grin I wore from my thoughts of Holly and Matty must have still been evident because Joe questioned me about it.

"What's up wi thee?" he asked. "Thas done nowt but smile since tha walked in. As tha gorra woman or summat?"

I did a brief translation in my head of what Joe asked. He wanted to know what was up with me and if I had a woman. He knew what I was doing and smiled at me. As was usual, from now on, he would rein in the accent a little more.

"Yes," I told him. "I have a woman, and she's beautiful, smart and caring. I am a lucky man."

"Well, of course she's a beauty if she's a Yorkshire lass. We've got some good-looking women 'round here. You should gerra a ring on her finger afore she gets away."

"She is much younger than me, though, Joe. She has a lot to see and do before she'll want to settle down with me."

"How do you know? Have you asked her?"

"Well, no. But she is barely nineteen, and I am…a lot older. There might be some who would object."

"So, let 'em. It's nowt to do with anyone other than you and her. Some people objected to my wife marrying me. Said because I was twenty-two years older than her, she'd regret it in years to come when she was looking after an old man. But it didn't work out that way in the end. My Janet died twenty years ago. I was seventy-four, and she was fifty-two. She had lung cancer, yet she'd never smoked a day in her life. So she wasn't left nursing an old man; it was me who did the nursing. She was so frail at the end."

Tears glistened in his tired blue eyes, so I placed my hand on the back of his and gave it a quick pat. Joe was old school and wouldn't appreciate a hug. Even a manly back-slapping hug.

"So you see, Sergei, you never know what life will bring.

And if you gerra chance at love and happiness, grab it wi both hands and never let go."

"I intend to do just that, Joe, but I must be careful. She lost her grandmother two weeks ago, so she has a lot going on in her head right now."

"Do I know this lass?" he asked.

"Yes, I saw you at her grandmother's funeral. And Holly just told me she and her grandfather went with you to pick Meg up when she was a puppy."

"So, it's young Holly that's got you smiling! It was a shock to hear what happened to Beryl. She was such a lovely woman, so kind-hearted. I'd only seen her a few hours before she died. She'd fetched me a few bits from the shop before she called in to see me. Beryl used to pop in with Matthew on the way home from school. She'd done so ever since my Janet passed away. Beryl, Janet, Moira, and Joyce at the flower shop used to play bingo three times a week at the old bingo hall in Rothley. It's not there now, of course; they made it into flats a few years ago. But they were as thick as thieves, them four.

"They were a great help when Janet got ill. Especially Beryl. It makes you wonder if there's anyone up there"—he gestured with his finger pointing upwards—"because for such a lovely woman to be taken so soon, and after all the loss she's had to deal with in her life—leaving them poor bairns with no other family… Well, it's just terrible."

"I know. Life has been cruel to them. But Holly and Matty have me now. I shall make sure they are well cared for and will want for nothing."

"You know the most precious thing that anyone can give, Sergei?"

"Yes, it is love," I answered confidently.

"No, it's not love. Although it is important. The most

precious thing you can give someone is your time. You can love someone from afar, but it won't mean very much to the other person unless you take the time to show them and make memories with them. Because soon enough, your time will be done, and memories will be all that's left. Think on that, young-un," Joe said as he lifted his glass to take a drink.

"Wise words," I told him before beckoning Yuri over. He came from behind the bar carrying a dog bowl with Meg written in bold pink letters on the side.

He knelt down next to Meg while she ate what looked like pieces of cooked chicken and liver. I shook my head and smiled at him. He was such a softy where animals were concerned, especially dogs. If it wasn't for him travelling so much with Gregor now that the cold war wasn't an issue anymore, I think Yuri would have a house full of dogs.

"Yuri, I might need you to do me a favour next weekend."

"What is it, Sergei?"

"I might need you to babysit for my girlfriend's little brother. He's seven years old, so you do not have to change nappies or anything."

"You have a girlfriend?" questioned Yuri. "Since when? And what is her name?"

"Since today, but we met a few days ago. Her name is Holly, and her brother likes to be called Matty. They are living with me at my flat because their boiler broke, and they have no heating or hot water at their home."

"I see," said Yuri, smiling. "When can I meet them? I could come around tomorrow evening. Gregor has a meeting in London in the morning, but we are flying there and back as early as possible. He does not wish to leave Chloe for long now that she is pregnant."

"Okay, I will expect you tomorrow evening. But not too late; Matty has school on weekdays."

"Of course. I shall buy him a gift. What does he like?"

I told Yuri about Matty's obsession with The Knights of Dellot and the stickers he collected before bidding him, Joe, and Meg farewell as I left for my shift at Night Movers.

Chapter Thirteen

Sergei

Before starting work, I went over to Nik and Gina's cottage. I'd taken my blood supplies there on Friday because I didn't want Holly or Matty to discover them. I knew I'd have to tell Holly what I was soon, but I wanted her to be comfortable around me and with our relationship before I did so. She needed to trust me, but the events of her recent past meant she was wary of men and their intentions. I'd seduced her this afternoon when I knew I should have given it time before we took that step, but I did not regret making love to her. I only regretted having to leave her and Matty on their first night in my flat. But with everyone away, I had to come in.

Sunday nights were always busy in the warehouse, getting everything ready for the supermarkets the next day. We had a tremendous demand for tubs of chocolates and other sweet goods with Christmas being so near.

While taking my fill of blood, I thought about the

upcoming festivities, of how different this time of year will be for me now that I have Holly. I usually spent it with Yuri and Viktor, and I would still like my friends around, but I had to make Holly and Matty my priority. I couldn't wait for Christmas morning, and seeing their faces while they open all their gifts from me will make my heart sing. But Holly and Matty will feel the loss of their beloved grandmother keenly, especially on this first Christmas without her.

I had a lot to think about to make this Christmas a special one for them, and for us as a new family. A lot of things to consider. Maybe I should buy a Santa Claus outfit for Christmas Eve? Like the one we have at the orphanage that Cezar wears when we hand out the children's gifts. Maybe I could persuade Holly to dress up as Mrs Claus?

I wrapped up the two empty blood bags and took them out to the dustbin. While I did so, I heard Keeley's Volvo turn into the lane that led to the cottages. I waited for the vehicle to pull up outside their cottage before making my way over. While a tired-looking Keeley and Josh got out of the front of the car and said hello, I opened the back door and greeted a very sullen Daisy.

"Whatever is the matter, little one? You look so sad."

"Uncle Sergei, I was poorly and couldn't go to the dinosaur museum. And when I woke up, I got some spots and Mummy said they were chicken spots. But I don't think they look like chickens at all," sobbed Daisy.

"They're chickenpox," mumbled Keeley as she took out the keys to the cottage.

"Maybe she means chicken nugget spots?" I suggested. I watched Daisy contemplate my words for a moment while we studied the pink spots. She turned and nodded enthusiastically.

"Yep, that's what they look like. Mummy, you got it

wrong—I've got chicken nugget spots. You know everything, Uncle Sergei. When I grow up, I'm going to marry someone just like you," Daisy announced while giving me an Eskimo kiss.

"I thought you said you wanted to marry someone just like me," Josh said, a little put out.

"Aww, don't worry about it, love. She told both Yuri *and* Dan she was going to marry someone just like them last week," Keeley told him.

Josh put their luggage down and went to fill up the kettle.

"Sorry you were left so short-staffed in the office this weekend, Sergei. I can come in later once we've all eaten and got Daisy settled, then you can take off for the night. Have you heard from Nik at all?"

"He rang last night. Gina's aunt had to have her hip replaced, and they are trying to get her into a rehab centre to help her become mobile again. Gina's sister is going over to stay near her aunt for a couple of weeks, so hopefully, they will be back by Wednesday."

"I'm not allowed to go to the manor while Daisy has chickenpox," Keeley said. "Gregor doesn't want me going near Chloe in case she catches it. It's not good for pregnant women to come into contact with anyone who has the virus."

"Chloe will be protected by Gregor's...*blood*." I whispered the last word with my hands over Daisy's ears. She pulled them away and told me I was funny.

"I know, but I think I'd be the same as him in this instance. I just wouldn't take the risk," replied Josh.

"When Nik comes back, I'm thinking of taking a few days off," I told them. I kissed the top of Daisy's head before turning to leave.

"Are you planning a holiday?" Keeley asked.

"No, but I would like to spend some time with my girl-friend and her little brother," I replied, trying to stop myself from smiling so they would know I was serious.

"You have a girlfriend?" Keeley asked excitedly. "Do we know her? Is she from the village?"

"Yes, she's from the village, and maybe you do know her. Her name is Holly Fraser."

I couldn't hide the pride in my voice.

"Beryl's granddaughter?" Josh queried.

"Yes."

"Sergei, she's way too young. What is she, seventeen? Eighteen?" he asked.

"She's almost nineteen," I replied defensively.

"I felt terrible for being away for Beryl's funeral. Gina did, too. I still can't believe she's gone. Poor Holly and Matty. They must be devastated." Keeley sighed and shook her head, her eyes downcast. Then she looked back up at me and said, "Look after them both, Sergei. As far as I'm aware, they have no other relatives. Just Moira and her family."

"But what about her age, Keeley? How will someone so young react to the knowledge of what Sergei is? What we are?" Josh questioned with obvious concern. "Does she know already, Sergei?"

"No. I haven't told her yet. Our relationship is still so new, and she has her grief to deal with. Holly and Matty have been living in a cold house for the past week because their boiler broke, and she couldn't afford to fix it, so I have moved them both in with me where they can be warm and comfortable. And rest assured, Keeley, I will look after them. They are my family now."

Keeley smiled and followed me to the door. She kissed me on the cheek before I left.

"What was that for?" I asked, looking back at Josh's grumpy face.

"Because I know you'll be good for them, Sergei. And… I know you're so much older than me, but I feel like you're like my younger cousin with his first girlfriend or something. I could just pinch your cheek right now and tell you how cute you are." She giggled and pinched my right cheek before declaring, "Look, Josh, our boy is all grown up."

I swatted her hand away and sprinted over to where my Lexus was parked. Keeley was still giggling and waving as I drove away.

Chapter Fourteen

Sergei

It was almost midnight by the time I left work. Thankfully, Maggie had drafted in one of our daytime office staff to assist with the Sunday evening rush. We'd needed all the help we could get with the extra Christmas stock levels and deliveries.

Josh came in around eleven. After a brief rundown of what we'd just sent out, he sat at his desk and went through the goods-in orders that were being brought here on Tuesday. The warehouses were almost at capacity, so we'd need to create space for all the extra stock.

I'd also dealt with a transportation request from an immortal based in Manchester. He wasn't happy about having to travel to Leeds/Bradford airport to board his flight to Rome. Nevertheless, he accepted the terms of business and was scheduled to fly out next week.

Josh never mentioned anything about Holly, and I was glad of it. I didn't want to argue with him, but I wouldn't put up with him saying anything else about Holly's age or our new relationship. She was mine—end of story. I would tell her about my immortality in my own time when I felt it was right.

Maggie was happy for me. I think she felt the same as Keeley. She knew that Holly and Matty had very few people in their lives to call their own, but she could also tell that it was more than that for me. More than wanting to provide them with a home and family. She had been around immortal men long enough to see that when we made up our minds about a woman, we would hold her in our hearts forever.

There had been a light snowfall earlier in the evening and combined with the frost, it made this pretty rural village glisten in the bright moonlight. The winters in Russia were often extremely harsh, with heavy snowfall for days or sometimes weeks. Over the years, it was less so. Possibly due to global warming? Who knows? But the last few years have seemed so much milder than they were in the last two centuries, although still extremely cold and snowy.

My flat was across from the Red Lion, and I noted that all the lights were off in the pub, so there was no lock-in tonight.

I turned in to park behind the shops. There was a row of garages that belonged to them, and as Chloe now owned all three properties—courtesy of Dodgy Dave the butcher—I could have used one of them. But I preferred to park the Lexus near the steps that led to the flat.

I carefully climbed the steep metal steps, which were slippery due to the frosty snow. When I opened the door,

Boris darted out into the ice-cold night before I could stop him. Damn! I'd be out with my torch searching for him later. No way would I leave him outside when the temperature was below freezing.

After closing the door as quietly as possible, I took off my coat and shoes in the small hallway. The sound of running water and intermittent sobbing came from the bathroom, so I went to investigate.

I found Matty with half of his fitted sheet in the sink, trying to wash it with soap and water. When I took in his full appearance, I could see his pyjama bottoms were wet, and his shoulders shook with heavy sobbing. Matty was so busy with his task that he hadn't noticed me standing there. I didn't want to scare him, so I knocked lightly on the open bathroom door.

Matty spun around quickly and dropped the soap on the floor as he did so. His little face was pale, and his eyes were red from crying.

"I'm sorry, Sergei," he sobbed before hiding his face in the crook of his arm.

"You have nothing to be sorry for, Matty," I told him. Bending down to his level, I added, "You had an accident, that's all. It happens to lots of boys and girls your age. I remember it happening to me when I was seven. So do not worry yourself, little one, and do not shed any more tears."

My heart ached for this little boy and what he must be going through.

Gathering Matty in my arms, I hugged him until his tears subsided. After drying his eyes, I gave him some loo roll so he could blow his nose, then I took both his hands in mine and asked him to look at me.

"So, Matty, we need to get you out of these wet pyjamas and into dry ones. I will run you a bath so you can get a quick wash, and while you do that, I will put the sheet and your wet pyjamas in the washing machine. When you get out, we can have a cup of warm milk and a biscuit and sit and chat until we are sleepy. Does that sound like a good plan?"

Matty nodded but didn't smile. He was wary of me, and I wasn't sure why. I leaned over the bath to put the plug in and then turned on the taps.

While I ran the bath, I chatted to him about how work had gone tonight and about all the extra tubs of chocolate we'd loaded onto the lorries. I told him I preferred sweets and jellies to chocolate, although I did like chocolate, too. When I'd run enough water in the bath, I asked him if he needed me to help him in. He shook his head and looked down at his feet before asking, "Are you going to make us go back home?"

"Is that what is worrying you, Matty? You think I won't want you to stay because you wet the bed?"

He nodded, then said, "I wanted to wash the sheet and put it on the radiator to dry so that you wouldn't know. Holly couldn't hear me in the bathroom because I closed the door to the room where she's sleeping. I knew she'd be upset, and I worried about what you would say. I was going to stay awake for the rest of the night so it wouldn't happen again."

"That would have been a silly thing to do, Matty. You would have been tired at school tomorrow if you had done that. And you wouldn't have been able to learn anything new if you were tired."

"But at least I'd get to come back here and stay with you," he said, tears falling once again.

"Matty, I want you and Holly to live with me from now on, and it doesn't matter if you wet the bed or not. So don't you ever worry about having to leave. Promise me that if this happens again, you come to me or Holly and let us know. You can come and tell me anything. You don't have to keep any secrets from me, ever. Now, let's get you clean and dry, then we can have our hot milk and biscuit."

Matty took off his pyjamas and climbed into the bathtub. I handed him the soap and told him he could use my body wash if he wanted. Then I picked up his wet pyjamas and the sheet and took them to the washing machine, leaving the bathroom door ajar so I could hear him if he needed me.

I walked into Matty's room to strip the rest of his bed and give the plastic shower curtain a wipe-down with a wet cloth and antibacterial spray.

As his bedding was dark green, I thought it would be okay to wash it with his navy-blue pyjamas. I was much more careful about separating dark colours in the wash since the recent disaster I had with red pillowcases and white boxer shorts.

Gina taught me how to operate the washing machine in Nik's cottage. Before she moved in with him, Nik did all the washing when I stayed at his home, and my housekeeper did it when I was back in Russia. I now considered myself quite domesticated and was keen to show Holly I could manage all manner of household chores—a good boyfriend in every way.

Once I'd set the washing machine going, I poured some milk into a pan and put it on the lowest heat. I heard Matty climbing out of the bathtub, so I made my way to the bathroom to make sure he was okay. He was wrapping himself in one of the extra-large, cream-coloured bath sheets. I had to stop myself from laughing when he tried to walk to the spare room.

"Come on, little one, let me carry you to your room," I whispered. "We don't want to wake your sister up. I bet she's all grouchy when she's tired."

"Sometimes she is," admitted Matty. Giggling, he added, "She was snoring when I closed her bedroom door."

"Is that what that sound is?" I asked, feigning a shocked expression. "I thought someone was sawing wood in there."

Matty giggled again. The sound was heart-warming—a soothing balm that touched my soul. I wanted to hear that sound more often, because the sound of his tears crushed me. But grief is a complex emotion that has its own time-line, and the way each individual deals with it is different. I couldn't take away all his grief, but I would do whatever I could to lessen the boy's suffering.

I made sure he'd dried himself fully before putting on clean pyjamas, then I took clean bedding out of the cupboard and made his bed again. Taking Matty's hand in mine, I led him into the sitting room.

"Matty, can you remember what your nightmares are about?" I asked as we finished our hot milk. He'd sat next to me on the sofa and yawned one after the other, so I knew he was sleepy.

"Yes, but I don't like to talk about them. They aren't nice, Sergei," he mumbled, shoulders slumping.

I rubbed his back, telling him, "When I was your age, I didn't have a mum and dad, so I lived at an orphanage with my cousin, Nik. One day something happened that put Nik in danger, and even though I was terrified, I ran out to help him. But helping him put me in danger too, and although we managed to stay safe, we were both lucky to survive."

I would not go into detail about the time that men from the next village had come to the orphanage to capture young boys to take as slaves or worse. I didn't want to add to his fears.

"Did you cry?" he asked.

"Not at the time it was happening, but I did afterwards. And I would often wake in the night, shaking and crying. Sometimes I wet the bed, too. When I started talking about my fears and feelings—about what happened that day and in my nightmares—I began sleeping better. I learned it wasn't good to keep my fears locked away. My uncle, who looked after us at the orphanage, taught me a valuable lesson. Would you like me to share that lesson with you, Matty?"

He nodded reluctantly. Taking our empty cups, I placed them on the floor beside the sofa, then I lifted him sideways onto my knees so he could look at me while I spoke.

"Can you tell me where on your body your fears begin?" I asked.

At first, Matty appeared confused, his brows knitting together in a frown. Then he tapped the top of his head.

"That's right, Matty. Whether your fear is because of something very real that has happened to you, or something you are worrying will happen in the future, your fear grows because of thoughts and possibly memories that are whirling around in your head. And the more you think about them, the more your fears grow, until they are much too big to be stored up here anymore," I told him, rubbing the back of his head.

"Where do they go then?" he asked.

"They spill over and go down into your body. Someone who has great fear or worry will hunch their shoulders and often shake if their fear is strong. Working further down your body, your heart can feel as though it is pounding so hard it will beat out of your chest. Then lower down, your belly will feel like it's turning over and can make you sick. So it makes sense that things can happen even lower than your belly. Like making you wet the bed. But talking about your fears and worries can stop them from building in your head and spreading down your body."

"What if your head and body are already full of them?" he asked.

"The more you talk about them, the more room you will make in your head. The fears that have spread down your body will rise back up until they only affect your thoughts. Instead of keeping those thoughts and fears in your head, if you share them with me tonight, they'll spill out into the air around us and won't stay trapped in your head."

"But what if they end up in your head instead of mine? That won't be good for you, Sergei." Once again, his brow furrowed, showing his worry for my wellbeing.

"If I open a window, those thoughts and fears will fly straight out and blow away," I assured him.

He considered it for a moment, then said, "Okay, I'll tell you, but we have to open the window first."

Standing with him in my arms, I drew back the curtains and let him open a small window at the top of the frame. Then we sat down on the sofa and waited until he was ready to speak.

"My grandma went out to get something from the shed. She said she'd test me on my spellings when she came back in, and if I got them all right, I could have some of the apple pie and custard she'd made earlier. So I started learning them. She was gone for ages, and I was getting hungry, so I went to find her. She was lying on the path near the shed, and I was shouting, 'Gran, are you all right?' But I saw blood around her head and in her hair, and her lips and cheeks weren't pink anymore. They had blue in them—like when you have one of those blue lollypops from the shop. Her eyes were open, but she didn't look at me when I shouted at her or when I shook her. She looked like she wasn't a real person. Like she was one of the wax people we'd seen in the waxwork museum we went to. Her mouth was open a bit, and I could see her teeth. I kept shaking her, but she wouldn't move."

Matty started crying, but I didn't try to stop him. He needed to let it all out, though it hurt to see him do so.

"I don't know why, but something in my head told me she was dead. That this was what dead looked like. But I couldn't be sure, so I ran back into the house and rang the ambulance number, just like Grandma had taught me.

"I told the woman on the phone that my grandma was dead, but I don't think she believed me. She asked me lots of questions about her to see if I could get her to wake up and stuff. But I said no, she can't because she's dead. She told me to get a blanket to keep her warm, so I did. Then I ran as fast as I could to Aunt Moira's."

"Is that what your dreams are about? The day you found your grandma?"

"Sometimes. But sometimes I have a different one, like tonight."

"What happened in tonight's dream, Matty?" I asked, brushing back the blond hair from his tear-filled eyes.

"It starts off nice, like normal, I mean. Not scary or anything. Me and my grandma are walking to school. She's holding my hand while we cross the road outside the school gates. I can hear different noises, like cars on the road and my friends on the playground. But when she bends down to kiss me goodbye, she looks like she did when I found her on the path. She has the blue on her face, and her eyes are staring; her hand isn't warm anymore and…and…"

He was shaking now, his tears falling one after the other. I hugged him close but said, "Carry on, Matty. Tell me what happens next."

"All the noises around us stop, and she says in a funny voice, 'I'm dead, Matty. Dead.' I can see the blood in her hair, and I try to get away, but she won't let go of my hand. I shout for help, but no one is there anymore. Then I cry and shout for her to get off me, and I feel myself peeing—but then I wake up and I've done it in bed."

I held him tighter while he rode out his tears, stroking the back of his head, wanting to soothe him somehow. To find his grandmother like that—to see what he saw that day—is something he would never forget, unless… Unless I could replace some of his memories. Or change his perception of them using mind control. I tried to think of the best way to go about it. How to keep the facts of his grandmother's death the same but change his memory of them?

I let him calm down for another minute, then I asked him to look at me. Holding his face in my hands, I said, "The day your grandmother died, you remember learning your spellings like a good boy, then you went outside to find your grandmother."

I made sure his eyes were completely focused on mine before continuing.

"When you saw your grandmother on the path, you noticed she had her eyes open, looking up at something in the sky. You looked up but couldn't see what she could see because some angels—guardian angels in particular— appear only to the person they are assigned to. You noticed that your grandmother looked so pretty, with pink cheeks and lips. She was smiling, and you wondered if she was smiling at her angel or if she was smiling because she was going to see your grandfather and your mother again.

"You knew she had bumped her head, but you didn't see much blood, so you didn't think she'd hurt herself much when she fell. You called the ambulance and spoke to the lady on the phone and told her that your grandmother had died. Then you covered her in a blanket and ran to your aunt Moira's. As you were running, you thought you heard your grandmother whispering in your ear. You are sure she told you she loved you so very much, but it was time for her to be with your grandfather again. You knew that this was a special message just for you, one that you keep safe in your heart for always.

"In your dreams—when your grandmother walks you to school—when you get to the school gates and she bends down to give you a kiss, she looks just like she did when she was alive and well. Her warm hand lets go of yours, and she waves to you as you run into school. You will remember her warm hand in yours and that beautiful smile of hers every time you feel sad."

I broke eye contact with him before asking, "Now tell me, Matty. When you dream about your lovely grand-mother, what is it you see?"

Matty smiled and told me all about his *walk to school* dream with his grandmother; how she smiles at him and bends to kiss his cheek before he waves goodbye and walks into school.

Sometimes, outside influences can make mind control harder to perform, but on a young, innocent, trusting child, it is easily accepted. I only hoped it would be enough to help him with his nightmares and memories of his grand-mother in the long term.

Matty yawned loudly. Despite him telling me he wasn't tired, I picked him up and carried him to the bathroom so he could use the toilet before bed. When he finished in there, I tucked him up in bed and wished him pleasant dreams, kissing the top of his head before I left him.

After closing the window in the sitting room, I picked up our cups from the floor beside the sofa and carried them into the kitchen. The washing machine had finished its cycle, so I took out Matty's bedding and pyjamas and put them in the dryer.

I desperately wanted to climb into bed beside Holly, but I didn't want to wake her. She needed her sleep, so I did the right thing and left the bedroom door closed.

Scratching sounds and meowing came from outside the door of my flat. When I opened it, a very moody Boris ran inside. Obviously, the female he was courting had stayed in tonight—probably due to the cold weather—so my Boris had decided to come in and get warm.

I grabbed a blanket from the cupboard in the hallway and lay on the sofa with him. He pawed and padded the shirt I wore before settling down to sleep on my chest.

Chapter Fifteen

Holly

I woke up warm and toasty and forgot where I was for a moment. Then I realised I was in Sergei's flat, in his bed, and I was alone. Had he come back home?

He'd texted that he might leave work early, so once Matty was tucked up in bed, I had a hot bath, dried my hair, put on my nightshirt, and lay down for half an hour. That was at 10 p.m. last night. It was now 8 a.m.

I jumped out of bed and dashed across the hallway to Matty's room, but on opening the door, I found he wasn't in bed. I also noticed that someone had changed his bedding.

Oh, no! He must have wet the bed. But how did…

"Good morning, my angel," Sergei bellowed from behind me, making me jump. Matty leapt out from behind him, laughing loudly.

"We're running late, Matty! I need to get you some breakfast and get you dressed," I told him, my heart pounding hard in my chest.

"I've already had my breakfast, Holly. Sergei made me eggs and soldiers. I'm going to get dressed while you have your breakfast, then Sergei's going to take me to school."

"Wash your face and brush your teeth first, remember?" Sergei smiled, ruffling Matty's hair when he raced past us towards the bathroom.

"I don't usually sleep in like this, Sergei. I'm so sorry."

"Why should you be sorry for sleeping in? You obviously needed it." He pulled me into his arms and placed a chaste, gentle kiss on my lips.

"Matty is my responsibility, so I should have made his breakfast. And I see he has fresh bed linen on, and his pyjamas are different. He wet the bed, didn't he?"

"That happened last night before midnight, so I took care of it. Matty and I had a good long talk about what was causing his nightmares. Getting it all off his chest may have helped him."

He ushered me through the flat until we reached the dining table, where he pulled out a chair for me to sit.

"What did he tell you?" I asked.

"I found Matty trying to wash his sheet at the sink in the bathroom; he was worried I wouldn't let him stay here again if I knew he'd had an accident. He was trying to stay awake for the rest of the night so he wouldn't do it again." Sergei shook his head before sitting down next to me.

"Holly, I could not bear his suffering and worry, so once he'd had a bath, we sat and had a little chat about all his worries, fears, and the nightmares he's been having. A lot of it was to do with what you told me. About the day he found your grandmother's body. But somehow, in his sleep, what he saw that day invaded his everyday life. I won't go into it all with you—I sincerely hope I never have to. If sharing his fears and nightmares has helped him, then I think we should leave it there."

I opened my mouth to protest, but I was silenced by Sergei's finger against my lips.

"No, Holly, do not push this any further today. I understand your concern, but Matty is happy this morning. If he has another nightmare and wets the bed tonight, then I will tell you what he told me. But I pray that his fears no longer spill into his dreams. I could not bear to see him so upset again."

Matty came running into the room with his school uniform in complete disarray. "Holly, I can't get the zip up on my trousers, and something's wrong with the buttons on my school shirt."

Looking at his school shirt, I could see that he'd buttoned it wrong—with the second button being placed in the first buttonhole. The trousers, however, had to come off so I could release the material from the teeth of the zip.

"I think you need to take a bit more time putting your clothes on, little one," Sergei remarked. He poured me a cup of tea and asked, "How would you like your eggs, Holly?"

"I bet she'd like them with soldiers like we had," Matty said with a grin.

Sergei smiled fondly at Matty. I could see he held genuine affection for my brother; he wasn't just being kind to him because of me.

After Sergei placed two poached eggs on toast in front of me, he helped Matty put on his coat and collect his schoolbag.

Monday was dinner money day, so I grabbed my bag and ran to the door after them.

Sergei wouldn't accept the money I had in my purse, but I kept insisting he take it. When I tried to put money in his coat pocket, he grabbed my wrist and held it still. Before I could object, he said, "A man must provide for his family. You and Matty are my family now, so I will provide."

Matty grinned and took hold of Sergei's hand while I… well, I just stood there, mute, while Sergei and Matty kissed me goodbye and set off walking down the steps. Before they got to the bottom, I heard Pam and Chloe—from Chloe's Flowers and Gifts—chatting as they came out of the back of the shop. As soon as they noticed Sergei and Matty, they said hello and approached them. Sergei pointed me out, so I waved at them.

"Hi, Holly," yelled Pam and Chloe in unison. They both wore the same knowing smirks when they looked from me back to Sergei, and it was then I realised how this must look. I was in my nightwear at Sergei's flat early in the morning. What would they think of me? Of my timing, of…

"Holly, we've got new Christmas decorations being delivered today if you want to pop down for a look and a cuppa. They should be here this afternoon," shouted Chloe. "You can have first dibs on what comes in."

"Okay," I shouted down to them.

Even though the icy wind was biting at my bare arms and legs, I stood there transfixed while watching Sergei and Matty walking down the street until they were no longer in sight. Matty hadn't let go of Sergei's hand while they chatted and walked away.

I could get used to this: to having someone else share our lives. But that's what worried me. What if Matty and I got used to Sergei's presence, and then he left us? What if he decided it wasn't what he wanted anymore?

I was confused. I liked Sergei. He was kind, generous, and so good-looking he almost made me drool with just a glance. But I didn't really know him.

I went back inside and cleared away the breakfast plates. While washing them in the sink, I thought back over the last few days. From the first day I met Sergei, I felt a connection with him. Like something within him called to something within me. Obviously, I was attracted to him. I mean, who wouldn't be? Seeing him shirtless was like a gift bestowed by the heavens. I wanted to touch, kiss, and lick every muscular area of his body. And that smile... His smile lit up my world.

I was falling so hard for Sergei. But whether it was my distrust of the opposite sex because of my ex, or just me being wary in general, I felt as though there was something very different about Sergei. Something that wasn't obvious but was important all the same.

Once I'd finished washing up, I went to get a shower. It was great to feel the hot water flowing over my skin, and even better to feel the warmth of the room when I'd finished. Hopefully, the boiler repairman could fix the problem at Gran's today. Although I had to admit, I'd be sorry to leave here.

I wrapped a towel around myself and made my way to the bedroom. Once again, I jumped in shock when I saw Sergei lying shirtless on the bed.

"Bloody hell, Sergei, you're doing a good job of scaring me today."

"I disagree, my love. However, if you had dropped your towel, I'd have considered it a job well done." He raised one eyebrow and gave me a sexy grin.

I wanted to give him some witty comeback, but none would come to mind, so I tutted in admonishment and tried not to smile.

Taking my brush from the mirrored dressing table, I sat on the edge of the bed, facing away from him, beginning the laborious task of untangling the ends of my hair. I'd washed and semi-dried it last night, but because I hadn't put the required effort into drying and styling it before I'd fallen asleep, I awoke to frizzy hair that wouldn't tame without help.

My hair is thick and has a natural half curl/half wave, which, if not tamed with the right products at the point of blow-drying, can become frizzy and unruly.

"Let me do that for you," Sergei commanded, taking the brush from my hand as he moved to sit behind me, his legs on either side of mine.

"Why?"

"Why not?" he replied.

When he gently brushed through the ends of my hair like he'd just watched me do, I re-adjusted the towel, making sure it was tucked in tight under my arms.

"That won't save you from me, my love," he whispered in my ear. He was watching my facial expressions through the dressing-table mirror, his eyes hooded. Warmth spread through my body and a heaviness settled in my breasts and between my legs as he gazed at me through the mirror, still brushing my hair.

He put down the brush and hooked his legs underneath mine, opening them wide and pulling the towel apart as he did so.

"Sergei, what are you doing? We need to get ready. I have the repairman coming to Gran's today, and I need to go through some more of the files we started yesterday," I told him, trying to pull the towel back around myself.

"No, Holly. Do not cover yourself. I need to see the beautiful body I was fantasising about all night. We have plenty of time before we need to be anywhere, and I intend to spend every minute of it touching and tasting you."

Sergei grabbed a fistful of my wet hair and tugged my head backwards. He whispered something in Russian before trailing his tongue around the shell of my ear and down my neck, making me shiver with both desire and nervousness. I had zero confidence in myself and was unsure how to play this game of seduction, but Sergei was a master. I didn't stand a chance, not when my body was so openly receptive to his touch.

He turned my face towards his and kissed me softly on the lips, causing my heart to skip a beat. I couldn't fight what was inevitably going to happen here, so I let go of the towel and placed my hand behind his head.

I twisted slightly so I could deepen the kiss in a more comfortable position, flicking my tongue against his when he opened his mouth. Sergei groaned and held me tighter. His chest muscles rippled against my bare shoulder, and I let myself go lax in his powerful embrace. I expected him to unhook his legs from mine and roll me over onto my back, so I was surprised when he stopped kissing me and sat me back upright.

Sergei wrapped his hand around my throat and whispered in my ear, "*Watch.*" Then he moved his hand from my throat and up to my chin, positioning my face so I could see us both in the mirror. With his legs still hooked inside mine, he spread them wider. My breast, tummy, and the glistening lips of my sex were on full display. I tried to close my legs but his were unmoving, leaving me fully exposed.

To hide the most intimate parts of me, I placed my right hand over my mound and my left arm over my breasts, feeling both embarrassed and vulnerable. Sergei grabbed my left hand and placed it against my side, but instead of doing the same with the right, he put his hand over mine and said, "Show me."

"Show you what?" I asked, observing his face through the mirror, growing more aroused every time I felt his lips and breath against my ear.

"Show me how you touched yourself when you tried to make yourself come."

"What? No, I can't do that!" I struggled against him once again, but there was no give in his grip. I watched the blush spread through my body; my embarrassment was clear to see.

"Yes, you can, my love. I demand it. I want to know everything about you, and I need you to tell me what works for you sexually. I want to see and feel all of you as you come apart in my arms, and I want to share that sight with you."

"Sergei, I can't. It didn't feel right when I tried. It's never felt right until you." Tears pooled in my eyes, and I couldn't hold his gaze.

He slid his hand underneath mine and pressed against me, his fingers seeking my entrance and stroking with the lightest touch. I was already wet, but when he touched me down there, my body's response was automatic.

Sergei's touch felt different now; his strokes became firmer, the palm of his hand against my mound pressing harder. I gasped, then moaned, both from the feel of his hand and his hot breath against my ear.

I glanced at the mirror, and our eyes met. Sergei's hand stilled, and apart from our heavy breathing, so did everything else. I waited for him to continue what he was doing, but he didn't move at all.

I looked down at his unmoving hand, willing for him to touch the part of me that was aching for him.

"Show me," he demanded. I hesitated, but only for a second. Then I pressed my hand against his and forced it to move up and down. Sergei smiled. It was a slow, satisfied smile. Combined with that sexy gaze, it triggered something deep within me. I wanted this. Wanted to feel myself come over his hand and mine.

I became bolder in my movements, taking two of his fingers and rubbing the side length of them against my clit. Sergei gave me some slack in the grip he had on my legs so I could rock against his fingers, creating just the right amount of friction to start the climb to orgasm. With each rub and rock motion I climbed higher, hitting the peak with a loud "Oh God!" My head fell back on his shoulder as the most exquisite orgasm rolled through me, my body undulating against his.

While still in the throes of orgasm, Sergei began moving his hand again, doing the same as I'd just been doing.

"This time, you watch," he whispered. I lifted my head from his shoulder and looked in the mirror.

Sergei slid his fingers to my opening and slipped one inside. I cried out once again, pushing against his hand to take him deeper. He added a second finger, and my head rolled back as my body surrendered to him. But Sergei didn't want that.

"Watch, Holly." He said it with a growl this time, sending tingles throughout my body. My nipples tightened to painfully hard points, and I cried out in frustration when he removed his fingers from inside me.

He slid them high inside my cleft and rubbed them over my clit as I had done. I was panting hard now, my chest heaving. His left hand cupped each breast, his thumb stroking the fullness.

"Please," I begged, glancing down at my nipples.

"You want me to touch your nipples, Holly?" he asked.

"Yes, so much," I gasped. I needed to come again, and it was almost there, but I couldn't quite hit the point that would take me all the way.

"I will give you what you need, my love, then you will see through this mirror the most beautiful sight a man could ever behold."

He pressed down harder against my clit and grabbed my left nipple, pulling and twisting to the point of near pain. I saw the moment the orgasm slammed into my body, my mouth opening, eyes wide. A red flush appeared on my neck and chest and the wetness my body created glistened between my legs and on Sergei's hand. Then my eyes became hooded and glazed, and all I could see was the way my body jerked against his lap as I rode out my orgasm to the end.

Feeling totally spent, I closed my eyes for a moment, enjoying this time of peacefulness and bliss. My body felt boneless, and I wondered how long it would take before I could stand and support myself. If this was foreplay, then I didn't have the strength for sex.

Sergei unhooked his legs from mine, then he lifted me in his arms and laid me on the bed, my head on a pillow. I heard him unzip his jeans and opened my eyes to see him standing beside the bed. His jeans had a large damp patch to the right side of the zip, and when he pulled them down,

I noticed he wasn't wearing boxer shorts. His cock sprang out and slapped against his belly when he bent to remove his jeans and socks.

"No underwear?" I asked with a lazy smile. I didn't find the size of him as daunting as I had yesterday. In fact, I felt my girly parts tingle with anticipation.

"I took a shower this morning; my clean clothes were in here and I didn't want to wake you. But that is the last time I venture out without boxers this winter. Little Sergei was most unhappy without the extra covering."

I laughed, both at his words and his serious expression. "There's nothing little about him, I can assure you of that."

He raised his eyebrows and smiled before lying next to me.

"I wanted to come in here and sleep with you when I got home last night, but I didn't want to disturb you," he said as he kissed me on the tip of my nose.

"Thank you for taking care of Matty. I'm glad he could talk to you about what was troubling him, but I wish he would've talked to me, too."

"Well, we did not want to come in here and awaken the sleeping dragon," he said.

"What do you mean?"

"Matty said you were snoring, but surely that was the sound of a fire-breathing dragon. I was positive there was nothing human about the sounds that came from this room last night."

"I do not snore," I yelled indignantly.

"No? Then it is as I first thought—you were in here sawing logs. I looked for them when I came in, but you hid them well, my love," he said, glancing around the room and laughing at me.

"Well, if I snore *that* loudly, you won't want to sleep next to me, will you?"

"I'll be sleeping next to you every night from now on, *angel moy*, but I'll pop in some industrial-strength earplugs before we turn out the light."

"Oh, you… I do not snore," I insisted as I slapped his bare arse and then rolled away from him.

"Oh, no. If you get to slap my ass, Holly, then it is only fair I get to slap yours," he declared, trying to roll me over onto my belly.

"Nope, you deserved it for calling me a sleeping dragon."

I wriggled away from him, giggling when he tickled my sides.

"Ah, so my Holly is ticklish," he said, pinning my arms above my head with one hand while he used his other to carry on tickling me.

I laughed so hard I thought I might pee myself. I've always been extremely ticklish on my sides, and even more so on my feet.

I had to abandon a pedicure at the hotel spa because I couldn't stop laughing when the beauty therapist touched my feet. And Sergei was relentless with his tickling.

I spun over to escape, but his tickles changed to a loud stinging slap that covered both my arse cheeks.

"Oww," I yelled, trying to get away from him, but with his hand still pinning mine above my head while he straddled my legs, that was impossible.

"Oh, did that sting, my love? Perhaps I should kiss it better?"

"What? No, you can't do that," I protested.

Sergei ignored me, peppering soft kisses across the

cheeks of my bottom, which turned into licks and nibbles the further down he went.

He let go of my hands and lifted my hips in the air. I thought he was going to take me from behind, so when he slid underneath my legs and fastened his mouth over my sex, I cried out in surprise and utter bliss.

Sergei pulled my hips down and speared his eager tongue inside me. I begged for more and he groaned against my lower lips—the sensation making me gasp with pleasure.

I couldn't believe how quickly he'd made me throb so hard between my legs. He suckled at my clit, then flicked his tongue rapidly against it. The throbbing became more intense, and I knew I was about to come. But instead of bringing me to that anticipated orgasm, he stopped and lifted me higher, pushing me down the bed towards his waiting cock. I slid down on it slowly, gasping at the fullness I felt as he stretched me. When I'd taken him all the way, I had to pause for a moment while I got used to his size. He was watching me closely, not moving, just staring deep into my eyes.

I moved with a slow rock and grind of my hips, but I had to stop when I felt a slight pain deep inside. Adjusting my position made it feel much better, yet Sergei halted my movements, lifted me up, and then pulled me down towards him. I expected him to kiss me, but he held me close and said, "I'm sorry I hurt you. I should have better prepared you to take me."

He was stroking the damp hair out of my face and was looking at me with such concern. I think I fell in love with him just then. The feelings he evoked within me were overwhelming. I kissed him in a gentle, open-mouthed, sensual caress, trying to show my feelings that way instead of with words. Words wouldn't have been right at this point in our relationship.

He wrapped his arms around me, continuing our kiss, which was making me wetter than when he'd made me touch myself earlier. How was that even possible?

I rocked against him, grinding my throbbing clit against his length. Then I lifted my hips and slid down steadily onto him, and this time, there was no pain.

I rode him like a woman possessed, grinding my clit against him every time I took him deep, gripping his forearms while I took what I needed from his body. I gasped, moaned, and cried out his name as I came hard around him. Seconds later, I felt him pulse inside me when he found his own release. His eyes squeezed tightly shut, and he must have bitten his lip because a trickle of blood ran down to his chin.

I leaned forward and gently wiped the blood away from his mouth with my thumb. He opened his eyes, grabbed my wrist and brought my thumb to his mouth, licking the blood away. I felt it even more now—that we were connected in some strange way. Not just boyfriend and girlfriend, but something far more than that.

Maybe it was me being young and silly, falling in love with someone older than me, more experienced. Or maybe we were soulmates and destined to have the kind of love that people write stories about.

I lay down against his chest, my head on his shoulder. He kissed my hair and wrapped his arms around me once more. I liked the feel of him holding me; it made me feel at peace. He was still semi-hard inside me, but I didn't have the energy for more sex. I stayed in his arms a few minutes more, then suggested we get cleaned up.

We showered together—which took a while due to all the kissing and cuddling—then we dressed and ate a light lunch, followed by yet more kissing and cuddling before heading over to my gran's house to meet the repairman.

Chapter Sixteen

Sergei

I noticed a change in Holly when we pulled up to her grandmother's house. She became distant, as if distracted by something. Perhaps she was secretly hoping the same as I? That the boiler was unrepairable, and they would have to stay with me. I'd been contemplating using mind control on the repairman to make him say that the boiler couldn't be fixed, or that he needed some obscure part that would take months to order. I just needed enough time to have her fall in love with me, and that love had to be deep enough to withstand the revelations of my immortality.

On entering the cold hallway, I once again saw my breath fog in front of my face, and I knew I couldn't risk them coming back to this house without heating and hot water. If Holly could not cope with my immortality and all that it involved, I'd have to make sure that she and Matty were warm and comfortable. I'd ensure their home was properly maintained and would provide for them financially.

They would have a good life—even if that life did not include me.

Holly made us both a cup of tea and went to sit in the living room with the gas fire on. I sat next to her on the sofa and waited for her to speak. She took a few hesitant breaths, as if she had something to say. Something important. But the words weren't coming. Either they would hurt to say them or hurt me to hear them. Maybe both. After ten more silent seconds, I could stand it no longer.

"What is it, *angel moy*? What words are you so hesitant to speak?"

"I don't enjoy being back here, Sergei. This was my home: the one I shared with my family for most of my life. But without my gran, it doesn't feel like home anymore. It's like *she* was the home, not this house. Does that make sense?"

The relief that spread through me was instant. She didn't want to come back here, so there was hope for me, and for us as a family. I needed to be forthright—to seize the day and tell her I wanted forever with her and Matty.

Placing my tea on the small coffee table, I turned to face her. Before I could utter a single word, I heard a vehicle pulling up outside. Holly heard it too and got up to look through the window.

"It's the repairman; I hope it won't be too expensive to fix. I'm glad you're here with me, Sergei, because I don't have the first clue about things like this." She gave me a quick kiss on the cheek, handed me her tea, and then went to open the front door.

After turning off the gas fire, I waited for the repairman to enter.

Holly told him about the water and heating failing, and how they'd been managing. She said she hadn't been able to find the manual for the boiler, though she knew her grand-mother had it serviced around this time every year. The repairman nodded and confirmed this. He told us either he or his partner had been the ones to check and service it over the last four years.

He set to work removing the front panel from the boiler—which was in the kitchen—while my sweet angel made him a cup of tea. Then we left him to his task and went back to the living room. Now was not the time to talk to Holly about our future, not with the repairman present. So instead, as I had done so yesterday in her bedroom, I looked at all the photographs scattered about the room.

There were lots of a younger Holly, many of them with whom she informed me was her grandfather. She pointed out photographs of her mother as a child; Holly's resem-blance to her was uncanny. The same colour blonde hair and blue eyes ran through them both, and they had the same smile.

Most of the ones of Matty were with Holly, either playing on the swings and slide at the local playground or building sandcastles at the beach.

There were a few photos of her grandmother as a young woman with her daughter on her knee, and also one on her wedding day. She was extremely pretty, and I told Holly that. It made her smile.

It was such a shame that the beautiful young bride expe-rienced such tragedy in her later years.

Holly brought out two photograph albums and talked me through the photos that detailed her and Matty's life so far. It was clear to see that she was much happier talking about her life with her grandparents than the time she spent with her mother, so I didn't ask questions. I just let her speak and tell me where each one was taken.

They'd only been on one holiday since Matty had come along, although they used to go yearly to the Yorkshire coast before that. Her grandmother used to pay into what Holly called a tote every week at the community centre, where she played bingo, which enabled them to go on all the trips they ran. She said they usually went to one of the Yorkshire or Lincolnshire seaside resorts by coach, and during December, they would go to a Christmas market. This year's Christmas market trip was to York, and her grandmother had collected her and Matty's ticket on the day she'd passed away.

I could see that although Beryl Fraser had very little, she had done her best for her grandchildren. Both Holly and Matty were kind, loving and extremely loyal, all thanks to their grandmother's utter devotion to their wellbeing.

The repairman cleared his throat and tapped a screwdriver on the door to get our attention.

"I'm sorry, Miss Fraser, but the boiler is unfixable. They stopped making parts for these boilers after they discontinued them five years ago. I attended a call out last week in which the boiler had the same fault. We tried for two days to get the part we needed, but there just aren't any about."

Holly's shoulders slumped as she let out a heavy sigh. I put my arm around her and asked, "So we'll need to fit a new boiler?"

The repairman nodded. "Yes. And I know it's a bad time of year for this to have happened—with it being winter and with Christmas around the corner—but as I've said, there's no way to fix this one."

"It is not a problem," I told him. "Are you able to supply and fit another one for us?"

"Sergei, that will be expensive. I can't just say yes to a new boiler," Holly protested.

Ignoring her, I asked, "How much are we looking at?"

"Is this a three-bedroomed property?" he questioned.

"Yes," replied Holly. "But I can't—"

"Holly, do not worry about the cost. I'll take care of it for you."

"No, Sergei. I can't let you do that."

"You can, and you will. Please, Holly, let me help you and Matty. It would make me very happy to do so."

I looked back at the repairman. "You were saying?"

"To supply and fit a new combi boiler will be two thousand."

"And how soon could you do that?"

"I could probably get it done for you a week on Wednesday. We're busy at the moment, as you can imagine. If we get Friday's job done quicker, I might make it on Monday. In the meantime, I can leave you a couple of convector heaters."

"That will not be necessary," I told him. "They'll be staying with me. Now, how do I pay you?"

"Three hundred deposit and the rest on completion. Cash or card, either is fine. I have a machine in the van."

I took the money out of my wallet and handed it over. Holly stood there looking so out of place—a spectator instead of the decision maker. She wasn't happy about it, but either way, this house needed to be warm, so it had to be done.

I took hold of Holly's hand while the repairman wrote out a receipt. Her hand felt limp in mine, but I would not be deterred. I took the receipt and placed it in my wallet, then shook the man's hand.

Once he'd gathered all his tools together, he handed me his card, and Holly walked him to the door. She appeared bewildered but also angry. I put the kettle on again, thinking a fresh cup of tea would calm her down. It's what my British friends did whenever there was a crisis, and I was willing to try anything to avoid an argument.

I made sure I had my back to her when she approached. Taking two tea bags out of a lidded pot with *TEA* written on the side, I popped them into a floral teapot and filled it with boiling water. Holly took the milk out of the fridge and passed it to me, so I thanked her.

So far, so good.

I finished making the tea and handed her a cup.

"Thank you," she said in a clipped voice.

"You are welcome, Holly."

My tone must have mellowed her because, after a long sigh, she said, "Sergei, you shouldn't have done that. It wasn't your decision to make, and it's too expensive."

I put down my cup and turned to her. "Holly, by the time he installs the new boiler, you could afford it anyway. You'll have another week's wage going into your bank account."

"For what, though, Sergei? I haven't earned it. When I should have been working, you took Matty and me to lunch. Then yesterday we mostly talked and…did stuff in your flat. You took me to lunch, and then we came back here. We ended up in bed together, like we did this morning when we should have been working. And just now, you paid the deposit and agreed to have him fit a new boiler. I can't get my head around it, Sergei. It feels like you've taken over my life, and I'm not comfortable with it. It's not right."

"I don't want to take over your life, Holly. I want to share it with you. Just like I want you to share mine. You *and* Matty. I want us to be a family."

Leaning back against the counter, I said, "Some people don't believe in soulmates, but I do, and I believe you are mine. I have fallen for your smile, your strength of character, and the way your beautiful blue eyes light up when you know Matty is happy. You never think twice about putting his needs above your own. I have great respect for how you tried to keep it together for his sake when you were so obviously struggling with everything that had happened to you. I love your determination and your willingness to work and not take anything for granted, and I admire the fact that you still want to be independent and pay for things yourself. And even though you know full well that I can afford to spoil you and Matty, you don't want to take advantage of that fact."

I took the cup of tea out of her hand and placed it on the counter, then I pulled her towards me. We were chest to chest, but as she was much shorter than me, she had to look up to keep eye contact.

"I also love your curves, the feel of your breasts as they press against my chest. I love how your sexy ass looked in that black skirt you were wearing yesterday. That view kept Little Sergei hard far too long for it to be healthy."

She giggled at that statement; as if I was joking. I was not.

"I love your hair. That beautiful blonde colour is like a halo surrounding your head. An angel sent down to Earth to grant me happiness."

I brought my lips close to hers but didn't let them touch.

"And I love this mouth—when your soft, full lips press against mine and the sounds that come from it when I'm deep inside you. I love making love to you, and I look forward to many years of waking up with you in my bed."

I was going to carry on listing everything about her that had come to mean so much to me over the last few days, but she kissed me into silence. Her kiss was soft but effective, and soon I had her pinned up against the wall, my hands roaming over her belly and up to her breasts.

"You are perfect, *angel moy*. I could never part with you, even if you wanted to leave me. I've fallen hard and fast, but I've never been happier. Please say that you and Matty will stay with me?"

"I would love to stay with you, Sergei. I'm falling for you too. I know it's way too soon to feel as strongly as I do, but I can't help it. Promise me you won't break my heart. Everyone leaves Matty and me, so promise you won't do that to us?"

"I won't ever leave you, my love, that you can be sure of. You and I will be together for eternity if you wish it so. There is so much I need to tell you, so much about me and my life. We'll visit my home in St Petersburg, and my apartment in Moscow. I want to show you where I lived in Romania for the first fifteen years of my life, and I'd like to introduce you to all the people I hold dear—my family, of sorts. They will take you and Matty into their hearts and will be *your* family, too."

I kissed her again, sliding my hand around her back to her bra. Before I could unhook it, she stopped me.

"No, Sergei, not here. Take me home and make love to me there."

She said home. My home. Her home too, until my cottage is ready. Our cottage. Mine, Holly's and Matty's. Our family home. Well, our home here in Yorkshire, anyway. They will share all those other homes that belong to me, too. For it is true what Holly said about this house and it applies to all others. When you are part of a family, it is the people that make a house a home, not the building itself.

I kissed her once again before backing away and adjusting Little Sergei into a more comfortable position.

"Very well, my love. Let us go home. Before we get there, I will call to pick up my sticker book from the shop, and more stickers, too. I hope to get a powerful knight in my first two packs."

Holly shook her head and smiled. "You don't have to do it, you know—buy him stickers, I mean. Matty's just happy that you want to spend time with him. He's not a child you have to buy things for to make him like you."

"I know, but I'm not doing it for that reason, Holly. The Knights of Dellot is something I am genuinely interested in. I never had things like that when I was a child."

"Oh, of course. You wouldn't have got anything like that in the orphanage. I watched a documentary a few years ago about some orphanages abroad. They were so run down, and it was often three babies to a cot. I'm sorry if you had it rough there, Sergei."

Yes, we had it rough sometimes, but that's not what I meant when I said that. What I couldn't say was that they didn't have sticker books over two centuries ago when I was Matty's age. Any toys we had were carved from wood or stone, and as for books, we only had the bible. It was how we were taught to read. Marta—one of the few staff members—would often tell us Romanian folk stories, but the bible's miracles featured heavily in our schooling and story time.

Holly cupped the left side of my face with her right palm and held my gaze for a moment. She cared about my feelings, this beautiful angel standing before me, and I considered myself blessed by God to have her as mine.

Chapter Seventeen

Holly

After calling in at the local shop, we pulled into the Night Movers compound. I'd been here a few times with my gran when she'd forgotten something in her locker, and when she was dropping off something she'd knitted for one of the weekend girls. The whole site had grown over the years with what I understood was more warehouse space, and there were more lorries and vans in the parking bay.

Instead of pulling up outside the offices or canteen, Sergei drove down the narrow lane that ran past the office building. At the end of the lane, there were three detached two-story cottages. There was also a windowless, empty shell of what looked like the same type of cottage—the one that Sergei said he was having built.

"Come, my love, let me show you around our new home. The builders are waiting on the windows being installed before they continue, but you'll get an idea about the size of the downstairs rooms," Sergei said. He opened the door and walked around to the passenger side to help me out.

"Our new home?" I asked.

"Yes, our new home. Of course, if you and Matty don't like it, we can always find something else."

I kept telling myself, *"Be the voice of reason, Holly. This is too much, too soon."* Instead, I dismissed the negativity and allowed myself this moment of happiness and hope.

Sergei's enthusiasm for the cottage was clear to see. He told me what each of the rooms would eventually be, and he showed me how big the back garden was.

"It is big enough for a large trampoline and a wooden climbing frame for Matty. We could make it look like the castle from The Knights of Dellot. He'd like that. And my little Daisy could come over and play in it, too. She could pretend it was her fairy queen's castle. I'm sure they'll become great friends."

I nodded, unable to speak because of the lump in my throat. But for once, it wasn't through grief. I felt so happy I couldn't contain myself. I sobbed like a baby, and a poor, confused Sergei took me in his arms before quickly back-tracking over things he'd said to find out what was wrong.

"Nothing's wrong. I just feel so happy," I mumbled before the tears started back up again.

Sergei held me in his arms until I had to step away and blow my nose.

"I'm sorry for all the crying, Sergei. I bet you think I'm such a baby."

"Nonsense, Holly. Your emotions being so close to the surface is not a bad thing. And I would rather see tears of joy than tears of sadness, but you should never apologise for either. If you feel something so strongly, let it show. It does us no good to hide our emotions continuously. It causes stress and cravings for chocolate and sour fizzy jellies. Not good if you already have a sweet tooth."

He said this so seriously, and it added to the giggles his words had caused.

I didn't know if Sergei realised how funny he was, but I was so grateful for it. His playfulness and his ability to make me smile were something I treasured. But it was only part of the reason I'd fallen in love with him, and it seemed like every hour I spent in his company made me fall even harder.

"Come now, let us go home and get warm. I bought a chicken we can roast, and I have potatoes and vegetables, too. You can show me how to make Yorkshire puddings to go with them. Matty will be hungry when he gets home, and he needs his vegetables to grow big and strong. We can go to the supermarket tomorrow and stock up on all the things he likes," Sergei said while ushering me out of the doorway of my new home, his arm around my shoulders, pulling me close.

Before he could open the door to the Lexus, I heard someone call his name. Keeley Saunders waved from the doorway of one of the cottages, beckoning us over.

"Hello, my Keeley. How is the fairy queen today?" Sergei asked as we made our way down the path.

"She's all right, but she's developed even more spots overnight. I picked up a couple of bottles of calamine lotion to help with the itching, but there isn't anything else you can give them for chickenpox, unfortunately."

"Be careful she doesn't pick at them when they scab over, or they'll leave a scar. I have a couple from when I had chickenpox," I told her.

"That won't be a problem for Daisy," said Joshua York as he came to stand behind Keeley. He was one of my gran's bosses at Night Movers and had always been friendly whenever we'd bumped into him in the village. If Gran had heavy shopping bags, he'd give her a lift home and help her carry them in. But right now, Josh was looking at me warily, and it was making me nervous.

"Come on in out of the cold, Holly, and I'll put the kettle on. I'm so sorry I missed your gran's funeral. I'll go to the cemetery and lay flowers on her grave with Daisy at the weekend," Keeley said.

"Thank you," I replied in a quiet voice. I didn't want to talk about anything that would take my happiness away.

"We cannot come in just now. We must hurry back to make what you strange Yorkshire people call tea. It is confusing that you call the meal you serve early in the evening tea, when you also take every opportunity to make the drink known as tea. On entering Yorkshire, all foreign visitors should be given a handbook with all your Yorkshire sayings and oddities," Sergei said.

Keeley laughed and gave him a playful slap on the arm. "Oi, stop mocking us Yorkshire folk. You know you're an honorary Yorkshireman, anyway."

Before Sergei could reply, Joshua asked, "Have you been crying, Holly? Has Sergei upset you?"

"Josh!" Keeley admonished. "Don't be rude."

"Yes, I mean no, I mean… I have been crying, but Sergei hasn't upset me. Not at all."

Sergei's arm tightened around me a little more. He looked at Josh and asked, "Why would you ask that, Josh? You know I would never upset her."

"Not intentionally," Josh replied.

"Not ever," declared Sergei, glaring daggers at him.

"Shut it, Josh. I don't know what's got into you," Keeley stated.

"Have you told her yet, Sergei?" Joshua asked.

"My relationship with Holly has nothing to do with anyone but her, me, and Matty. We are a new couple with many things to talk about, but I will not be dictated to by you or anyone else as to how quickly we do that."

Sergei was so angry, and their confrontation and words had me confused.

I took a couple of steps back, and Sergei's arm dropped away from me. He glanced at me with a sad smile before stepping up to Joshua.

"You see, Joshua, it is you that has upset Holly and made her anxious. How does that make you feel, my friend, to upset my woman like this?"

Joshua looked apologetic as he glanced at me, but he glared back at Sergei.

"I'm sorry, Holly. Josh didn't mean to upset you," Keeley said while elbowing Josh in a move that looked so slight yet knocked him into the doorjamb.

"She's too young," groaned Joshua, rubbing his side.

So that's what this was about. He thought Sergei was too old for me. Crazy as it seems, I hadn't asked him his age. I assumed he was in his thirties, but maybe he's a little older. Forty perhaps? That would make him twenty-one years older than me, which is a lot I know. But he doesn't seem that much older. And anyway, what does it matter? As long as we are happy and he treats me well, our age difference shouldn't be an issue.

I stepped back up to Sergei and took his hand in mine before addressing Joshua.

"Don't make assumptions about me because of my age, or anything else you think would prevent me from having a loving relationship with Sergei. As he said, it has nothing to do with you. Sergei is mine, and that's all anyone needs to know. So in future, I suggest you keep your opinions about us to yourself. Come on, Sergei, let's go home."

I tugged on his hand, but he seemed rooted to the spot, and when I looked up at him, he was grinning like a Cheshire cat.

"You claimed me in front of others. You claimed me as yours and defended what we have. I love you, my strong, beautiful angel."

Sergei took me in his arms and kissed me. The soft, open-mouthed kiss was full of the love he felt for me.

"I love you too," I whispered between kisses.

Someone cleared their throat behind us, and I turned to find a teary-eyed Keeley and a smiling Joshua.

"I'm sorry for upsetting you, Holly," said Joshua sheepishly. "You are right; I had my worries. But from what I've seen, I think they're unfounded, and I hope you'll both be very happy together."

He held out his hand for Sergei to shake, and I stood there watching while he and Sergei came together in a brotherly, back-slapping hug. Joshua congratulated him and said in a voice so low I almost missed it, "Keeley and I will look after Matty when you decide to Bond."

"Thank you. We would appreciate that," murmured Sergei. He glanced my way with a look that spoke of pure lust. I hadn't the faintest idea what they'd been talking about, but if that look was anything to go by, I assumed it was something naughty.

"Just don't let him and Matty near blue chalk dye," said Keeley.

"I have told you time and time again, Keeley. It was supposed to wash off. Ask Yuri," Sergei grumbled.

"But it didn't, did it? And she had her school photographs two days after. If it wasn't for Beryl's mixture, she would have had to miss them. And those poor blue ponies," Keeley added, shaking her head.

"The ponies aren't blue anymore. Yuri went to check on them two weeks after it happened. He said the owners seemed a little disappointed because they'd had requests that the blue unicorns appear at birthday parties and charity events. They're even considering using the dye again now that they know it eventually washes off." Sergei stuck his tongue out at Keeley, then said, "Let's go, Holly. We really must leave before Keeley gives all my secrets away."

Keeley stepped out of the doorway and hugged us both. Before she pulled away from me, she whispered, "Look after him, Holly. He's a good man and will love you to the end of time if you let him."

I took Sergei's hand as we made our way to the car. We'd have to talk about everything that had happened here today because I felt there was something I was missing. I wanted to know what Joshua York meant when he said he'd look after Matty while Sergei and I Bond. And why did everyone keep going on about blue dye?

Chapter Eighteen

Holly

It took thirty seconds from Sergei locking the door to our clothes coming off. He apologised for his cold hands when he freed my breasts from the confines of my bra, but I didn't care.

We hadn't even made it out of the hallway before he was kneeling in front of me with his head between my legs. After he'd made me come that way, I wrapped my legs around him, and we had sex against the wall. Then he bent me over the sofa and took me from behind before making love to me on the rug in front of the fireplace.

Sergei was an energetic lover, and though I had youth on my side, I was aching. I wasn't just tender between my legs but also around my hips and thighs. I winced when I took his hand and let him pull me to my feet, and he immediately apologised for being so rough. To my surprise, he lifted me up and carried me to the bathroom so we could get cleaned up.

Sergei switched on the shower and got in behind me. We didn't have long before we had to pick Matty up from school, so he washed us both, and we dried off quickly.

As we were dressing, Sergei took a call from the Petrov offices in Russia, so I grabbed the chicken and vegetables we'd discarded in the hallway and took them into the kitchen. After a quick search through the cupboards, I found the pots and pans I needed to make our tea.

I hadn't realised Sergei was behind me until I winced again when I bent down to put the chicken in the oven.

"What is wrong, *angel moy*?" Sergei asked as he took me in his arms.

"Nothing's wrong, Sergei. I'm sore, that's all."

It was embarrassing to admit I wasn't used to this much action, which was stupid considering he'd seen parts of me in the mirror earlier that I hadn't looked at before today.

My blush must have given me away because he said, "Ah, I see what the problem is, and it is something I can help with."

"You mean we won't have sex for a few days?" I asked, trying not to sound disappointed.

"No, *angel moy*, that would be impossible. Your body is too tempting. But if you take a little of my blo… if you let me kiss you all better, I am certain it will take the pain away."

I laughed and pushed him away, then turned to wash my hands so I could prepare the vegetables.

"You were about to say something rude, weren't you? But you saved yourself by saying you'll kiss me better. Trouble is, Sergei, your kisses lead to rude things, or at least make me think of rude things."

"Just one kiss, Holly, and I promise you will feel better. Come on, *angel moy*; indulge me a little."

"I've indulged you far too much already, Sergei Petrov, but go on, one last kiss before I peel the veg."

He kissed me slowly, a sweet yet sensual caress, and like always, I was lost. The taste of him changed suddenly and became slightly metallic. I was about to pull away, thinking he'd accidentally bitten his lip or tongue, but then the taste became sweeter, like honey.

Oh, bloody hell! I wanted him again. I was turning into a nymphomaniac!

When Sergei finally ended the kiss, I was breathless and desperately aroused. He looked at me and smiled that sexy-as-sin smile that did nothing to calm my libido. He brought his face towards mine again, but instead of kissing my lips, he trailed his own up my neck, lingering at the pulse point that was throbbing in unison with my pounding heart.

"I know you are wet for me, my love, but we do not have the time right now for me to give you what you need. Later, if you are still awake when I return from work, I promise I will fulfil any desires you have."

"How do you keep on doing this to me, Sergei? I didn't know it was possible to feel this randy all the time."

"This is all your doing, *angel moy*. You drive me crazy with how much I want you."

I liked the sound of that. His words gave me a confidence in myself that I'd never had before.

"I love you," I whispered.

"I love you too, *angel moy*. But for now, I will give you the English saying, 'I will love you and leave you,' for I must collect your brother from school."

"No, you can't. They won't let you pick him up if they don't know you. I'll have to go with you and let them know it's okay for you to collect him."

"I do not think that will be a problem, Holly. His

teacher, Miss Lynton, and Jackie, the classroom assistant, were very sociable when I dropped him off this morning. In fact, they asked if I would consider talking to the class about how people from St Petersburg celebrate Christmas. Miss Lynton gave me her personal mobile number and told me she would be happy to meet up with me beforehand to discuss it."

"Did she now?" I muttered through gritted teeth.

"Yes, she and Jackie were keen to hear all about our traditions."

"Oh, I bet they were. Are you going to do it?" I asked, trying to hide my jealousy.

"I thought it would be nice for Matty if I spoke to his class about our festive traditions. It is good for children to learn about different countries and cultures, Holly. Obviously, I know nothing about the British education system, but I will need to find out more if I am to help with Matty's homework. Anyway, I must go now and collect our boy from school, or he will think we have forgotten him."

Sergei gave me a quick peck on the cheek and grabbed an apple from the fruit bowl before he left. I watched him out of the window while I peeled the potatoes. He was fastening his coat as he set off walking to school.

Sergei looked like sex on legs, even from way up here. He glanced up at the window and gave me a wave, and it felt like I had butterflies in my belly.

Our boy. That's what he'd called Matty. And he wanted to help him with his homework and be involved with his schooling. I bet Miss Lynton will love that!

Sergei is such a great guy, so selfless and kind. So loving. He's perfect in every way. No wonder the staff at school were making a play for him. Miss Lynton's so pretty, as is

Jackie. But Sergei's mine. I won't let anyone take him from me.

———

Fifteen minutes later, Sergei and a smiling, red-cheeked Matty came strolling into the flat. Boris got up from my lap to push his head against Matty when he gave me a hug.

As was the norm before Gran died, Matty talked a mile a minute about his school day. He also reminded me that Sergei said we could choose some Christmas decorations for his flat. I'd forgotten about Chloe's invitation to look at the new Christmas items she'd had delivered.

Sergei gave me a peck on the lips before pulling me up from the sofa and telling me to get my coat and shoes on. Chloe's shop was below the upstairs flat we were in, so I thought I'd forgo my coat, but Sergei made me put it on, telling me he needed to keep me healthy and safe.

On entering the back of the shop, Sergei gave Chloe and Pam a shout to let them know we'd arrived. They greeted us warmly and made a tremendous fuss of Matty. Pam put the kettle on, and we all followed Chloe into the new extension to her shop, which used to be part of the butcher's. The room had recently been plastered after they'd knocked through from Chloe's. Once it was finished, it would give them so much more room to display the gifts and seasonal decorations she stocked.

I particularly loved the scented candles and always bought Gran some to put with her Christmas and birthday presents.

Chloe told us she was waiting for new shelving and the till area to be finished before this part of the shop would be open to the public, but she was expecting the work to be done by next Monday. Both Chloe and Pam were incredibly excited about the extension and told me all about their future plans.

There were boxes along the floor and on a display table. Sergei went through them, taking each decoration out of the box carefully and asking Matty and me if we liked them. Of course, Matty said yes to every one of them, but I favoured the more traditional decorations above modern, whacky-coloured stuff.

Gran bought a few new decorations from here last year, so I asked Chloe if she had any other items in stock from that range. She checked her paperwork and then glanced around the room before selecting a large cardboard box from the floor.

Pam took a pair of scissors from her apron pocket and opened it for me. The pretty baubles and berry decorations were protected by layers of foam packaging sheets, which she placed in an empty box.

"Is this more to your taste, my love?" Sergei asked as he came to stand behind me.

He kissed my cheek and wrapped his arms around my waist. "Pick anything you want to decorate our home. Personally, I like anything Christmassy, but my decorating skills are sorely lacking. Perhaps it could be my job to select our Christmas tree. Even *I* shouldn't be able to get that wrong."

"My gran bought some of these last year," I told him as I held out the red apple baubles and bunches of realistic-looking red berries. "Would it be okay if we brought some of our decorations from Gran's house? I mean, we can add to them if you want, but I'd like some familiar things around us if we aren't staying at home this year."

"My angel, you can have anything you want, both you

and Matty. And if you would rather we live at your grand-mother's house until the cottage is ready, or if you just want to move back to your gran's, we could do that. Whatever you decide is fine with me. As long as our little family is together, I don't care where we live."

Matty came to my side and hugged us both. I heard a collective *"aww"* from Pam, Chloe, and Michelle, Chloe's other assistant, who'd brought through a tray of hot drinks, and juice for Matty. I blushed at having an audience for our sweet and loving moment, but I was pleased that Sergei wasn't one of those guys who was embarrassed to express his feelings in public.

After going through a couple of boxes of decorations and telling me to pick out whatever I wanted, Sergei took Matty back up to the flat so they could go through the new stickers he'd bought. I asked him to keep an eye on the chicken and told him I'd be up to put the vegetables on soon.

Truth be told, I felt a little nervous in the company of Pam and Chloe. I didn't know Chloe all that well, but I'd known Pam for years. She'd worked in this shop with the previous owner, who was one of my gran's best friends. I knew they were going to question me about my relationship with Sergei, but I wasn't sure I wanted to discuss it with them.

I'd fallen in love with him in double-quick time, although I knew it made little sense to give my heart and trust to him so soon. But it felt right to me, and that's all that should matter.

Chapter Nineteen

Sergei

Matty and I had been going through the latest Knights of Dellot stickers I had bought, and I was carefully sticking them into the album. I thought Matty would raise the roof when we found the knight Harbard, who carried an enchanted shield. Matty didn't know anyone who had a Harbard sticker, so he was extremely excited to share the news with his friend Jamie.

There was a knock at the door, and seconds later, I heard Yuri shout, "Hello!"

Yuri and Gregor walked into the flat and approached the table.

"Matty, these are my good friends, Yuri and Gregor. Yuri, Gregor, this is my boy, Matthew, but you can call him Matty."

"Hello, Matty," said Yuri as he came to sit beside him. He held out a large carrier bag for Matty to take. "I bought you a gift; I hope you like it."

"Thank you, Yuri," replied Matty. He looked at me for reassurance.

I nodded, so Matty opened up the bag and yelled, "*LEGO!*" He scrambled off the chair and pulled the large box of Lego out of the bag. It was a city airport set, complete with a plane.

"Wow! Look, Sergei, it's got an aeroplane. I can't wait to build it," Matty said with a beaming smile.

"I love Lego," Yuri told him. "I have lots of sets at home. Here, take a look at these I've built."

Yuri took out his phone and showed Matty photos of his collection of Lego buildings, modes of transport, and various other structures.

I remember when he first got into Lego. It began around forty years ago when we'd been stuck in an airport in West Germany. They cancelled our flight due to heavy snow, so we were stranded at the airport for the night. A little boy had brought along his Lego to keep him occupied while travelling, and when we all got settled down on the floor of the airport to wait out the winter storm, Yuri ended up next to him.

He was hooked from that moment on. He said it was a great stress reliever, and as Yuri rarely seemed stressed, it must be true. I didn't have the same fondness for it, but I'd learn to love it for Matty's sake.

"What are you doing?" Gregor asked, gesturing at the stickers and albums on the table. Matty left the Lego and climbed back on the chair to show them our stickers. He explained all about The Knights of Dellot and which ones were his favourites. Out of another carrier bag, Yuri pulled out a sticker book and four packs of stickers.

"Sergei told me all about your collection, and the knights sound very interesting, so I bought a sticker book and some stickers to get me started. Will you help me, Matty?" asked Yuri.

"Aww yeah!" Matty yelled as he fist-pumped the air.

Gregor watched with amusement while Matty chatted away enthusiastically to Yuri. He smiled at Matty and seemed interested in his descriptions of all the knights.

"You should get yourself a sticker album too, Gregor," said Matty after he'd questioned him about the knight Dallin.

"Oh, I'm not one for collecting stickers, Matty. I am a very busy man," he replied.

"I'd have thought you would have done one to put away for the baby in case it's a boy," remarked Yuri, giving me a sly wink.

"Good idea, Yuri!" I stated with a nod. "I bet Alex will start collecting them for Rory when he gets back from his holiday. It will be a nice thing to do, from father to son. It shows he was thinking about him."

"Yes, something to put away for when he is older. And much easier to get on board with than the ones we started collecting for Daisy," grumbled Yuri. "I swear they did not make any Tilly the purple fairy. No one seemed to have any."

"Ah, yes, the fairy queen stickers. I didn't even get my sticker book half full. Now you can't buy them anywhere," I told them.

We travelled miles from the village to get the rest of the stickers we needed for Daisy's "*Ellie the fairy queen*" collection, but we just kept getting the same stickers over and over.

"That's why you have to do swaps," said Matty. "There's nearly always someone who has a sticker that you need.

Sometimes you have to swap three of yours if they have one that you *really* want."

Yuri nodded his agreement.

Gregor cleared his throat, then said, "Perhaps I should buy a sticker album. Yuri, go to the shop and purchase a sticker book and all the remaining sticker packs they have left."

"Can't you go, Gregor? You said I was off the clock now," replied Yuri.

"I changed my mind." Gregor smiled, then winked at Matty. "And while you are there, you can bring back cakes and chocolate for us. I assume that going through all those stickers is going to be hungry work."

Matty's eyes grew wide. He readily agreed with Gregor that it would indeed be hungry work. I reminded him we'd be having a roast chicken dinner later, so he couldn't eat too many goodies.

While Yuri was gone, Matty explained all about the knights' superpowers.

"Is that why you like them so much?" questioned Gregor.

"They are so cool," said Matty. "They're strong and save people and the earth, *and* have powers. That makes them heroes, and that's why I like them."

"You know, Matty, being strong and having power doesn't make you a hero," Gregor said softly.

Matty looked confused. "What *does* make a hero, then?"

"A hero is someone who is selfless. That means he or she does something good for someone that doesn't benefit themselves," Gregor replied.

Matty still looked confused.

"Your grandmother was a hero," I told him. "She used to visit Old Joe in the village and get him some shopping.

She looked after him because he hadn't any family around, and she knew he wasn't very strong."

"I know Old Joe," replied Matty. "Gran used to make him a cup of tea and take him soup when he was poorly. She used to do his washing sometimes, and we'd take his dog out for a walk. I held her lead."

I nodded and smiled. "Then you are a hero, too, Matty. It didn't benefit you or your grandmother to help him and Meg, but you did it anyway, just to be kind."

"But don't you have to save someone's life to be a hero?" he asked.

"If you do something for another person, whether it is helping them do everyday things that make their life better, or if you save someone's life without thinking about your own, it still makes you a hero."

Matty was quiet for a while—as if he was contemplating what I'd just said. Every word of it was true in my eyes. And the more I learned about his grandmother, the more of a hero she became.

I looked towards Gregor to find him staring at me with a smile on his face.

"What?" I asked, not sure if this was indeed the real Gregor. He'd smiled at me three times in less than an hour, which was quite unlike him. Perhaps the normally *way-too-serious* Gregor had been kidnapped by aliens and cloned. A minute later and he was still smiling, and neither Chloe, Freya, nor Keeley was around. I found it most unnerving.

"I am happy for you, Sergei. It seems you are finally taking life and commitments more seriously," he said.

"I have always taken any commitments I have made seriously, Gregor."

"Sergei, sometimes you have done things without giving them much thought. You must admit that you've gone through life as if it were a game. But here you are now, with a family to care for, and you seem…more responsible. I am proud of you, my friend. And your grandfather would be, too."

"Give it a rest, Gregor. My grandfather would have been proud of me anyway. I work as hard as anyone else. Petrov Energy is thriving in the renewables sector, and I give my all at Night Movers. Just because I am not so serious all the time like you, it does not mean that I am not a responsible individual. My grandparents taught me that life is for living, to have fun and enjoy the time you have here on earth. And most of all, you should treasure the love of friends and family, yet always give more in return. I have stayed true to their teachings, yet you still judge me as lacking in commitment and responsibility."

I had deliberately kept my tone even, although I was angry inside. Matty was here, so it was not the time to argue.

"I did not mean to offend you, Sergei. It's just…with your grandparents gone and…" He looked down at the table and sighed. "I remember when Vasily brought you back to St Petersburg. You were fifteen years old and looked so much like your father when he was that age. I'd stayed with your grandmother while Vasily was away. We'd known about you from when you were born, but the war with the hunters had been so lengthy, and no one knew who they could trust anymore after some of our kind had turned on their own. All we knew was you were being kept safe with a relative. But there was still heavy fighting in the countries bordering Romania—Ukraine and Moldova especially. Bulgaria and Hungary had once been Born Immortal strongholds, but they'd been hit many times during that particular war, so were no longer considered a safe haven for us.

"Your grandparents knew your father was dead; they had each felt his passing. But they'd received word from one of his comrades of your birth. I had been in the first wave of Born Immortals that invaded the hunters' Romanian army after your father's death. It was the second time I had fought alongside Vasily, but it would not be the last. He was fearless in his quest to find you, and the hunters who got in his way were dealt with swiftly. But word reached us that their troops were once again about to breach Russia, and we had to go back to protect our own. Your grandmother and the staff at the Petrov Palace were competent, but as we had seen when they invaded before, if the hunters came in large numbers, there would be little hope of survival.

"You would have been seven years old the next time we came for you, but by that time, those who would have known of your whereabouts had fled, so we were looking blind in a country still heavily occupied by the hunters. Their numbers seemed to grow overnight, and you did not know who you were talking to when you asked for information. Vasily did not want to leave Romania that second time, but he was putting your life in danger every time he tried to find you. We had to go back to regroup and try to establish a greater immortal army.

"We travelled to England and recruited from there, as well as Ireland, Wales, and Scotland. Although at that time, nearly all those countries were fighting wars of their own. France and Italy had been picked apart by the hunters, so we had very few recruits from there. Spain, however, proved fruitful in our quest for reinforcements. When we had enough immortals join us, we set out to defeat the hunters who were occupying so many of the eastern countries.

"Your grandfather begged me to stay with your grandmother. I wanted to fight, but he wanted to be the one to bring you home. It took three months to defeat the majority of the hunters. Then he found you and brought you safely back to Russia. Nikolas' grandfather had been fighting alongside Vasily for weeks. When they discovered their grandsons were blood-related, it sealed their friendship for life.

"Your grandfather sent an envoy to tell us they were on their way home with you and would be bringing guests. He considered it safer for Nikolas and his grandfather to travel from St Petersburg on a ship we shared rather than buying passage from a Romanian port. Many of the immortal army came back with them and were given rooms at either the Antonov or Petrov Palace. Great friendships were forged during that war, and most remain to this day.

"So you see, Sergei, after all that, I cannot help but think of you protectively, like I would a younger cousin. Your grandfather always looked out for me, both as a young man and when I took the…"

Gregor glanced at a wide-eyed Matty, who was taking it all in.

"I appreciate what you are saying, Gregor, but you cannot try to dictate how I live my life. You and I are very different, and despite the closeness in our backgrounds, it does not give you the right to tell me that your way is the better way. I have lived many years and know that I cannot change who I am, not for anyone. Of course, you can make minor changes so that you fit in more with each decade or century, but who you are deep inside will remain. I lost a little of myself after my grandparents' passing, and the last few months have left me disheartened somewhat. Like I did not have a purpose. But I do have a purpose. I have those children in the orphanages who rely on what my company gives so they can have a brighter, safer future. We are making progress in the renewable energy sector, which will help the climate for generations yet to come. And now I have my family, Holly and Matty. What greater purpose does a man have in life than the woman he loves and his children?" I said with a nod towards Matty. "I consider myself truly blessed, my friend, and the only approval I'll seek from now on will be that of my family."

"I am happy for you, Sergei, and I only wish that Vasily could be here to see your little family for himself. Your grandmother would have adored Matty, I am sure."

"She would," I agreed as I ruffled Matty's hair.

"Sergei, what does immortal mean?" asked Matty.

I glanced at Gregor, who looked at me warily. Well, wasn't that great? He was the one who'd mentioned it, but it was down to Sergei yet again to sort it out.

"Well, Matty, immortal is a word that is used to describe being able to live forever. It's like the words eternal, everlasting, and infinite."

"So, is an immortal army made of soldiers that can live forever?" he asked with a furrowed brow. Trying to make sense of what he'd heard.

"Well, sadly, Matty, no one can really live forever, not even soldiers. We all have our time to die, though some of us live for a very long time," Gregor told him.

Good save, oh serious one.

"Old Joe was a soldier, and he's lived a very long time. Like nearly a hundred years. I don't think he was in the immortal army, though, but he's shown me his medals and let me place his poppy wreath on remembering Sunday," Matty stated proudly.

"Old Joe was in the British Army, and what a very

special moment it must have been for you to place the wreath on Remembrance Sunday," I told him. Matty's beaming smile made Gregor and me smile, too.

My phone beeped with a text message from Holly. She told me she was helping Chloe and Pam close the shop and would be up in twenty minutes, so I went to the kitchen to put the vegetables on. I checked the chicken and made sure we had gravy in the cupboard before going back to the table.

Gregor and Matty were chatting away about the super-powers each knight possessed. I had never seen Gregor so relaxed around children before. He had taken to Rory immediately, but he was only a baby. Daisy was a child who stormed her way into your life and commanded your attention, whether you liked it or not. I know Gregor adored her, but even at five years old, Daisy liked to think she was in charge. This had often caused a standoff between him and Daisy. She was similar to Chloe in that he never got his own way with her very often. It made for hilarious viewing.

How he was with Matty was very different. Their inter-actions were easy and kind of familiar—like they were old friends. Perhaps it was the knowledge that he would become a father himself next year that was making him this way? Or maybe it was because Matty was such an easy child to like? Either way, I had never seen Gregor Antonov this relaxed and interested in the company of a child in all the centuries I'd known him.

Chapter Twenty

Holly

The grand inquisition I'd been expecting from Chloe and Pam wasn't as bad as I thought it would be. They were mostly telling me how kind-hearted and funny Sergei was, but I sensed there was something else behind today's invitation.

I got the impression there was something they weren't telling me—like they both had a secret they wanted to share about him.

Sergei demanded to know all of my secrets, so if he was keeping something from me that could affect our relationship, I wouldn't be happy.

After helping them unwrap the decorations in the boxes, I brought the flower buckets in from outside so they could close the shop. Chloe told me she was expecting a baby late in the spring, so I didn't want her lifting anything heavy. She said she was getting married in the chapel of her fiancé's palace in St Petersburg and told me it wasn't very far from

Sergei's palace. She asked if I thought Matty would consider being a pageboy, but all I could hear in my head was that *Sergei lives in a palace.*

Was he some sort of prince? Is that what the secret was? Did Russia even have a royal family?

I knew he was rich. I mean, Petrov Energy was huge. Maybe all the wealthy people of Russia liked to own a palace?

I found it hard to imagine Sergei in a palace. He was quite at home in his flat, and the cottage he was having built wasn't all that big. It seemed that Sergei had two sides to him: the wealthy businessman and the man who was content to live in a flat above a flower shop and walk my brother to school. I wondered why Sergei had turned his back on that other life. I knew he was still the decision maker in Petrov Energy *and* his other business dealings, but he was currently working the night shift at an import/export company in Yorkshire. It didn't make any sense.

***

Chloe and Pam came back to the flat with me, and I found two unfamiliar men sitting at the table with Matty. Both men immediately stood and greeted us. Sergei came out of the kitchen wearing an apron with ducks on it. He put an arm around me and introduced me to his friends, Gregor and Yuri.

Chloe immediately went over to Gregor and kissed him. He gathered her in his arms, then took my hand and kissed the back of it.

"I am very pleased to meet you, Holly. Your brother and I are having a most enjoyable time with our new stickers."

"Gregor got Caspian in his first pack," Matty declared while high-fiving Gregor.

Before I could remark on the man's luck, Yuri enveloped me in a hug.

"I am so pleased to make your acquaintance, beautiful Holly." Yuri placed a kiss on my cheek before letting me go.

"Hello," I said, my mouth as dry as the Sahara. Both men were utterly gorgeous. Gregor had an intimidating yet sexy James Bond look about him, while Yuri appeared more casual but could pass for a model. Just being in the presence of these three gorgeous male specimens left me hot and bothered. Sergei spun me around to face him and kissed me full on the lips before whispering in my ear, "You are mine, *angel moy*, do not forget that."

I looked him in the eyes and replied, "Perhaps you could let Miss Lynton and Jackie know that."

Sergei smiled. "I only have eyes for you, my darling. You and that chocolate cake that Gregor bought."

I went into the kitchen with Sergei and noticed he'd made Yorkshire puddings.

"I thought you didn't know how to make them," I remarked, peeking at the well-risen puddings through the oven door.

"Yuri, Gregor and I did an internet search and took the recipe from there. I was certain the mixture wasn't the right consistency, but they're looking like those my Gina makes when I stay with her and Nik."

"Loving the apron," I told him.

"It belonged to Chloe's aunt. I think it suits me!" Sergei stated.

I leaned against the open doorway and glanced over at the table. Chloe sat on Gregor's knee, and they were going through more of the stickers with Matty. Yuri was trying to explain to Pam, without success, I might add, that The Knights of Dellot had nothing at all to do with King Arthur and his Knights of the Round Table. It was almost like an extended family scene—as if we did this all the time. It was so surreal yet comforting all the same.

I offered to make everyone a drink, but they all declined and got up to leave.

To my surprise, Yuri and Gregor had each bought a Knights of Dellot sticker book, and both offered to do swaps with Matty. They said goodbye and promised to call him when he got home from school tomorrow. Matty hugged them and promised Yuri he'd let him help with the Lego set he'd bought him.

Pam kissed Sergei on the cheek when she said goodbye. She seemed quite fond of him—almost in a sisterly way.

I like Pam. She's always so friendly and fusses over Matty whenever she sees him. Her husband, however, is a miserable sod. He used to drive the school bus, and I don't think I've ever seen him smile. They seem so ill-suited as a couple.

As we waved goodbye and watched them make their way down the metal steps from the flat to the car park, I noticed how affectionate Gregor was with Chloe. How he held her hand, then pulled her against him and kissed her lips when they got to the car. And how he opened the door for her and helped her inside, kissing her again before she fastened her seat belt. Their love for each other was obvious, and Gregor's loving yet gentlemanly behaviour was something you wouldn't normally see around here.

Yuri and Pam walked around the corner arm in arm, chatting away about the Red Lion's Christmas decorations. The pub usually has a large Christmas tree with multi-coloured lights outside, but someone stole the lights from it last year. There was a rumour going around that it was Darren Crossley and the rest of his yob friends, but as always, nothing was ever proven.

Back inside the flat, I helped Matty pack his stickers away while Sergei plated up our meal. I noticed he'd placed a portion of everything we were eating today inside a plastic tub. I asked him if he was taking it to work with him for later, but he shook his head and told me it was for Old Joe and Meg. He said he liked to take him a meal to warm up at least once a week. He'd bought him a microwave for that very purpose.

I refrained from asking Sergei any questions while we ate our meal. I doubt I could have got a word in, anyway. Matty was chattering away about all the fun he'd had doing his stickers with Gregor and Yuri. Then he went on about hunters and an immortal army. I told him I didn't want to know. It was hard enough keeping up with all the knights and their superpowers without starting with something else.

Chapter Twenty-One

Sergei

Holly and Matty had been living with me for four days by the time Nik and Gina arrived back from Ireland. I'd told Nik over the phone on Tuesday about finding the one I would Bond with, and he told me how happy he was. I could also hear the relief in his voice, and that pained me. It meant that no matter how many times I told him I didn't love Gina in that way, he hadn't believed me.

Alex and Julia were thrilled and supportive from the start. When Josh told Alex he'd had reservations about Holly's age, Alex reminded him that because he hadn't pursued Julia when she was eighteen, he'd almost lost her forever.

Freya was also happy I'd found my angel, but she said something that made sense when we spoke. It also disturbed me.

Freya thought I'd only developed those feelings for Gina because I met her when I was emotionally vulnerable. It was when I'd come over to stay with Nik, less than a week after I'd lost my grandparents.

Gina has a way about her that puts everyone at ease. You also feel valued and safe, which makes no sense at all as she is barely five foot four. Nik had fallen for her and had been telling me how wonderful she was. Freya's theory was that Gina had arrived in my life when I needed a distraction from the pain that grief had caused.

I worried that I could be Holly's distraction from her own grief and that the love she said she felt for me wasn't real.

Of course, over the years, Gina has become a great friend to me, and the friendship kind of love I feel for her is very real. But I don't want that from Holly. I want the deep, heart-and-soul love that Pamela talked about. The type of love my grandparents shared. I was determined I'd be a boyfriend that Holly couldn't help but love.

I arranged for Nik and Gina to come over and eat with us before Nik's shift on Thursday evening. Holly had gone overboard with the food in preparation for their visit, making a terrific number of tacos and fajitas. It was a good thing she had made so much because Gregor, Yuri, *and* Dmitry had joined us when Matty came home from school.

All three came with stickers for Matty, and as always, Gregor brought the lady of the house a gift. He presented Holly with a sparkling silver evening bag from some designer I'd never heard of. She thanked him profusely and made a big fuss about receiving it, but she seemed uncomfortable about accepting such an expensive gift. He told her that beautiful women should be surrounded by beautiful things. Standing beside her, I told him there was nothing more beautiful than my angel.

Holly served Gregor, Yuri, and Dmitry at the same time as Matty, and they all complimented her on her cooking. As I watched them eat their fajitas, I marvelled at how different my life had become recently. Before Holly and Matty had come into my life, I'd felt quite lonely. My immortal friends had little time to spend with Sergei then. But now…it was like Holly, and especially Matty was a magnet to their steel. But just because spending time at my flat had now become popular with my immortal friends, it did not mean I'd abandon the human ones who'd made my last few months in this village bearable.

On Sunday, I was taking Holly, Matty, Pamela, and Old Joe to a Christmas event at the local garden centre. There would be a craft market, festive food and drinks, plus a Santa's Grotto. I had already discussed with Matty that he'd need to send a letter to Santa. I wanted to know what was on his Christmas list so I could go shopping for it.

Holly was another matter altogether. I asked her what she wanted for Christmas, but all she said was, *"Just you, Sergei."* I made a joke and said I would wrap a red bow around Little Sergei for her. From the way her pupils dilated, I think she liked the idea.

When Nik and Gina arrived, Gregor, Yuri and Dmitry said their goodbyes. Nik laughed at the fact that all three of them were collecting stickers like Matty, but the *"you are a fool for not realising how cool these are"* look they all gave him had made him curious.

Holly and Matty already knew Gina, but I introduced

them to her and Nik all the same. Gina took Holly in her arms and hugged her tightly, asking how she was doing, while Nik shook Matty's hand and questioned him about his day.

Nik had seen Holly in passing over the years, but he hadn't spoken to her before today. Once Gina was done hugging Holly, Nik took her hand and kissed the back of it. He asked, "What's a pretty girl like you doing with the likes of Sergei?"

"I am a catch, Nik. How could she resist?" I told him, winking at Holly and gaining a smile.

We sat down to eat, and after discussing the next steps in her aunt's hip replacement recovery, Gina told us stories about Holly's grandmother. Apparently, Beryl had been the go-to person in the village for knitting and had crocheted baby blankets for Gina's children.

Gina also told us quite a few funny stories involving Holly's grandfather, Jock. There was one in particular that made us all laugh out loud. It had involved Jock, Old Joe, Ken Fearn, a beer barrel, and roller skates. From all the funny stories Gina told, I was sure I could have been good friends with Jock. Some of his escapades rivalled those of Nik and me over the years.

The Victoria sponge cake Holly served up for dessert was delicious. My angel definitely knew her way around the kitchen, and her baking was exceptional.

I couldn't stop looking at her tonight. She had a glow to her cheeks, which could have been because of the wine Gina brought. Her blue eyes were glassy, and those full lips had been begging me for a kiss. So I did just that. When my lips met hers, I let them linger longer than I intended and only stopped when Matty yelled, "URGH, kissing again."

"I was thanking her for making this wonderful meal for us, Matty."

"Thank you is something you say, not kiss," he pointed out.

Nik and Gina laughed at him, and Gina asked if he had a girlfriend at school. Matty made a few noisy protests and said girls were weird, and he didn't ever want a girlfriend.

"But what if a girl at school was really nice and collected the same stickers as you?" Nik asked.

"None of the girls collect *my* stickers, and even if they did, I wouldn't let them be my girlfriend. No way. They collect stupid fairy stickers and play with dolls. And they're *always* telling on the boys to all the teachers and dinner ladies. Like Natalie Wells. She told on Jamie for kicking the ball over the fence, but it was an accident."

"You know what, Matty? I'm going to remind you about this conversation when you are fifteen. Let's see how you feel about having a girlfriend then," I told him. Nik chuckled at the disgusted face Matty pulled.

When Matty began yawning, Holly told him it was time for bed. I'd been testing him on his spellings earlier, so he didn't have any homework to finish.

I was finally having a night off now that Nik and Alex were back in the office, and I was looking forward to settling down with Holly and watching a movie. To my dismay, I'd had to work every night since Holly and Matty came to live with me. It couldn't be helped, I knew that, but it was certainly not ideal.

Nik and I carried the plates into the kitchen while Gina topped up her and Holly's wine. Their conversation became louder the more they drank, but it was good to see Holly so relaxed. Nik closed the kitchen door behind us.

"So, you've found the woman you want to Bond with.

Can you feel the difference between what you said you felt for Gina and what you feel for the one who's meant to be yours?" he asked.

"Why does everything have to come back to that one conversation?" I replied angrily. "I told you I no longer loved her in that way."

"What if I told you I was in love with Holly? That I'd wanted to sleep with her?"

I felt a tingling behind my nails as my claws threatened to extend. Why the fuck was Nik trying to provoke me?

"We've had a great evening, Nikolas, yet you are spoiling that with the point you're trying to make. I will not let you goad me into an argument in front of my family. They've been through enough recently and do not need to feel frightened in their own home. I suggest you make your excuses and leave."

"Sergei, I would never upset your family, and I don't want an argument. I just... I wanted you to know how I've been feeling since the day you told me. Why I had to distance myself from you as much as I did."

"You did not believe me when I said I no longer felt that way?"

"Yes, kind of, I..." Nik sighed and looked up at the ceiling before glancing my way again. "I know my Bond with Gina is everything it should be. Our love for each other is unbreakable; it's infinite. But I can't help wondering... What if she'd known you had feelings for her before we Bonded? Would she have preferred you rather than me? You're a better man than I am, after all."

"Don't be ridiculous," I told him. "You only have to say my name to have people rolling their eyes. Gregor has always thought me irresponsible, and Alex barely tolerated me until recently."

"That was their problem, not yours. You are funny; you like children and animals, and you commit more time to the orphanages than I do. You always know what to do in a crisis and how to get a positive result—even if the way you do that is bizarre. Okay, so you can get a bit bloodthirsty, but you'd never hurt your friends. You're the type of man that women like to go for because you don't give a shit about showing how you *really feel* and all that other emotional crap they like. If Gina had known how you felt about her, I'm sure I wouldn't have her now."

"Nikolas, you are wrong. I am not a better man than you. I make mistakes because I often do things without thinking, and everyone knows that. Although I have patience with children, animals, and the elderly, I find I have little patience for those who annoy me, and my temper often gets the better of me. My vampire side is harder to keep hidden because of all this. You are much stronger than me in that way. You always have been.

"You knew you had found your woman, yet you could not have her at that time. Instead of leaving to wallow in pity, you stayed around and waited for her to be ready. I wouldn't have the strength to stay around if Holly belonged to another man. And before you found Gina, you never had a shortage of women to warm your bed, even though you never did the *emotional crap.* You'd give them a smile and raise one eyebrow, and they would be yours for however long you wanted them. I could never do that."

"Well, that is true," Nik admitted, adding, "I've always been better looking than you."

"Oh, I wouldn't go that far, Nikolas."

"I've always had more muscle than you, Sergei," he said while flexing his biceps.

"This is true," I confirmed while flexing my own in comparison. "You also sing better than me, Nikolas."

"Sergei, anyone can sing better than you. You've never been able to hold a tune."

"But I have a much bigger cock than you, my friend, and do not deny it."

"It's not a cock, Sergei; it's a birth defect. I think all the cells got confused when you were developing in the womb and tried to grow another limb instead."

I laughed at his words. He'd always made fun of how large I was.

"You are jealous, Nikolas. Admit it. You wish you were as big as me."

"Fuck off, Sergei. Who in their right mind would want a cock that comes with a government health warning?"

"I hope you two are doing the washing up," shouted Gina.

"Yes, Gina, we are slaving away in the kitchen while you are getting drunk," I yelled back.

Looking at my friend, I asked, "Are we good now, Nikolas? Can you let what I told you go?"

"Yes, I can. You have Holly now, which makes it easier. I saw how you were with her at the table. Needing to touch her, even if it was just brushing your fingertips over hers. The way you looked at her like you could never get enough…"

"I can't," I admitted. "She is addictive. I meant it when I said I didn't know how you lived without having Gina all those years. If Holly decides she doesn't want to be with me, I'll be devastated."

"That won't happen, Sergei. You can see in her eyes how hard she's fallen for you."

"But I have seen the truth in what Freya said about Gina and me. What if it is the same for Holly?"

"What do you mean?" Nik questioned warily.

"She pointed out I first met Gina just after I lost my grandparents. She has a theory that my feelings for Gina and the love I thought I felt…it was not true. And I only thought I felt that way because of my grief. I think she may have been right. No, she *was* right. I see it all so clearly now. I was drawn to Gina's goodness and kind, comforting nature. It wasn't anything like the love I feel for Holly and never was in all those years."

"And you think it's the same for Holly?" Nik asked.

"I don't know. But until I am sure, I dare not tell her about my immortality. If her feelings aren't genuine and are only there because of her grief, the knowledge that I am a vampire could make her leave me. I do not think I could live without her and Matty in my life, Nikolas. I would see them well taken care of, but I could not be near them knowing I'd not be part of their everyday lives."

"I'm sure she's wrong, Sergei. When did Freya tell you this?"

"This morning."

"So you weren't questioning Holly's feelings before that?"

"No." I sighed heavily and began washing the dishes.

"Sergei, I would ignore what Freya said. Women like to think they're always right, but they aren't. Don't tell Gina I said that, though."

"I won't."

Chapter Twenty-Two

Sergei

By the time Nik and I came out of the kitchen, Holly and Gina had consumed their second bottle of wine. I knew my Holly rarely drank alcohol, so the fact that she was having trouble standing didn't surprise me. Matty was laughing at her obvious clumsiness and said, "Sergei, I think you're going to have to carry her to bed. She can't even stand up straight."

"I can," mumbled Holly. "Look!"

Holly stood and immediately started swaying.

"See, straight as an arrow," she slurred.

I caught her before she fell back on the sofa. She smiled and closed her eyes. "You caught me, Sergei; you didn't let me fall. I love you!" Holly went to kiss me but ended up head-butting me instead.

"Oww," she cried. "Why did you move?"

"I didn't," I groaned, loud enough to be heard above the combined laughter of Matty, Nik, and Gina.

"I think it's time we were off," Nik said, grabbing his and Gina's coats. "I think it'll snow again tonight, and I promised Josh I'd call in at work and look over tomorrow's goods-in paperwork."

"We're running out of space," I told him. "All those Christmas items are taking over the warehouse."

"It'll be like this until the week before Christmas. It's crazy. The shops are only closed for one day."

"We need to work out the office Christmas rota," I told him. "Don't forget that I'm travelling to Romania a few days before Christmas. Will you be coming with me this time?"

"I'd love to go, Sergei," slurred Gina. "I want to see where Nik grew up, as well as give out gifts to the children."

"What do you say, Nik? I'm taking Holly and Matty, too."

"I'll have a word with Alex and Josh to see if they can fill in for me. I haven't been for a few years, and it would be good to see the improvements to the building."

"The renovations are going extremely well. You will notice such a difference, Nikolas. I'm debating whether to rebuild the chapel next to the old orphanage. Of course, it's no longer needed since they built the new church in the village. The original plan was to demolish what was left after the earthquake. I wish I'd acted sooner and not let it go to ruin, but our main concern was keeping the children safe. I can't help thinking that Petre would be disappointed if we didn't rebuild it."

"Sergei, I don't feel well," moaned Holly. "The room is spinning."

"Come on, my drunken angel, time to get you in bed," I said as I kissed her cheek. "Matty, there is a bucket under the sink; bring it to the bedroom. I think we might need it."

Chapter Twenty-Three

Holly

This hangover should have been the worst in the history of hangovers! But apart from having a strong taste of blood in my mouth, I didn't feel as bad as I thought I would. I felt around the inside of my mouth with my tongue, wondering if I'd bitten my lip in my sleep, but it didn't appear so.

I couldn't believe I'd got so drunk. Thinking about my behaviour last night was mortifying.

I was sure I'd finished being sick after the second time it happened, but no! My body wasn't stopping until my stomach was completely empty. What made it worse was that every time I retched, my head felt like it would explode.

Sergei's side of the bed was empty, and when I looked at the time, I could see why.

Shit, it was 9 a.m. The flat was quiet, so I assumed Sergei had taken Matty to school. What must they think of me?

Poor Sergei had been up with me through the night

every time I was sick. He'd held my hair back when I'd hugged the bucket he'd placed by the side of the bed, and surprisingly, he didn't berate me for drinking too much. He'd emptied the bucket each time and brought me a wet washcloth to wipe my face. I bet he was going to be angry with me. I'd totally deserve it.

After getting out of bed, I steadied myself for a moment before heading to the bathroom. On the bedside table, there was a note and a glass of water with two pills. The note read: *My dearest Holly. I thought I'd let you sleep in because of your delicate state last night. I will make you some breakfast when I get back from taking Matty to school. Until then, here are two paracetamol for the hangover. See you soon, love Sergei xxx.*

My delicate state? I'd hardly call throwing up in a bucket and yelling, *"I think I'm dying,"* delicate. Still, it was sweet of him to write that and take care of Matty this morning. Maybe he wouldn't be that angry after all. I'd only ever been drunk once before, and Paul yelled at me the whole time I was being sick. He'd been angry because he'd had to leave the party to take care of me.

I took the pills and drank the whole glass of water, which made the inside of my mouth feel almost normal. Well, less furry anyway. Making my way into the bathroom, I debated whether to have a bath or shower. Although I felt much better, I still wasn't one hundred per cent and doubted that would be the case until much later.

Looking in the mirror, I gasped in shock. I looked terrible. My normally pale skin looked even paler, and I had panda eyes from smudged mascara. Just great! My gorgeous boyfriend had seen me throwing up while looking like a reject from a Halloween movie. Why was the universe so against me?

I decided on a shower, and by the time I got out, I felt

much better than before. I wrapped myself in a towel and brushed my teeth, glad of the minty taste of my toothpaste.

When I stepped out into the hallway, I heard the radio from the kitchen, which told me that Sergei had returned. So, after putting on my bathrobe, I made my way towards the kitchen.

Frankie Valli and The Four Seasons had been one of my gran's favourite groups, but hearing Sergei sing along with the radio to "Big Girls Don't Cry" might have made her change her mind. Even Boris walked away in disgust.

Sergei seemed oblivious to my presence as he buttered toast and tended to the eggs he was poaching. I watched as he used the butter knife as a microphone, belting out the chorus while he did a little dance. Despite the horrific sound, I couldn't help smiling. I said nothing but kept watching, almost sure he hadn't seen me. But when the song ended, he turned to me and asked, "Would you like tea or orange juice, my love?"

"Orange juice, please. You didn't have to make me breakfast, Sergei. You've done enough already by getting Matty to school on time."

"I enjoy taking care of Matty. And it is my duty as your boyfriend to take care of you."

"Well, thank you, anyway, and I'm glad you're not angry with me. I'm angry with myself, though. I don't know what I was thinking, getting drunk like that. It's not like me at all."

He put my breakfast on the table and then came towards me, taking me in his arms gently.

"I could never be angry with you, *angel moy*. Not even if you ate my secret stash of sour jellies. You let yourself go last night and drank a little too much wine. So what? You were enjoying reminiscing about your grandparents, which is a positive step in the grief process. I was here to take care of you, and no harm was done. Here, sit and eat," he said, gesturing to the plate of poached eggs on toast.

I sat and did as I was told, enjoying the perfectly poached eggs, until Sergei said, "Besides, you said the sweetest things before you threw up."

I put down my fork, ready to question him, but Sergei shook his head and pointed at my breakfast. So once again, I began to eat.

"You told me you loved me," he said, smiling. "Then you said you wanted to marry me."

I stopped chewing and stared at him, trying to remember what else I'd said, but I couldn't recall much of anything before being sick.

"When I started undressing you, you asked me if I was going to make you come."

I could feel my cheeks heat from embarrassment, so I took a gulp of my orange juice to cool down.

"When you told me you were desperate to give me a blow job but were afraid you'd choke on my *monster willy,*' I found that both amusing and arousing." Sergei laughed out loud, then winked at me suggestively. He was enjoying this, I could tell.

My full-body blush was an invitation to create more teasing, so I needed to say something that would stop him in his tracks. I tried to think of something witty, but my brain wasn't functioning properly. In the end, I told the truth.

"I'm surprised you haven't been pushing for one because you've gone down on me a lot."

His laugh stopped abruptly, and he glared at me.

"I give you pleasure because I want you to have it—to see you experience the deep satisfaction that an orgasm can bring. I do this because you are mine, and I love you.

Admittedly, there are also selfish reasons for me to do it. I love the way you taste, especially when you come. I love it when your thighs begin to tremble and the sounds you make when you go over the edge. Holly, I don't pleasure you with my mouth so that you'll do it in return. Do you believe me?"

"Yes."

I believed him, but it wasn't what I was used to. My ex demanded oral sex from me often, yet rarely gave it back. And he was never any good at it. Not like Sergei.

"I want to do it. Give you a blow job, I mean. I want to know how you taste. But you *are* big, Sergei, so I doubt I could take much more than half of you—although I'm more than willing to try."

His breathing became heavy, and I thought he was about to pin me to the table and fuck me senseless, but a very odd thing happened. His eyes developed a red ring around the iris. I gasped in shock and ran to him immediately.

"Sergei, are you all right? Your eyes… They went red!"

"Do not concern yourself, *angel moy*. I am well. It's just something that happens occasionally." His tone was placating, but it didn't work.

"Sergei, your eyes turning red is not something that should '*just happen occasionally.*' I'm pretty sure it shouldn't happen at all. I mean, I'm no medical expert, but I'm sure that's something you should be worried about. You could be going blind. We need to get you to a doctor."

"*Angel moy*, your concern is touching, but I can assure you it is unwarranted. It is common amongst my people for this to happen."

He sounded like he wanted to say more but stopped, gauging my reaction.

"Your people? Do you mean your family had this, too?"

I was confused. I'd heard about lots of things that ran in families, but eyes turning red wasn't one of them. I'd be doing one hell of an internet search later.

"Yes, my grandfather had this happen to him often," he told me. He smiled as he touched my damp hair. "Now, come on, eat your breakfast. We have a lot to do today, so you'll need your strength."

Sergei picked me up and carried me back to my chair. I ate my breakfast in silence, watching as he fed Boris in the kitchen. But I couldn't leave it there. I just wasn't satisfied with the answer he'd given me.

I took my half-empty plate into the kitchen, and he tutted at the amount of food I'd left.

"I couldn't eat it, Sergei. I'm worried about you."

"There is nothing to worry about, *angel moy*. Please believe me when I say that I am perfectly fine, and this is simply something that happens with heightened emotion. It is not common, but there are a number of men and women in the world that have this occurrence."

"Sergei, I've lost so many people close to me for so many different reasons. I couldn't lose you too; it would break my heart completely."

"Do not fret, my love; you will not lose me. I could never leave you. Not unless you wanted me to go."

"Promise me, Sergei?"

"I promise."

Chapter Twenty-Four

Holly

After taking a phone call from his staff at Petrov Energy, Sergei began looking for something in the paperwork I'd gone through a few nights ago. When he was done, the room looked like the aftermath of an explosion in a paperwork factory.

"Sergei, those files were in the specific order you asked me to put them in. I can't understand how you couldn't find what you were looking for," I grumbled, picking up the discarded papers.

"I know, but I swear the figures I needed were in one of the first three folders."

"We really need a proper filing cabinet, but you have to promise to go through the files one at a time and put them back when you're done. You're such a tidy person in your everyday life, Sergei, but your lack of organisation with your paperwork is going to cause you problems."

Sergei nodded in agreement. "You are right, *angel moy*, yet I always find what I need in the end."

"But it's time-consuming, and I can't understand your method of organised chaos. I doubt anyone could. How do you get on at Night Movers?" I asked, thinking we could use their filing system if he was more comfortable with it.

"I have Maggie. And the new girl, Liz, is very good at making me stick to Maggie's system when she isn't around. She frightens me sometimes. She can hold a stare longer than Nik and grips the stapler in such an aggressive way when we annoy her. I have often thought she might throw it."

"Perhaps that's what I need to do here, then? Scare you into keeping your paperwork in order."

"My angel, you are too sweet to be scary," he said mockingly.

"I could always withhold sex," I told him, smirking at the shocked expression on his face.

"That is going *too* far, my love. Now go and get dressed. We will shop for a filing cabinet immediately."

I laughed as I left the room, and he swatted at my bottom when I passed him. I knew he'd follow me, and sure enough, not two minutes later, he walked through the door.

"Sergei, I can't have sex. Although my hangover's just about gone, I'm not ready to bounce around on the bed," I declared, wagging my finger as I backed away.

"The floor, then?" he questioned with his right eyebrow raised.

"Sergei…" I yelled, laughing as he pulled at the belt on my robe, bringing me flush against him. "You know what I meant."

"Sshh, my love. You cannot threaten to deny me your

body and expect me not to crave it. Let me taste you and satisfy my hunger."

His words, the tone of his voice, and his expressions made me hot and wet. I could tell by that slow, sexy smile of his that he knew he had me, and he'd got me to a point where I craved him in return. He unsnapped the buttons on his jeans and repositioned his erection, which had escaped the top of his boxers by a few inches. *Unleashing the beast*, I thought to myself, trying to stifle the giggle that was desperate to escape.

"What is it you find so amusing, my love?"

The way he said *my love* told me there'd be no place for humour in this encounter.

"Sergei, why do you never call me your angel in here?" I asked, gesturing around the room.

"I have no need of an angel in the bedroom, Holly. Your halo and wings are not welcome here," he answered in all seriousness.

After slipping the robe off my shoulders, he took my hand and placed it inside his boxers. "Touch me, Holly; feel how much I crave you."

Sergei's mouth met mine in an almost brutal assault of lips and tongue. I grasped his hard length, and it grew even bigger in my hand. My need for him was overwhelming, and I could sense nothing but Sergei and my increasing desire for him.

Seconds later, I was on the floor with my legs spread wide, his face between them—biting, sucking, licking at every inch of my sex. I climaxed quickly and rode out the tremors while gripping his hair, keeping him captive until I was sated.

He rose to his knees, removed his T-shirt and pushed his jeans and boxers down his thighs. His face was shiny with the evidence of my orgasm. He licked his lips and chin, not wanting to waste what he'd wrung from my body.

I was throbbing inside, needing to be filled. Sergei lifted my right leg high and kissed my calf before placing it against his chest. He ran his cock over my sex, lubricating the length, and when he finally surged inside me, I cried out with pleasure and relief.

His thrusts were hard and deep, his grip on my leg almost painful. This wasn't making love—it was hot, intense fucking, but it was no less beautiful.

It surprised me to know I could take him this deep. Occasionally, his thrusts caused a small bite of pain, but it was a pleasurable pain, and the rest were...perfect.

"Touch your breasts, Holly," Sergei commanded, his voice gravelly.

I hesitated for a moment, but the look he gave me brooked no argument. I trailed my hands around the full globes until Sergei shook his head and growled out a harsh, "No. Not gently. Firmly. Push them together. Yes, like that. God, Holly, you don't know how much I want to slide my cock between them right now. That's it, tug at your nipples. Harder, Holly."

And that was all it took to make me fly, my orgasm slamming into me, taking my breath and coherent thought.

"Holly," Sergei yelled as he found his own release. I felt it hit me deep inside and welcomed it all. A tiny part of me wished I'd become pregnant from this encounter—by a man I'd only been with for a week yet loved so very much.

Chapter Twenty-Five

Sergei

We needed to buy Matty a car seat suitable for his age, so we went to a store called Halfords. It sold a variety of car seats along with some car essentials—such as batteries, oil and light bulbs. The store also sold bikes, and I saw a great one I could buy Matty for Christmas. We didn't have time to look for one for Holly and me, so we decided to come back another day.

After leaving Halfords, we went to an office supply store in Doncaster and bought a filing cabinet, an all-in-one printer/copier/fax machine, and various office supplies that Holly thought she would need.

Due to our bedroom activities this morning, we didn't have time to go food shopping before picking Matty up from school. But my angel was determined, efficient and well organised, despite me trying to distract her with kisses and touches. I couldn't help it. Every time Holly bent over to grab something, I had to squeeze her shapely ass. She admonished me for doing it, but it was her fault for having such a sexy ass. I could scent my come on her from earlier, and it pleased me. It was as if I'd marked her as mine to warn others away.

She *was* mine, of that there was no doubt. I'd stopped worrying about what Freya had said. I was sure that Holly's feelings for me were genuine and not enhanced by grief. Even if they were, I would not care. I would take her love, no matter how real, as long as she stayed by my side. But I'd yet to tell her I was immortal and drank blood regularly. That could change everything.

Several times, the opportunity to tell her I was a vampire had presented itself, but I had not done so. Well, that is not entirely true. A few nights ago, we lay in bed discussing our lives. She had asked about my age, and I told her I was forty-four in human years. She laughed as though I was making a joke and questioned if I was an alien. I'd said, *"No, not an alien; I am a vampire."* She'd laughed again and asked, *"Do you want to bite me, vampire?"* I answered her truthfully. *"More than you could ever know."*

So many times, I've had to rein in my instinct to taste the blood that flows through her veins. I wanted—no—I *needed* to take my time in introducing her to my world. I had to know in my mind that I'd done everything just right so I didn't mess up the best thing that had ever happened to me.

Both Alex and Gregor had offered their advice, but their circumstances differed greatly from mine. They'd both had time to build a solid friendship with their women, and both Julia and Chloe were older than Holly. They also didn't have a young child to care for and protect, so I ignored their advice.

Alex told me not to let Holly's age get in the way of making her mine. He said he'd not claimed Julia because he wanted her to enjoy her youth and have the kind of experiences with her human friends she could look back on for many years to come. But then she'd met someone and married him, and if not for the tragic accident in which she lost her child, her marriage might have lasted.

Alex said I should claim Holly and Bond with her without fail because time passes slowly when you are without the one you love, and who knew what could happen to our human women without our protection? Julia could have lost her life in that car accident. Then Alex would never have known what it was like to have her love.

I chanced a look at Holly as we drove to pick Matty up from school. She was humming along to a tune on the radio while looking out of the window. Holly glanced my way and caught me watching her, and she smiled. My heart skipped a beat. I smiled in return and placed my hand on her thigh.

"Do you realise how much you mean to me, Holly? Do you know how lost I'd be without you and Matty in my life?"

I needed to spend this weekend being the most perfect boyfriend Holly could ever wish for. She had to know I'd spend eternity making her smile. Our family of three could be so happy together, despite me being a vampire.

I hoped that Holly would have a child with me one day —a companion for Matty. I'd love to be a father to the boy. Holly was more like a mother to him than a sister anyway, so I secretly hoped I could slip into that role.

I pulled into the nearest side street to Matty's school. Parking outside the school was almost impossible, so I wasn't even going to try. Before getting out of the warmth of the vehicle, Holly leaned over and kissed me, whispering, "You mean the world to me, too."

Chapter Twenty-Six

Holly

Sergei always held my hand or had his arm around me whenever we went out somewhere, but as we stood waiting for Matty outside the school doors, I leaned into him a little more. I wanted to show Miss Lynton and Jackie that Sergei was taken. I didn't know I had such a possessive streak. Maybe it was because of what happened with my ex? Or maybe it's because I know that what I have with Sergei is special? Either way, I was determined that the pretty teacher who dared slip Sergei her telephone number knew that he was mine.

The door to Matty's classroom opened, and Miss Lynton began calling out children's names who had someone waiting for them. When she saw us, she waved us over but didn't call out for Matty. I instantly tensed, knowing something was wrong. Sergei picked up on this and pushed past her to search for Matty.

"Mr Petrov, I—"

"Where is Matty?" Sergei asked, the panic clearly audible in his voice.

"He's here," shouted Jackie from over in what the children call *the quiet corner*.

Sergei stalked towards them, his complete attention on Matty. He lay on a carpeted area, his head resting on his coat.

"What's wrong, Matty?" Sergei asked as he picked him up.

"I don't feel well," he replied in a quiet, teary voice. He laid his head on Sergei's shoulder and closed his eyes.

I turned to Jackie to ask questions, but Miss Lynton interrupted.

"Matthew said he didn't feel well at around half-past one. I thought he might be tired after playing out at lunchtime, so I told him he'd feel better if he lay down for a while in the quiet corner."

"Matty just told me he didn't eat his lunch because he felt sick," Jackie said as she picked up his coat and reading bag.

"And yet none of you called to tell us our boy was ill," bellowed Sergei. We all flinched, including Matty.

"I'm sorry, little one. I did not mean to alarm you," Sergei told Matty in a soothing voice. The glare he directed at Miss Lynton cut off any other words she was about to give as an excuse.

"The secretary has my number," I told her. "You should have called me straight away. I would have picked him up earlier."

"You know how children are sometimes. It's Friday, and they get tired when they're running around in the play-ground. Unless they have a tummy ache that makes them sick, we find it helps if they just have a bit of a rest. More often than not, they bounce back right as rain after half an hour," Miss Lynton replied, trying to defend her actions.

"Well, clearly, that didn't happen with Matty," I countered. "If he ever becomes ill again while at school, I need you to call me straight away."

I was angry, but I didn't want to waste any more time discussing this when I needed to get Matty home.

Sergei took Matty's coat and draped it around his shoulders. Matty had his arms around Sergei's neck. His eyes were closed, and his face was flushed. I took Matty's reading bag and headed to the door. Miss Lynton dashed to open it for Sergei.

"Mr Petrov, have you thought any more about coming into school to talk to the children about Christmas in Russia?" she asked. "You have my number if you want to call and discuss it."

Sergei point-blank ignored her as he strode out of the classroom with Matty in his arms. I would have loved to stay and gloat about that, but I was worried about my brother and wanted to get him home as quickly as possible, so I could determine what was wrong with him.

I had to hurry to keep up with Sergei as he strode to the car. He was cursing about having not parked outside the school, but with how quickly he moved, it didn't take too long to get to the car.

Being only five foot five, my legs would never have the same long strides as Sergei's, and he was already buckling Matty into his new car seat by the time I got to them.

I felt Matty's forehead and could tell he had a temperature.

"Matty, do you hurt anywhere? Do you have a sore throat or bellyache?" I questioned.

"No, I just don't feel well," he whispered.

"Do you have a headache? Does your neck hurt?" I asked, thinking about the symptoms of meningitis.

"No. Can we go home now, Holly? I'm really tired."

"Yes, we'll get you home and tucked up in bed after you've had some medicine."

I looked towards Sergei and told him I'd need to call at Gran's to pick up a bottle of Calpol.

"I think we should take him to a doctor," Sergei said as he started the car. "Do you go to the medical centre in the village?"

"Sergei, you can't get an appointment that quickly. You have to phone at eight in the morning to see if they have an emergency one; otherwise, you have to wait a week or two."

"What? That cannot be right. Surely they will see a child if they are ill?"

"No, they won't. Not if there are no more emergency appointments."

"Well, let me speak to them. I guarantee they will see him straight away," he said, convinced that they would.

"Sergei, let's just get him home and give him some Calpol. It's a paracetamol medicine for kids. I've got some ibuprofen medicine for him, too. So if we call into Gran's and—"

"The pharmacy is nearer. We will collect it from there. The sooner he has the medicine, the sooner we will find out if he needs to see a doctor."

He seemed so anxious while driving us to the pharmacy. Sergei was clearly upset about the fact that Matty was ill.

"I'm sure he'll be fine, Sergei. They nearly always say it's a virus and give it up to forty-eight hours. I know the signs to look out for with meningitis and septicaemia, so as long as we check for them while he has a temperature—"

"That's it!" Sergei declared as he stopped the car. "We

are going to see a doctor. You cannot talk about such serious illnesses and expect me not to panic."

After calling at the pharmacy for some Calpol, Sergei managed to get Matty in to see a doctor. I was impressed. Not only did he get the receptionist to give us an emergency appointment, but he also got her to bring Matty a glass of cold water. The receptionist he spoke to was one of the biggest battleaxes in the village and was never so accommodating. I half expected to see a news crew outside filming such an impossible feat.

By the time we saw the doctor, the Calpol had started to work, and Matty's temperature had cooled. As I'd guessed, the doctor said it was probably a virus. He advised us to keep up with the paracetamol medicine and to get him to drink plenty of fluids. Nonetheless, Sergei demanded he give Matty a full examination, just to be on the safe side.

When we arrived back home, I sent Sergei into the kitchen to put the kettle on while I helped Matty change into his pyjamas. It seemed like he was reluctant to leave Matty's side, but I told him that warm blackcurrant cordial might help Matty feel better, so off he went to make some.

Sergei sat next to Matty on the sofa and kept feeling at his head. It was almost as if he'd not seen anyone with a virus before. He was so protective of Matty, and it was obvious he cared a great deal about him. Matty was enjoying the attention, and he smiled when Sergei called him his boy. But then again, Yuri and Gregor called him their boy, too. My brother had never had a strong male influence in his life, so I thought it would do him good to have them around him.

Matty had a bowl of soup with a slice of bread, which went a long way in convincing Sergei that he wasn't seriously ill. He hadn't been able to relax since we entered Matty's classroom. After bringing today's purchases in from the car, he sat on the sofa watching cartoons with Matty until bedtime.

After another dose of medicine, we put Matty to bed but left the door open so we could hear him if he needed us. Sergei had wanted him to sleep in our bed with us, but it just wasn't practical. He said if Matty needed to get in with me, he would sleep on the floor beside us. Sergei also told me we'd need a larger bed to accommodate the three of us —in case Matty ever got ill again.

I informed Sergei it was highly likely that Matty would get ill again because he was only seven, and all school-age children had bouts of tonsillitis, sickness bugs, and yearly coughs and colds. The prospect of all that happening made him even more anxious.

Honestly, with the way Sergei was reacting, you'd have thought he'd never been ill a day in his life.

Chapter Twenty-Seven

Holly

"I'll go to the supermarket and stock up with food for the rest of the week. If you make a list of everything you think we'll need, I will make sure I get what is on it… Holly, are you listening?" Sergei asked.

I rubbed my eyes, trying to push away the fog of sleeplessness, then coughed a little to clear my throat before I answered, "Yes, make a list for the supermarket. On it now!"

I left the table, my breakfast barely touched. Sergei grabbed hold of my arm as I cleared away our plates. "Leave it, Holly. I will see to those. Why don't you lie down for an hour? You hardly slept a wink last night."

"Neither did you, Sergei. Yet here you are, wide awake as usual. I don't know how you do it."

I didn't know how anyone could be such a morning person after tossing and turning all night. We'd both been listening out for Matty, and as neither of us could sleep, we talked well into the night about our plans for the future.

Sergei wanted to take me and Matty to St Petersburg after we visited the orphanage in Romania. We'd filled in the passport forms and the nurse who did the medicals and organised the blood donor days at Night Movers had countersigned the passport photos.

Sergei was going to take them to the post office today and do the *check and send*, so we'd get them back quicker. I couldn't wait to see all the places that Sergei had talked about and Matty's face when we were flying.

I'd have loved to go out shopping with Sergei and Matty today, but although Matty didn't have a high temperature anymore, he was still unwell. And thinking about it, I didn't feel so good either, although that was mostly because I was overtired.

Sergei had taken a phone call from Gregor earlier. In fact, all Sergei's friends had been calling to ask how Matty was since Sergei had let them know he was ill.

I wasn't used to so many people caring enough to enquire about Matty and me. We'd had no other relatives other than my gran, although we'd always called Gran's best friend Auntie Moira. But since being with Sergei, we'd developed a whole new family of sorts. And now I'd got used to them, I found I quite liked it.

Gregor had asked if Matty was feeling better and if he could speak to him.

Matty had spoken to Gregor like he was one of his friends at school, and I realised after a while they were discussing swapping stickers. But what I hadn't realised before today was that Matty was an extremely savvy negotiator. Gregor needed a sticker that Matty had so he could fill a page, but my brother wouldn't let him have it unless he could swap him for two powerful knights that Gregor said were hard to come by. When Gregor tried to renegotiate and swap for one sticker, Matty said, *"Gregor, the terms of my swap are non-negotiable. However, if you'd like to reconsider my offer or come up with terms I find more agreeable, I'll hold off from trading that sticker with Yuri."*

My jaw dropped, and I sat there wondering when my little brother had been replaced by a businessman.

Sergei was thrilled, although when Matty handed the phone over to him so he could sort out Gregor's sticker, I could hear the man himself proudly saying that his influence was why Matty had negotiated so well. He'd ended the call by saying, *"Sergei, when he is older, I will steal your boy away so he can come and work for me. If he's this good now, he'll be a winner in the boardroom."*

Sergei had laughed before telling him, *"No, my friend. When my boy becomes a man, he will take over Petrov Energy and do great things."*

Before Sergei left, Matty came running out of the bedroom with Gregor's sticker. He scratched his tummy and the back of his neck after handing it over.

"Holly, I've got some spots and they're itchy," Matty said as he lifted his pyjama top to show me. There were four randomly placed spots near his belly button, and two on the back of his neck.

"I think they're chickenpox," I declared. Sergei agreed.

"Daisy has them, too. She calls them chicken nugget spots. Keeley has been putting some white lotion on them. Can you remember what she said it was called? If you add it to the shopping list, I'll pick some up," Sergei said while putting on his coat. I added calamine lotion to the shopping list, along with several bars of chocolate and ice cream.

"I have a craving for something sweet," I told him, then added doughnuts to the list, too.

"So I see, my love." He bent to whisper in my ear. "I have a craving for you."

Sergei kissed me, then ruffled Matty's hair before he left, telling him not to scratch at the spots.

———

About an hour after Sergei had gone, the reason why I wasn't feeling so good and was craving chocolate became apparent.

I got my period.

I searched through my toiletry bag, holdall, and shoulder bag, but I couldn't find any tampons or pads. My periods weren't particularly heavy at first, but I needed something. I folded up a wad of toilet paper, which would have to do for now. Although I didn't want to take Matty out today, I contemplated a slow walk up to Mr Singh's shop.

When I got to Matty's bedroom, he was fast asleep on the bed, his stickers in his hands. I felt his forehead to check if his temperature had come back up, but he seemed okay.

While prising the stickers out of his hands, I noticed a few more spots had appeared on his arms and lower back. We wouldn't be able to go to the Christmas market at the garden centre tomorrow after all, not now that he had chickenpox. Matty would be so disappointed.

I covered him up with his duvet and gently kissed his cheek before heading to the kitchen. While waiting for the kettle to boil, I picked up my phone and debated whether to call Sergei to get him to add tampons and pads to the list, but I was too embarrassed.

After making a cuppa, I called Sergei anyway to find out how long he'd be. I could walk up to Mr Singh's when he got back.

Chapter Twenty-Eight

Sergei

Dropping the stickers off at Gregor's gave me a chance to have a bag of blood. I needed it after yesterday. The fear and stress I'd felt when I found out Matty was ill was almost unbearable. I'd been so angry with his teacher that I'd felt my fangs begin to emerge, and my eyes had flashed red. Luckily, it went unnoticed.

When Matty was well enough to go back to school, I'd have strong words with Miss Lynton about her duty of care to my boy and the rest of the children in his class. I also found it so wrong that I'd had to use mind control to get Matty an appointment to see a doctor. In my mind, if a child is ill, they should be seen immediately.

I considered hiring a doctor who could care for my human family if they became ill with something my blood couldn't cure. After discussing it with Gregor, he agreed it was for the best. He told me he worried constantly about

Chloe and the baby and said he'd ask Keeley to look into it for us.

The supermarket was enormous, and I had difficulty finding things that were on the list my Holly had prepared. I could not wait until we opened the supermarket in Rothley. The one I was at now was in Barnsley, and because it was a Saturday, the roads in town were extremely busy.

While looking for ice cream in the frozen food section, I took a call from Holly.

"Hello, my beautiful angel. Are you feeling any better? Is Matty okay?"

"Um, yeah, I'm okay, and Matty is sleeping. I just called because I wondered how long you'll be. I need to pop out for a while as soon as you get back."

"Where do you need to go, my love?" I asked, wondering about the nervousness I could hear in her voice.

"I need to call at Mr Singh's, that's all," she said. There was something she was hiding from me. Her voice gave it away.

"Holly, I'm at the biggest supermarket I have ever been to. If they don't carry whatever you need here, I doubt Mr Singh will. Now tell me, what is it you need?"

I heard her sigh before saying, "Sergei, I need… No, I'll wait until you get back."

"Holly," I almost growled down the phone. "Do not do this. You said you would not keep secrets from me."

"I'm sorry, but this is really awkward. I just got my period, and I don't have any tampons or pads. You probably think I'm being immature, but I feel so embarrassed about asking you to get them. As I said, I'll go to Mr Singh's shop when you get back."

"Nonsense, Holly," I chided, relieved that there was nothing to worry about. "I am your boyfriend; you should not be embarrassed about discussing anything with me. I know your body intimately, after all."

"Sergei!"

I chuckled when she said my name in that way. No doubt my words had made her blush. My angel is adorable. She has an innocence about her that is so appealing, but when we make love, she becomes a wanton, sensual woman. She is perfect.

"Now go and take a warm bath, my love, then put your feet up. Switch your phone on silent and catch up with your sleep. I will buy you what you need, and I'll make sure the ice cream is an extra-large tub."

"Sergei, let me tell you what I need. I prefer—"

"I know what to buy, my love. Now do not fret; I will finish my shopping and be home soon."

"But—"

"See you later, *angel moy*," I told her before hanging up.

She seemed to want to protest or something. Maybe she thought I'd be embarrassed to purchase such items? Well, she would be wrong. I am, as popular media puts it, *"a modern man."* I am not the type of person to shy away from things such as this. Women deal with it throughout their reproductive lives, so their men should also step up when needed and help with these matters. Even if it is buying the necessary products or supplying them with a hot water bottle for their pain, as my grandfather did for my grandmother when it was her *"time of the month."*

I made my way over to the aisle that said *feminine hygiene* and was immediately overwhelmed by the number of products and brands available. There was an entire aisle dedicated to the necessary items. Four long shelves containing hundreds of products to help deal with the monthly curse.

Shit! I hadn't expected so much choice. Holly had said tampons and pads… Well, that was a start, I suppose.

I looked at the shelf containing tampons and recognised a brand I'd seen advertised on TV. I immediately bypassed that brand. From what the adverts had depicted, that brand was for women who liked to skydive and go mountain biking, so I dismissed those. I would certainly not allow my angel to parachute out of a plane, and she'd mentioned in Halfords that she did not own a bike.

I carried on looking at the various boxes of tampons and was shocked to find they came in sizes. I hadn't realised that the size of a vagina would matter when it came to a woman's periods, but from what I could see, it did.

They came in four different vagina sizes, which were mini, regular, super, and super plus. I assumed that the mini ones were for young girls who'd just started their periods, and the super plus ones were for women who had a large vagina. Like I imagined women who had big babies whose birth weight topped the world records would have. I'd read the pregnancy book Julia brought to work; it said in there that the vagina shrank back to its normal size after giving birth. But Nik and I had Googled *"world's heaviest babies"* to tease Julia with, and I would imagine vaginas having a hard time shrinking back after parting with the babies in those photographs.

I decided my angel would be a regular. Holly's vagina was a tight fit, but then most were for me. Just as I was about to pick up a box, a petite woman came to a stop at the side of me and placed a box of super plus in her shopping trolley.

I could not believe it. She was even shorter than my Holly, who is around five foot five, and this woman was so thin. It seemed impossible that she would have one so big. She looked up and smiled at me. I smiled back. Bless her. It felt good to know she was happy, despite having a super plus-sized vagina.

I watched her walk to the end of the aisle where she met who I assumed was her husband. He, too, was short in stature and slightly built. I looked down at his crotch, hoping for the man's sake he had enough of a package to make it count with his woman. But from what I could see, it did not appear to be the case. I glanced up to find him watching me staring at his crotch. *Damn!* He must have realised I knew the couple's dilemma. I gave him the most sympathetic look I could manage, but he scowled at me before turning away.

Male pride! He did not like the fact that I knew he could not fill his wife.

I put the regular tampons in my shopping trolley and began my search for pads. Fuck! These were so confusing, but they seemed to go by weight. To my knowledge, many women were sensitive about their weight, so I'd imagine that most women would not admit to buying the ones that said heavy. Some pads also had what looked like teardrops on the front. They must be for when the pain was so bad it made them cry. This was even more confusing. I was unwilling to admit defeat, but I did not want to disappoint Holly and bring her the wrong ones. So, taking out my phone, I called her to ask which ones she wanted.

I waited for her to pick up, but it went straight to voice-mail. So I called again, but still, she did not answer. I'd told her to have a bath, then switch off her phone and rest, so she must have done just that. Shit! What was I going to do now?

I looked at the many packs of pads or *towels*, as they also seemed to be called, and the entire experience bewildered me. Row upon row of coloured packets stared back at me, taunting me with my lack of knowledge and the fact that whichever I chose was probably going to be wrong.

I began to sweat, and I realised I must have been down this aisle for at least ten minutes. If I didn't choose soon, the staff might get suspicious.

To be on the safe side, I contemplated buying one of each pack. But if I did that, I'd need another trolley. I could not do this on my own; I needed help, so I called Gina.

The phone rang for what seemed like ages, then suddenly Nik answered.

"What can I do for you, Sergei?"

"Nik, I need to speak with my Gina."

"She's in the shower."

"Nik, this is very important. I need you to take the phone to her now."

There was no disguising the stress in my voice, and the worry in Nik's tone was evident.

"Sergei, tell me what's wrong. Is it Matty? Has he got worse? Do you need me to come over? Hang on; I'm just getting my car keys."

"No, Nik, just get Gina. This is not something you can help with." I carried on scanning the shelves and discovered… "Fuck! These have wings. What the hell?"

"Sergei, are you at the airport?"

"No, Nik, please, just get Gina," I begged. This was too much. I needed to get out of this place.

"I'm not getting Gina until you tell me what's wrong," Nik yelled.

I did not want to discuss this with him, but I knew he'd not be moved. So I took a deep breath and said, "I'm in the supermarket. Holly has her period, and I have to buy her some tampons and pads, but I don't know which to choose."

There was such a long silence that I thought the line had gone dead, but then I heard Nik clear his throat and say, "I'll put Gina on."

After explaining to Gina what I knew about tampons and my reasons for choosing regular, I had to put up with her howling with laughter down the phone for nearly two minutes before she would help me.

"Sergei, tampons and pads have nothing at all to do with the size of a woman's vagina. It's about how heavy their period is. For instance, if blood flow is light, you'll choose between mini and regular. But if the flow is heavy, you choose super or super plus. The difference between each one is based on how much absorbency they're able to hold.

"Regular is a good choice for at the start or at the end, but if her middle days are heavier, then Holly might need a few super ones."

I added a pack of super to the trolley and felt like such an uneducated fool for my earlier miscomprehension.

"Now, on to pads. Should I just buy the ones that say normal and only have two teardrops? Or should I buy the ones with more teardrops in case Holly has a lot of pain?" I asked.

I picked up the ones that said they had wings and wondered from the picture on the back where they stuck the wing parts. Their legs, maybe?

"Sergei, those aren't teardrops; they're meant to represent drops of blood. Again, it all comes down to absorbency and flow. For those that cater to a heavier flow, the more drops you'll see. I'd get the ones that show two drops or say normal, then a pack of night-time ones and maybe some liners for use with the tampons, just in case."

"LINERS," I yelled. "Seeing the ones with wings was puzzling, but now you mention something that sails on the ocean. Gina, I wanted to show Holly I was a good boyfriend—one that she'd like to keep. But I didn't think it would be such a hard task."

I was thoroughly exhausted, and I realised I was not a *"modern man"* after all.

"Sergei, if you buy what I told you, you'll be fine, trust me," said Gina, and I could tell by the sound of her voice that she was trying not to laugh.

"Okay, but you have to tell me again what to buy. The moment you said liners, I forgot everything else. And, Gina?"

"Yes?"

"I'll be stopping by for blood on my way back. I am much too stressed to go straight home without it."

Chapter Twenty-Nine

Holly

I was surprised to see two policemen in the churchyard. They were taking a statement from the vicar regarding the vandalism and graffiti on some of the graves and headstones. I heard them mention Darren Crossley and his gang of thugs, and I hoped the police had enough evidence to arrest them. Luckily, my grandmother's grave hadn't been targeted, but I felt so sorry for the families of those that had.

After visiting Gran's graveside, my best friends Gemma and Marie came inside the church to light a candle with me. I knew if they hadn't been in the middle of exams, they would have been here for the funeral. Both had been back to offer their support when they found out she'd died, but I hadn't seen them since.

We kept in touch by calls or texts, but I hadn't felt comfortable talking to them about Sergei before yesterday. Mainly because I wasn't sure how they would react to me living with him so soon. And the fact he was so much older than me.

Sergei was at the supermarket when I spoke to them yesterday. I explained about the boiler being broken and how it made sense for me and Matty to stay with my new boyfriend until it was fixed. I didn't tell them I planned to stay with him permanently.

When Gemma and Marie saw Sergei for the first time, their jaws almost hit the floor. He was wearing a pale blue shirt and grey jeans and could have graced the cover of a magazine. His dark brown hair was still damp from the shower and looked almost black when under the light. Those deep brown eyes framed by the longest lashes were just so captivating, and when those full lips curved into a smile, I genuinely thought Gemma and Marie would start drooling.

He charmed them both with his friendly manner and sexy Russian accent, and it took forever to get them to the door so we could set off to the churchyard. But then Yuri walked in with more stickers and Lego for Matty and started the whole ogling and swooning process once again. I hadn't got them to stop talking about *"the sexiest men they had ever seen"* until we got to Gran's grave.

We all shed a few silent tears as we relived memories from our childhood—how Gran would take us out for the day or when she would put the paddling pool out in the summer. We always ended up at my house somehow. Gran never got fed up with having everyone over, even when we were being noisy and demanding picnics and parties.

Gemma and Marie said that Gran would have approved of my relationship with Sergei, and that pleased me. I just wish she was here for me to talk to about everything like I did when she was alive. She always gave the best advice, no matter what the subject was.

Marie asked if Sergei and I would join her and her boyfriend this evening. They were having a night out in Rothley with friends, but I declined. I knew Sergei wanted to take me out this weekend, but with Matty being ill, we'd had to put our plans on hold. I told Marie we'd join them another time, and Gemma said if I could get Yuri to tag along, she would go, too.

Another reason why I hadn't wanted to go was because of Paul. I didn't fancy bumping into him when I had Sergei with me—not after the last time they met.

After calling in to say hello to Gemma's mum, I made my way back to the flat.

On opening the door, it was the noise level that hit me first, and when I walked into the living room, I thought a tornado had ripped through it. There were cushions and bits of cardboard strewn about the floor, and it looked like two old wooden clothes airers were holding up a bedsheet— as if to make some sort of shelter.

"Aha, me hearties," Sergei yelled, then a little blonde-haired girl ran out from the kitchen, squealing with laughter.

"Take that, you nasty pirate," shouted Matty. He chased Sergei out of the kitchen with what looked like a cardboard sword.

"What in heaven's name is going on here?" I asked, trying not to smile.

"Argh, it's me angel! I will kidnap her and sail away to the island of the lost treasure," declared Sergei. He lifted me off my feet, kissed me, and then spun me around.

"Oh, no, you won't. I will fight you for her," yelled Matty. He thrust his cardboard sword at Sergei.

Making out that he'd been stabbed with the sword, Sergei dropped to his knees and said, "That's it, I'm done for. You got me, Captain Matty."

The little blonde girl ran up to Sergei and threw her arms around him. "Don't die, Uncle Sergei. I love you," she cried, hugging him tightly.

"Don't hug him, Daisy. He's a pirate, and he's kidnapping my sister."

Sergei stood up quickly with Daisy in his arms. He swung her up and over his shoulder, then ran back to the kitchen.

"I've got another captive now," he yelled, tickling her feet as he did so.

"Come on, Holly, grab a sword. We need to rescue Daisy," Matty bellowed.

I laughed as I watched my brother and Sergei duel with cardboard swords until Matty's bent, then broke.

I heard the door to the flat open and close and turned to find Yuri entering the room with three large pizza boxes.

"Hello, Holly. How did it go with your friends?" Yuri asked while setting the pizza boxes on the table.

"It's always good to see them; it doesn't feel the same when we're on the phone. And I'm so glad that Darren Crossley and his gang of idiots hadn't targeted Gran's grave."

"What do you mean?" he asked, pulling out a chair for me to sit.

I explained about seeing the police interviewing the vicar in the churchyard and about the vandalism on and around random graves. Yuri uttered something in Russian that I believed to be a swear word because it sounded like the word Sergei yelled when he'd stood barefoot on a tiny piece of Lego this morning.

I looked up and found Sergei gazing at me with such concern. It appeared as though he was about to say something when Daisy ran to the table yelling, "PIZZA!"

Matty had certainly got his appetite back. He ate three slices of pizza and two slices of garlic bread. Daisy sat rubbing her tummy, complaining that she was too full to eat anything else. But when Sergei asked, "Does that mean you don't want any chocolate-covered strawberries?" she soon changed her mind.

Sergei beckoned me to the kitchen and closed the door behind us.

"I hope you don't mind me inviting Daisy to sleep over. Matty was upset that we couldn't go to the Christmas market to see Santa, so I wanted to do something to take his mind off it."

"I don't mind at all. You looked like you were having fun when I got back. But where's Daisy going to sleep? Matty only has a single bed."

"I thought we could put our mattress and his on the floor in the living room, along with the cushions from the sofa. Then we can all settle down and watch Christmas movies until we fall asleep. What do you think?" he asked, smiling.

"That sounds perfect, Sergei. Thank you for doing all this. A lot of men wouldn't go to all these lengths to make a child happy. Though if I'm right, this night isn't all about Matty."

Sergei's smile got even bigger. "You know me so well, *angel moy.*"

A large bowl of melted chocolate sat in a saucepan of hot water. Sergei had brought two packs of strawberries from the supermarket yesterday, so I took them out of the fridge and washed them. Sergei picked one up, dipped it in the melted chocolate, and then brought it to my mouth. It was heavenly. I moaned appreciatively, licking the chocolate from my lips. He dipped a larger strawberry this time and held it just above my mouth. I tilted my head back slightly, licked all the chocolate from the bottom, and then held the rest between my lips. Sergei brought his mouth to mine, then he took the strawberry and ate it.

"One day, when we are on our own, I will paint your body with chocolate, then lick you clean. I think I will enjoy chocolate-coated nipples," he said.

Sergei cupped my breasts through my T-shirt, brushing his thumbs over my nipples. I reached down to his jean-clad erection and gave it a slight tug.

"Perhaps you could save some of that chocolate for later, then when the kids fall asleep, we can sneak off into the bedroom so I can paint your cock with it before licking it clean."

Sergei uttered something in Russian before pushing me up against the door and kissing me roughly.

As always, Sergei had me hot and bothered within seconds. But now was not the time for fooling around, and when we heard Yuri and the children laughing loudly from the other room, we reluctantly broke away from each other.

Matty and Daisy looked so comical with their dreamy expressions and their messy chocolate faces. They'd thoroughly enjoyed the chocolate-covered strawberries and the marshmallows Yuri had brought.

I'd watched Sergei and Yuri take part in a stare-off for the last marshmallow before I snatched it away and ate it. I was quickly tackled to the floor and tickled mercilessly by

Sergei, and Yuri said he and I were now at war, so I was to be prepared.

It didn't take long for both Matty and Daisy to start yawning, so I took them off to the bathroom to brush their teeth while Sergei and Yuri brought out the mattresses and bedding.

I left them to their teeth brushing and went to bring their nightwear and the calamine lotion. The conversation they were having when I came back made me stop and listen behind the half-open door.

"Matty, do you think Holly will marry my uncle Sergei?"

"Oh, yes. They love each other and kiss a lot, and he holds her hand when they go out. We live with Sergei too, so they'll definitely get married one day."

"I'll be their bridesmaid because I'm very good at being one. I was a bridesmaid for Uncle Alex and Auntie Julia, and I'm going to be a bridesmaid for my mummy and daddy AND Auntie Gina and Uncle Nik. Ooh, will Sergei be your daddy when they get married? When my daddy said he wanted to marry my mummy, he got to be my daddy, but before that, I called him Joshua Bubbles."

"That's a funny name. I want Sergei to be my dad. I pretend he is when he takes me to school and when we go out somewhere. But Sergei will be marrying my sister, not my mum, so I don't know if I'll be allowed to call him Dad."

"Well, I'm not sure if it's the same if they marry your sister and not your mum. We'll have to ask them. I'm still going to be their bridesmaid, though, so I suppose I'll have to have another pretty dress."

Daisy let out an exaggerated sigh, as though getting a pretty dress was such a hassle. I almost laughed at her theatrics, but I also felt a little sad. I knew where Matty was coming from with wanting a father.

As a child, I'd always wished that my grandparents were my mum and dad, so Matty imagining that Sergei was his dad was something I could understand. He's a positive male role model, and Matty and I are lucky to have him in our lives.

———

After making sure that Matty and Daisy's chickenpox were covered with the calamine lotion, I got them ready for bed. We all went into the room to say goodbye to Yuri, and then Sergei put on the first film—*The Muppet Christmas Carol.*

It was my and Matty's favourite Christmas film, closely followed by *Elf*, which was the next film we watched while lying on the mattresses on the living room floor. Daisy fell asleep first, and just before the film ended, so did Matty.

Sergei used the remote control to turn the TV on silent. He lay on his side watching me for a few minutes, not saying anything.

"What are you thinking?" I whispered.

He traced his fingertips over my cheeks and lips before kissing them almost reverently.

"I'm thinking how lucky I am to have you as mine. You are so pretty, so angelic. But when we come together as one, you become a vixen."

"Which side of me do you prefer?" I asked. "The angel or the vixen?"

"Both," he replied, before elaborating with, "I find the whole package that is Holly Fraser extremely appealing. If you come to the bedroom with me, I will prove to you just how appealing I find every inch of you."

"Sergei, we can't. What if Matty and Daisy wake up? And I'm…you know… It's out of bounds for a few more days."

Sergei placed his lips next to my ear and whispered,

"Let me worship every inch of you that is not '*out of bounds,*' my love. I need you."

He kissed me full on the lips. It was slow and gentle until I opened my mouth and let him inside. Then it became more urgent, and I felt my nipples harden and stand proud. Why did I have to be on my period? Once again, Sergei had kissed me into the kind of wanting that could only be eased by having him inside me. But that couldn't happen, not tonight. I felt his half-smile against my mouth. Oh, he knew what he was doing to me. Perhaps it was time for some payback?

"Sergei, it's such a shame all that melted chocolate has gone. I would have had so much fun giving Little Sergei a chocolate paint job," I told him while running my fingers along his hard length.

"Holly," he growled. His whole body seemed to stiffen while he awaited my next move.

"Although, I could be persuaded to go for the healthy option—you know, chocolate-free..."

Sergei let out another low, throaty growl before throwing the quilt back and lifting me up. He put me over his shoulder and hurried towards the bedroom.

Less than a second after he closed the door, he dropped me to my feet and tugged my T-shirt over my head. My bra was next to go, and I quickly unsnapped the buttons on his jeans while he kissed me into a hot, needy mess.

"Lean against the wall," I commanded as I spun us around to change positions. Then I dropped to my knees, taking his jeans and boxers down in one go.

His cock sprang out and almost hit me in the face. Now it was here in front of me, only inches away from my mouth, I felt slightly nervous. I'd done this many times with my ex, but Sergei probably had women with more talent and experience than me do this to him. Women that were used to dealing with someone as big as he was. I worried that I'd disappoint him. Sergei must have picked up on my anxiousness.

"You do not have to do this, my love. You have the right to change your mind. I would never pressure you to do something that you didn't want to do."

He looked at me with so much concern and adoration that I felt something grow within me. A confidence of sorts. Not the type of confidence that someone who is sure of their abilities has. No. It was just enough to know that whatever I did intimately with this man, I would never disappoint him.

I pursed my lips and kissed the head of his cock. Sergei sucked in a breath. He hadn't expected me to carry on, and it made me more determined to give him pleasure this way. I licked the underside of his length from root to tip, circling the head with the tip of my tongue. When I heard Sergei groan in that sexy way of his, it spurred me on. I closed my lips over him and took him as deep into my throat as I possibly could without gagging.

"Fuck, that feels so good," Sergei whispered breathlessly. I kept up the momentum, trying to take him deeper each time. A slight gag created more saliva, which I used as lubrication when I wrapped my hand around him and fisted from the base upwards. Sergei placed his hand on the back of my head, but he didn't force it forward. I was grateful for that. It made me want to do more to make this experience as pleasurable for him as I could.

I took my mouth away from his cock and angled my head to the side so I could lap at his balls. Sergei groaned loudly and rocked forward slightly. The position left little room for manoeuvre; his jeans were still wrapped around his calves, so he couldn't widen his stance. I turned my attention back to his erection, which was weeping pre-cum, so I licked it up before taking him back into my mouth. With my hand around the base once again, I ran my mouth up and down him, keeping the firmest grip possible with my lips. I cupped and fondled his balls with my free hand while I sucked and licked at his cock.

"Holly, you are making me come. If you do not want this in your mouth, you can use your hand only."

When I didn't stop, Sergei muttered some words in Russian before gripping my hair tightly in his fist and holding my head still. He wrapped a hand over mine, withdrew his cock until only the head was inside and grunted, "Open your mouth wider."

Within seconds of me doing so, he came in rapid spurts on my tongue while he looked down at me and watched.

I closed my mouth and swallowed down his release while staring up at him. Sergei unwrapped his fingers from my hair and kicked off his jeans and underwear before dropping to his knees and demanding I remove the rest of my clothes.

"I have to keep my knickers on," I reminded him. He nodded, then smirked.

"I seem to recall you wore them the first time I made you come, my love. Let me see if I can do that again."

For the next half hour, Sergei proved repeatedly that he could indeed make me orgasm with my clothes on. Then we lay in each other's arms, just holding one another and enjoying being together.

Chapter Thirty

Sergei

"Keeley, your daughter has strange nocturnal habits. Several times I had to reposition her during the night. She went from having her head on the pillows to having her feet in my face, then Matty's face. And then she did something that looked like the front crawl and almost sleep swam to the bottom of the mattress."

I'd been awoken on and off throughout the night due to Daisy's constant moving. I'm surprised she does not wake up exhausted every day.

"She's always been like that, but she's even worse if she sleeps anywhere new," Keeley replied while helping Daisy put on her coat. "I hope she behaved herself last night. We'll have to have Matty stay with us sometime. If you fancy a night out or if you need time alone, just let us know."

"Thank you, Keeley. I'm sure Matty would love that. Having Daisy here last night was a lot of fun—even if she did let herself get captured by the evil pirate," Holly joked, so I did my funny pirate voice before grabbing Daisy again.

"Well, at least she's not changed colour this time," Keeley said as she poked me in the chest.

My phone rang with a call from the orphanage, so I excused myself and went to the bedroom to answer it. Holly and Keeley were chatting, and I wanted them to become friends. I thought it was important for her to have more friends in the village near her own age. Keeley was twenty-five, so only six years older than Holly. I also thought that maybe Keeley would be someone that Holly could talk to and confide in when the time came for me to tell her I was a vampire.

I knew I had to tell her soon, but I couldn't seem to find the right words to use. I had to reassure her that I would never hurt her and Matty. No matter how badly popular media portrayed us, we always protected those we held dear.

I sighed heavily as I sat on the bed. I could hear Holly and Keeley laughing over something that Daisy had said. Perhaps the fact that Keeley was also a Born Immortal vampire and was a mother to a young child would help Holly see that we live our lives just like any human can.

I apologised to the caller who rang me. It was Mari, one of the residential staff who cared for the children. She was the one organising the gift giving in a couple of weeks and was keen to tell me about the gifts my latest donation had purchased. I could not wait to see the joy on each child's face when they knew that Santa had left them a present.

Chapter Thirty-One

Holly

After waving goodbye to Keeley and Daisy, I gathered up some dirty clothes to wash. Matty and Daisy had left his room in a bit of a mess when they were playing with the Lego, so I told him to tidy it.

"I don't want to tidy up. I want to go outside," he whined.

"Well, if you tidy up your Lego and stickers, we can go for a walk to the swings. There's an hour left until school finishes, so there shouldn't be any children around. As long as you get wrapped up warm, I think it will do you good. But if you don't tidy your room, we won't go."

Matty reluctantly got up and went to tidy his bedroom. I set the washing machine going and searched under the sink for a duster. Sergei didn't have any ornaments, just a couple of photos in frames. One was of Daisy dressed as a fairy, and the other was of a baby boy who belonged to one of my gran's old bosses at Night Movers, so dusting in the living room didn't take me long at all, not like at my gran's. She had so many photos and ornaments that the dusting seemed to take forever.

I wondered what Sergei's other homes were like and if he had any input on how they were decorated.

"The sight of you bent over doing housework is giving me ideas," Sergei said in a low voice.

"Oh yeah, what sort of ideas?" I asked.

"You wearing a French maid's outfit complete with stockings and suspenders," he answered while running his hand up the inside of my thigh.

"My thighs are too chunky, Sergei. Stockings and suspenders wouldn't suit me," I told him.

"*Angel moy*, every inch of you is perfect. Do not put yourself down. I have become intimately acquainted with your thighs, and my favourite place in the world is between them."

I flicked the duster at him and laughed when he grabbed me and pulled me close. "I have to work tonight, but I will think of you constantly, my love, and hope the hours pass quickly until I am home with you again."

"Do you have time for a walk with us before you go?" I asked hopefully.

"I have a few hours yet, so let us get our coats and go now. There's an ice-cold breeze outside, even though the day has been so bright. It's like Moscow, but with much less snow."

The swing seats had been freezing, but although Matty was complaining of a cold bottom, he had a healthy glow to his cheeks, and he was grinning from ear to ear.

We made our way back to the flat and met Old Joe on the village green across from the Red Lion. Matty asked if he could walk Meg around the green, so Joe handed him Meg's lead, telling him it would be a big help.

Sergei told Joe he was worried about him slipping on the ice, so he'd grit the pavements from Joe's bungalow to the Red Lion before he went to work. Joe thanked him and said he'd appreciate that.

The noise of an engine revving and brakes squealing loudly halted our conversation; a car was racing through our village at breakneck speed. I thought it would carry on up the road, but it hit a patch of ice, which sent it towards the other end of the green where Matty was walking Meg.

I screamed out for Matty to run as I dashed towards him, but I knew he wouldn't be fast enough to get away. Instead of running, Matty turned and faced the car, crying out something I couldn't hear. I screamed, thinking the car was about to hit him, but out of nowhere, Sergei zoomed towards Matty. He managed to push Matty and Meg out of the way, but the car hit one of Sergei's legs and spun him over.

I yelled for Matty to get up, and when he did, I almost collapsed with relief. But Sergei was hurt, so I carried on running on shaky legs until I was a few feet from the car.

To my horror, the driver, Darren Crossley, revved the engine and reversed the car—backing over Sergei's lower leg.

I was screaming and yelling Sergei's name, but if he answered, I couldn't hear him over the engine noise as the car sped away.

Sergei appeared to have passed out; his eyes were closed, and he wasn't moving.

I dropped to my knees by the side of him, taking in the

sight of his injured leg. His jeans were torn, revealing deep gashes on his calf that showed two different-sized broken bones. The amount of blood spilling out of the wounds was terrifying, and when I looked up at his face, I could see blood coming out of his ear.

"Sergei," I cried, willing him to wake up. I searched in my pocket for my phone to call an ambulance and realised I'd left it charging in the flat. Matty took my hand and sobbed, "Please don't let him die. Please, God, make him well again."

I heard whining from behind me, and when I looked, I could see one of Meg's legs was bent at a strange angle. The poor dog was in pain, but when I reached out to gently stroke her head, she whined even more.

"Go to Old Joe and let him cross you over the road to the Red Lion to call for an ambulance," I told Matty in the calmest voice I could muster. We needed to get help fast, but I couldn't leave Sergei. I was shaking so hard I doubt my legs would've held me up.

Only seconds after Matty had gone, Pamela came running over and dropped to her knees in front of Sergei, closely followed by Chloe, who was calling Gregor, not an ambulance.

"Have you already called for an ambulance?" I asked, but she ignored me as she spoke frantically to Gregor.

"He needs blood, Holly," Pam declared. "Are you going to give him yours, or should I give him mine?"

I heard Chloe gasp loudly as she stared at Pam.

"You know!" she stated accusingly.

Pam didn't answer. She took some sharp scissors out of her pocket and made a small cut on her wrist. My mouth gaped in utter shock when she pressed it to Sergei's lips and urged him to drink.

For a moment, nothing happened, and I was just about to wrestle the obviously barking mad woman away from my boyfriend when, to my horror, Sergei opened his mouth to reveal long, sharp fangs before biting into Pam's wrist.

Sergei made a growling sound while sucking greedily, causing Pam to wince. His eyes shot open, and once again, I could see red around the iris that was bleeding into the brown.

"What is he?" I asked in a whisper.

"He's a vampire, Holly. But don't be scared; he won't hurt you," Chloe replied in a voice that was meant to be calming.

It didn't work. How could it? My boyfriend, the man my brother and I had been living with for over a week, was currently sucking blood from the wrist of someone he'd just bitten.

I swayed to my left, black floaty spots appearing in front of my eyes before the world turned on its axis and the lights went out.

———

"Holly," Sergei growled in a voice that certainly wasn't human. "Holly, speak to me. Tell me you and Matty are okay."

I looked up to find Sergei staring at me; his eyes still ruby red and his fangs on display. He'd rolled onto his side and had his arms around me. I became aware of even more people surrounding us, but I couldn't take my eyes away from Sergei.

Dmitry was telling him to let me go and to lie straight so he could set the protruding bones before he took any more blood. I heard him say that if he was to take more blood before the bones were set, he risked them healing wrong.

"Lie back, Sergei, and let him help you," I commanded, and after a few more seconds of looking at me, Sergei complied.

I couldn't look at what Dmitry was doing to Sergei's leg, but the pain it brought about was obvious. Sergei screwed up his face. He yelled out various Russian words, and his fangs grew even longer.

As soon as Dmitry said he was done, Gregor appeared beside me and handed Sergei a bag of blood—the type you see in hospitals when someone has a transfusion. Sergei's fangs pierced the bag, which he drained in less than ten seconds. Gregor immediately handed him another, then another, until five empty bags lay at my side.

At some point during the last bag, Sergei's eyes had returned to their normal chocolate brown, and as soon as the bag was finished, his fangs retracted.

"We need to get you inside," a deep voice said from behind me. "You've attracted quite a crowd. Alex and Josh are having trouble using mind control on them all."

"Mind control?" I questioned, alarmed. I turned to find Nik looking at me, unsure of what to say.

"Let's just get Sergei back to the flat, and he can explain everything. I'm sorry you had to find out this way, but what's done is done. I hope you're able to see past all this to the man you said you were in love with because that's who he is, despite the need for blood."

I watched while Nik picked Sergei up and Gregor helped him stand.

"I would advise not to walk on it for at least an hour," Dmitry said.

Nodding at Dmitry, Nik told Sergei to get ready, and then he took him over his shoulder in a fireman's lift.

I stood up and swayed again, my heart pounding in my chest.

"I have you, Holly," Gregor said as he put his arm around me. "It is the shock that's making you weak. You'll feel better after a cup of tea and something sweet to eat."

"He's a vampire, Gregor," I stated, pointing out the obvious.

"I know, sweetheart, but we are not bad people, I assure you. Now come, let us follow Sergei up to the flat. Gina and Pam have Matty, so you need not worry about him. Chloe has put the kettle on, so let's not keep her waiting."

"What about Meg?" I asked, looking back to where she'd been lying.

"You mean the dog? Yuri took her and her owner to the vet. I fear her leg may be broken, but I am sure Yuri will let us know when he can."

When we arrived back at the flat, Sergei sat on the sofa drinking tea, his injured leg supported by a chair. He looked up at me and held out his hand, but I didn't go to him. He dropped it back down to his side and looked away.

"Holly, can you explain what happened exactly?" asked Nik. I nodded in response and then relayed what had happened on the green. Alex Staithes and Joshua York had joined us and were cursing the fact that Darren Crossley had run back over Sergei's leg to get away.

"He's caused enough trouble in this village. If it hadn't been for Sergei's increased speed, he would have probably killed Matty and the dog. He needs to be stopped," Nik declared angrily.

"He will be," Sergei replied calmly. "I will see to that."

While the men began talking between themselves in low voices, Chloe passed me a drink and sat beside me at the table.

"So, how are you processing all of this, Holly? I can imagine you feel really overwhelmed. I remember when I found out that Gregor was a vampire. I thought he was joking, but nope. Those fangs, eyes and claws were real."

"They have claws, too?" I asked.

She nodded.

"Sergei will never hurt you, Holly. Remember that. Both your life and Matty's are precious to him. The reason why he was so hurt was to protect Matty, and he'd do it all again without a second thought. All of them would." Chloe gestured around the room.

"They're all vampires?"

"All except Dmitry, but he's what's known as a Born Immortal—meaning his mother was human and his father was a vampire. If he drinks human blood, he'll become a vampire too. Sergei will explain the differences between Born Immortal vampires and Made ones."

"You mean there's more than one type? What else is out there? Zombies, werewolves?" I questioned with alarm.

"I know it's hard to take in. Especially after something so shocking as what just happened."

I heard the door to the flat open, and Matty ran inside, closely followed by Gina and Pam.

"Sergei," Matty cried, throwing his arms around his neck.

"Matty, are you all right? You didn't hurt yourself when

I pushed you away, did you?" Sergei asked while checking Matty over for injuries.

"No, but I think Meg has a broken leg because I fell on her. Yuri put her in his car, and he's taken her to the vet with Old Joe."

"Matty, come on, leave Sergei alone. You're going to hurt him if you climb all over him like that," I cautioned.

It was true that I didn't want Matty to hurt Sergei, but I also didn't want Matty to be so near to him less than twenty minutes after I'd seen him drinking blood. I know everyone said he wouldn't hurt us, but I couldn't shake the image of Sergei with those red eyes and fangs.

"I'm not leaving him, Holly. Not ever. I don't care if he drinks blood. It's what gives him his superpower. Like when The Knights of Dellot drink from the magic fountain, or when Popeye has his spinach."

"Matty, it's just not the same. I need you to go to your room and—"

"No," he cried. "I know what you're going to say. You want me to pack my things so you can take me back to Grandma's house. He's my dad, Holly, and he was hurt today, so I'm not leaving him."

"Matty, Sergei isn't your dad. He's—"

"He's my hero!" Matty stated.

Chapter Thirty-Two

Sergei

"Matty, look at me," I commanded while stroking his head as it rested on my shoulder. He had his arms wrapped tightly around my neck, and I could feel the wetness of his tears when they soaked through my T-shirt.

"Please don't make me leave, Sergei," he begged.

I turned him to look at me and held his teary gaze for a moment.

"Matty, I love you very much. You know that, don't you?"

"Yes, and I love you, so I want to stay with you."

"You can stay with me, but for tonight, I think it would be a good idea if you went to stay at Daisy's house."

"Why?"

I needed to talk to Holly without interruptions, and it would be better if we were on our own to do that. I made sure I held his gaze for a few more seconds, then began to speak.

"Matty, you cannot wait to stay at Daisy's house tonight because she has lots of games that you can play. You can see that I'm perfectly fine, so you're not worried about me anymore. You did not see me drinking blood; I drank raspberry juice. You are going to your room to get clean pyjamas while your sister fetches your toothbrush. Nod your head if you understand me."

He nodded and then ran to his bedroom, asking Holly if it was okay to take his Lego.

"What did you do to him?" asked Holly anxiously.

"It is called mind control. He's perfectly fine; it does not cause any harm. I didn't want him to be worried and upset about my health. It is also important that he cannot recall me taking blood. The knowledge that my kind exists can be way too exciting for children to keep to themselves."

Holly shook her head. It seemed like she was about to say something but decided against it. Instead, she went off in search of Matty—no doubt checking if he was all right after the mind control I'd used on him.

"Sergei, I think it's best that we all get going when Matty comes out. You and Holly need time to discuss everything because it can't have been easy for her to find out like this. I remember how her mother died. Holly watched that train hit the car, knowing she couldn't save her, and for a moment, she must have gone through something similar today. You need to give her time to come to terms with everything that's happened. *And* what you are," Gina said. She bent down to kiss my cheek before taking Nik's hand in hers.

"I should have told her about my immortality days ago. I hope it is not too late now."

I hoped she would listen to my reasons why I didn't

share the fact that I was immortal so soon in our relationship.

No one commented. They just looked at me with pity.

Holly came out of the bedroom with Matty. He was all packed up for the night, and I thanked Josh for taking him for us. I could sense that Holly didn't want him to go, but she relaxed a little when Josh started talking about him and Matty taking Keeley and Daisy on at Hungry Hippos.

Gregor visibly relaxed when Matty and Josh left. Because Chloe was pregnant, he hadn't wanted her to come into contact with Matty and his chickenpox.

After saying their goodbyes, Dmitry, Gregor and Chloe left, too, closely followed by Nik, Gina, and Alex.

My angel leant against the doorway, watching me. She was probably waiting for me to speak, to make excuses as to why I didn't tell her I was immortal. But I couldn't find the words to start that conversation. The conversation that could lead to the woman I love telling me she no longer wanted me.

"Why, Sergei? After demanding I tell you everything and not keep secrets, why would you hide something so important?"

"Because I wanted you to fall in love with *me*—Sergei the man—before you saw me as Sergei the vampire. I wanted you to know that you and Matty are completely safe with me and to trust that I'd love and care for you both for eternity."

"Trust is built on honesty, Sergei, but you weren't honest with me, were you?"

"I did not lie to you, Holly."

"That's just semantics. You lied by omission, Sergei."

"I'm sorry. I know I should have told you about my

immortality, but I didn't think you would understand. You are so young; it's a lot to take in at your age."

"So my age was a factor, huh? Didn't stop you fucking me, did it?"

"Holly, do not make what we have into something sordid. You are nineteen next month; old enough for a physical relationship."

"Exactly! I am old enough to live alone, to raise a child, get married, have sex. Yet, despite all that, I'm not old enough to deal with the fact that my boyfriend is a bloodsucker? Come on, Sergei. That's a poor excuse for hiding the truth from me, and you know it."

"I also wanted to make sure your love was true. It was pointed out to me that you might only love me because your emotions are all over the place due to you grieving over the loss of your grandmother."

"So other people, who had no right to question my feelings, thought they could pass judgement on them? And you must have believed them for you to say you had to know my love was true."

Holly shook her head and sank to the floor. I took my foot off the chair, ready to stand, but she held up her hand to stop me.

"Don't, Sergei. I don't want you near me right now. I need to think about all this—to make sense of everything I've learned today."

"Are you going to leave me?" I asked, dreading the answer.

"I should. Our relationship is based on lies, Sergei. That won't provide a solid foundation for our future. I need to know I can trust the man I choose to spend the rest of my life with, and from where I'm sitting, you certainly don't fit that criteria."

"Then let me get everything out in the open, so there are no more secrets. Let me share with you the story of my life. I will warn you, Holly, not all of it is pretty."

"And will you swear on the lives of all you hold dear that every sentence you utter is the truth?"

"I swear that from now on, I will hide nothing from you unless you request it, *angel moy*."

"Go ahead, then."

I sat back and looked at her for a moment before I spoke. I wanted to see the changes in her expression to judge how she felt about what I told her. I suspected the first sentence would cause her eyebrows to rise, and I was right.

"I was born two hundred and ninety-three years ago in a small, secluded village in Romania. My father was a Born Immortal vampire—which meant he could walk in the sun without harm. My mother belonged to a family of what we used to call enchanters. The enchanters were sought out by vampires for several reasons, but mainly for cloaking. The vampire hunters would use seers to find out the location of immortals, but with an enchanter's spell or potion, they could stop the seer from locating them.

"My father was part of an army of vampires who banded together to eliminate the hunters. Or *The Hand of God*, as they were known at the time. They've gone by different names throughout the centuries; all have religious connotations, despite them being nothing but killers. Anyway, my father and his comrades followed the hunters into Eastern Europe, and they were destroying most of their strongholds. I'm told that he met my mother and knew immediately that she was his. The one he was destined to Bond with."

"What does that mean? I heard Joshua York mention that he and Keeley would look after Matty when we Bond."

"When an immortal meets someone they're destined to Bond with, it triggers something inside. It's like they recognise them as theirs. Their scent is familiar and intoxicating. Their blood calls to them."

"Is that how it was for you when you met me?" she asked.

"It was so much more than that for me, Holly. I'd never experienced anything so powerful. When I took your hand in mine that first time, I felt the connection—like I was bound to you already. And I could tell that you felt something, too, but you were confused as to what that was. Sometimes, if the human is open to it, they, too, can feel the stirrings of a Bond."

"I did feel connected to you somehow. When things got so serious between us so quickly, I kept telling myself that it wasn't right, but something inside me made me ignore it."

I nodded, glad that she'd admitted it.

"Humans call it *love at first sight,* yet love between humans can die. But when an immortal forms a Bond, it cannot be broken. They will love their Bonded one forever."

"Until the human dies?" she questioned.

"When a vampire and human Bond, they do it with an exchange of blood. It's usually done during sex and will connect the couple telepathically as long as each of them is receptive. The couple will sense each other's feelings, both good and bad, and will know when they are unhappy, hurt, or in danger. As long as the human continues to take blood from the vampire, they will not age, get sick, or die. A vampire's blood can do this for any human, whether they are Bonded to them or not. They just need to take a few drops per week to enable that to happen. So when Matty becomes an adult, a small amount of my blood on a regular basis will keep him fit and well and on this earth for as long as he wants."

"So you wouldn't want to turn us into vampires?" she asked nervously.

"Never, my love. A vampire who is turned or Made—as we call it—cannot walk in the sun. I am a Born Immortal. Because I was born to a vampire father and human mother, I could decide if I wanted to stay human or become immortal. By ingesting human blood as an adult, I became a vampire. A Made vampire is someone who takes in enough vampire blood at the point of death to make them immortal —usually after they've been drained of their own.

"Joshua is a Made vampire. Alex found him beaten and dying and saved him by turning him. Because Joshua is over two centuries old, he can stay in the sun without harm for a short time. But if he were not to take shelter after that, he would burn from the inside out."

"Sergei, did you want to be a vampire? Didn't you like being human?" Holly asked.

"There were two reasons why I took the blood. One of them was because I enjoyed my life, and I didn't want it to end. The second was you."

"Me? But you didn't know me then."

"I knew I would find you one day. I saw how in love my grandparents were and how the Bond worked for them. I wanted a family of my own with as many children as my wife would allow."

"Can you father children?" she asked. "You told me you couldn't get me pregnant; I thought you meant you were sterile."

"I'll be able to get you pregnant when we Bond—if you would want a child with me."

She remained quiet. To reply would have meant she was

considering the Bond, and it seemed my angel did not want to commit to that.

"Would you like me to tell you about my childhood, Holly?"

"Yes, carry on with your story. I'll try not to interrupt again."

"Ask whatever questions you wish, my love. I want you to know all of me. If there is something that needs further explanation, then tell me so."

She nodded and made herself more comfortable. I did not ask her to join me on the sofa. She needed the distance, and I respected that.

"Just before I was eight months old, the hunters invaded the villages surrounding where my family was living. As well as my father, there were two other soldiers of the vampire army who were living with their Bonded humans and children in our village. They decided that the women and children should leave so that the vampires could fight without worry for their safety. They were told that the hunters' numbers were small after suffering defeat not a month before, so the vampires were confident they would end them quickly. But they'd been deliberately misinformed.

"A human mate of a female vampire had been fighting alongside my father for several years. When his vampire was killed in battle, he went to pieces, as all Bonded mates do. He wanted to die and said he would sacrifice himself in battle. But his end never came. He resented the vampires who had their Bonded mates when he no longer had his, so he deserted them and went to the hunters with all he knew.

"My father was killed when they invaded the village, and my mother would have felt this through their Bond. She also knew that the hunters took great joy in seeking out and killing the human families of immortals, so she and the other two mothers took us to where we would be safe. My mother's cousin was one of the other two women, although Petre insisted they were sisters. He said they had the same father. Anyway, they took us to the orphanage that Petre, who was a priest, ran. They knew the hunters would likely identify them, but not their babies, so they planned to leave us there until it was safe to come back and get us.

"Only one mother came back for their child. My and Nikolas' mothers were identified two months after leaving us and were tortured in an attempt to find our location. But they did not succumb and were eventually killed."

"I'm so sorry, Sergei."

"It hurts to know she suffered, but I don't remember anything about her. I was barely nine months old when she left me."

Holly moved a little, as if to come to me, then she hesitated and stopped where she was.

"Perhaps you would like to get more comfortable, my love. You could be sitting there for a while."

My angel got up and came towards the sofa. She left a cushion's width of space and was careful when she sat.

"I didn't want to knock you. You know, with your leg, I mean."

"My leg is fine. It will be tender and a little weak for a few hours, but the break has healed."

Holly nodded. Again, she looked as if she wanted to ask questions, but she remained silent.

"Petre was a relative of our mothers. Nik and I called him Uncle, even though he wasn't. We were brought up in the orphanage like the other children so as not to arouse suspicion regarding our identities. Our mothers knew that our fathers had sent word of our births to their families, so they'd been confident that when the hunters were defeated, our grandparents would find us. As the years went by, we lost hope that would happen.

"When we were seven years old, Borya—a soldier from the immortal army—came to the orphanage and told Petre that my grandfather was looking for me. We were confident he would arrive within a few months, but he couldn't. A new wave of hunters descended on the borders surrounding Romania; it would have been unsafe to retrieve us at that time. So, Borya stayed with us for a while and made sure we were safe. He taught me and Nikolas how to hunt rabbits and fish, as well as showing us how best to defend ourselves against the hunters. He gave me a knife that had belonged to my father and told me to keep it with me always. It was only three weeks after Borya left that I had need of it."

I closed my eyes and tilted my head back. The images that came to mind were picture-perfect, even after all these years.

"A group of men came to raid the orphanage. There was little to steal apart from the cross and chalice in the chapel. But they weren't after material goods. They were after children—boys in particular. Orphaned boys made good slaves. The bigger, stronger ones were sold as farm slaves, and the smaller ones were used in the home. Sexual abuse was something I'd encountered before when a rich benefactor, who used to support the orphanage, came to visit. He'd expressed an interest in me, and being only five years old, I didn't know that the amount of physical affection he gave me wasn't right. He'd tell me I was his favourite out of all the children and would hug me and run his hands over my body. The first time he tried to put his hands down my trousers, Petre caught him. Even though my uncle was a priest—a man of God who preached to turn the other cheek—he took hold of the man and beat him bloody. After that day, the man withdrew his monetary support, which had been used to pay for protection from any gangs that might descend."

"Sergei, I don't know what to say to that. It must have been awful for you." Holly placed her hand on my arm, offering me comfort.

"Holly, I was a young boy who did not know any different. Thankfully, he did not get the chance to touch me underneath my clothes. From what I know about some of the children who've ended up at the orphanages over the years, I think myself very lucky."

"It's good that they have you and your company looking out for them," she said.

"I try to do my best, but what they really need are families. It's much easier to place babies, but not everyone wants an older child."

"Sergei, what happened when the gang raided the orphanage?"

"They were targeting the older boys and those that didn't look so weak. Nik had always been much bigger than me in stature. Even now, he has a more muscular build than most. It's just the way he's made. Because of this—combined with his height—he looked much older as a child, and on that day, the gang had him and several others in their sights. My uncle had been knocked to the ground and was not in a position to stop the men. I believe there were four of them in total. Nikolas hid, but not before one of them had seen him. They pulled him out from hiding, and even though Nikolas was punching and kicking him, he was no match for a grown man. He hit out at Nikolas a few times and knocked him to the ground.

"When he knelt beside him to tie his hands behind his back, I took out my knife and ran to them. I stopped just behind the man, grabbed his hair to pull his head back as Borya had shown me, and then slit his throat. Nikolas was covered in the man's blood and kept slipping when he tried to stand. So I helped him up, cut the rope that bound his hands, and then went to help the others. After seeing what I had done, two men came charging towards me. Nikolas threw stones at the men, which slowed them down, but they still came for me. I remember Borya saying if you were going to die, you had to be sure to take one of the hunters with you. Well, on that day, those men were the hunters, so I shouted out as loud as I could, *'If I am to die, I will take one of you with me.'* Even though I was still but seven years old, it made the men stop and think twice. *'I have already taken your friend. Which one of you should I kill now?'* I added, showing them the bloodied knife.

"The men didn't move for a few moments, and I couldn't bear the wait that would decide my fate. So I did something that was very stupid but paid off anyway. I charged forward, screaming loudly. To my surprise, the men turned and ran, and the third man let go of Daniil—the boy he was trying to take."

I expected Holly to be repulsed by the fact that her boyfriend had killed for the first time as a child, but that was not the case.

"You must have been traumatised, Sergei. To have to do something like that when you were so young… I don't know how you coped."

I said I would not lie to her, but I did not want to correct her, either. Yes, I was traumatised. The incident caused nightmares, anxiety and bed wetting. But it wasn't the fact I had killed a man that caused all that to happen. No. It was the fear that I may have lost Nikolas, who was more like a brother than a cousin. And the fact that other children could have been taken that day.

I realised we were defenceless in the orphanage, and I knew I'd have to be watchful and ready to strike should others come.

"I prayed every day that God would send my grandfather to me, but it took nearly eight more years for that to happen. I thought God hadn't answered my prayers because he was angry that I'd killed a man. But my uncle said that God forgives all sins of those who repent."

That was probably why God made me wait so long. I did not repent. Just as I have never repented of the other lives I've taken. Vampire *or* human.

Tears welled in Holly's eyes. She took my hand in hers and held it tight.

"I can't imagine how you ever get over something like that, Sergei. It was bad enough losing my mother. I remember feeling heartbroken, angry, anxious, and then numb. My head was a mess with different thoughts, feelings, and questions. If it hadn't been for Gran and Matty, I don't think I would have coped so well. It was like I had to be strong for them. I kept thinking I could hear my grandad's voice, and he was telling me that everything would be okay—that I had to be there to help Gran take care of Matty. So that's what I did."

"Just as you did when your grandmother died. We are one and the same, you and I. We always put others before ourselves," I said.

"Sergei, are there people still hunting you? I mean, do people still hunt vampires?"

"Not for over a hundred years," I assured her.

"So Matty and I will be safe when we travel with you?"

A valid question, one that filled my heart with joy.

"Yes, my angel, you and Matty will be safe. I will protect you with my life; it is worth nothing without you in it."

I pulled her into my arms and kissed her with love and passion. Worshiping her mouth with my own. When she broke away from the kiss, I felt the wetness of tears on my face—her tears combined with my own. Tears of happiness and relief.

Chapter Thirty-Three

Sergei

The door to my flat opened, then closed. Yuri entered the room, his shoulders hunched and his face ashen. From the look of him, I already knew the answer, but I asked anyway.

"How did it go at the vet's?"

"Meg was old, and the vet thought her heart was too weak to undergo surgery to repair her broken leg, so he said it was kinder to put her to sleep. Joe agreed. He didn't want her to suffer any more pain than she had already. Joe told her he loved her, and then he held her head and stroked her as she passed away. It was quick and painless for her, but fuck! It felt like a knife through my gut. Joe is devastated. He was brave at the vet's, but he cried in the car coming home. I made sure he was settled in the bungalow with a cup of tea, and Ken Fearn stopped by before I left, so he isn't on his own."

Holly went over to Yuri and wrapped her arms around him; he hugged her back and I heard him sniffle. I said nothing, but then again, what could I have said to make this any better? An old man had lost a much-loved companion who'd shared his life for fifteen years. She was his reason to get up in the morning.

Holly kissed Yuri on the cheek, dried her eyes, and announced that we all needed tea. When she went to put the kettle on, I looked Yuri in the eye and asked, "Are you up for doing this tonight, or do you want to wait until tomorrow?"

"Tonight," he answered resolutely. "They are still breathing, Meg is not. If you hadn't been there, they would have hit Matty and Meg head-on. Neither would have survived that.

"They've been committing crimes in this village for years, and because the British justice system is so lenient, they've got away with most of what they have done. Even robbing old folk in their homes. Joe told me they ran over you again in their bid to get away, so it is clear to see they have no remorse. For obvious reasons, we have not involved the police," he said, pointing at my leg. "I say we find them as soon as possible and end their existence."

"How do you suggest we dispose of their bodies?" I asked. I wanted them dead, but he seemed to have thought this through.

"Mel keeps two cans of petrol for the mowers in the outbuildings of the Red Lion. We could kill them, put them in their car, douse the inside and outside of it with petrol, then set it alight. What do you think?"

I heard a gasp, followed by a loud, clattering smash from behind me as Holly dropped a tray of cups on the floor.

I leapt off the sofa and ran to her as quickly as I could, but because of my protesting leg, Yuri got there first. He picked her up, ran to the kitchen, and set her at the side of the sink.

"Holly, there is hot tea on your leggings. I will pour cold water on them, then you will have to remove them carefully." Holly nodded and was crying silently.

I went to put my arms around her, but she shrank away from me.

"I heard you," she retorted. "You were talking about killing someone and setting fire to them in their cars. When you told me you'd slit that man's throat as a child, I thought it was a one-off thing. Are you some sort of serial killer? Do you enjoy killing people?"

I watched Yuri pour cold water over the areas on Holly's legs where the hot tea had landed.

"Let me help you, Holly, then we will talk."

She shook her head and batted Yuri's hands away before pushing off the counter to a standing position.

Holly was wearing a long jumper that ended mid-thigh, so her modesty was more than covered when she carefully peeled off her leggings. There were angry red marks where the hot tea had hit her, and I needed to take her pain away and help her heal.

"Who are you planning on killing? Do I know them?" she yelled.

"The man who nearly took your brother's life. The one who ran over me without a care and is the reason that Meg is dead. That man and those who hang around with him will never stop until they kill someone. And even then, only if the police can gather enough evidence. What's to stop him from hitting you and Matty when you cross the road to take him to school? Can you honestly say you'll feel safe in this village with him speeding around like he's in a Formula

One race? I will not rest until I know he is dead," I declared.

I stepped directly in front of her and held her gaze. "Holly, I love you and Matty. You are my world. If there is a threat out there, something that could harm either of you, I will eliminate it. Not only right now, at this minute, but throughout your whole lives—whether you choose to spend them with me, or not."

"How am I supposed to condone you killing someone to keep us safe?" she cried.

"You don't have to. Just don't hate me for doing so."

"Holly, hot tea has burned your legs, so you need to take some of Sergei's blood to help you heal. You will blister if not." Yuri folded his arms in front of his chest and did his squinty stare that said, *you will do as I say or else.*

"Please, Holly, let me help you. If your legs blister, you'll be unable to wear anything on them until they go. You could also scar. It won't take very much to heal them. Six or seven drops at the most."

I could almost feel the heat from the burns from where I stood, and I knew they were causing her pain.

"Fine, I'll let you help me. But please reconsider your plans."

"I will think about it. Now, I am going to bite into my wrist and place it at your mouth. I want you to suck, then swallow until I take it away."

"I thought you said I'd only need six or seven drops?"

"This is just in case. The burn could have gone deeper than it looks."

Wasting no more time, I bit into my wrist and placed it at her mouth. She hesitated when she first tasted my blood, then she closed her eyes and sucked. I watched her throat swallow and was instantly hard.

Yuri left the kitchen and closed the door behind him, leaving us alone. On the third swallow, I had to fight the need to tear off her underwear, lift her rapidly healing legs and fuck her into oblivion. By suck five, the scent of her arousal was so strong I could bear it no longer.

I tore my wrist away and replaced it with my mouth, kissing her hard and relentlessly. Wrapping her beautiful blonde hair in my fist, I tilted her head to the side and ran my lips down her neck until they reached her rapidly beating pulse point. My fangs emerged, and I was just about to bite her when she yelled, "No!" before pushing me away.

"I'm sorry, I should have asked. I just... Please forgive me, my love," I begged.

"You're about to murder someone, yet you want me to forgive you for going to bite me without asking?" Holly shook her head. "I think you need to reassess your views of what's right and wrong, Sergei, because they're seriously fucked up to me."

I took a step back and considered not going through with my plans, then I recalled the sight of the car seconds away from hitting Matty and knew I had to act.

Taking a deep, calming breath, I said, "I have to go. Please be here when I return. I love you, my angel."

And with that, I left.

Chapter Thirty-Four

Sergei

We drove to the outbuildings at the back of the Red Lion to collect the petrol before driving around to find Darren Crossley and his partners in crime. Yuri told me their names, but they were of no interest to me. He'd known of these people for some time due to hearing about their acts of burglary and violence from patrons at the pub, so he knew some of the places they liked to hang around.

We discovered them at the football field on the outskirts of the village. Yuri parked us down a lane behind some bushes so that no one would see the vehicle, which we realised was a good thing when the bus stopped just a few metres away.

A woman got off the bus and set off walking towards some nearby houses. We lost sight of her while the bus was pulling away, but once she came back into view, we noticed that one of the gang was following her. As he drew near, he raised his hand before sprinting back to the field.

"Yuri, this cannot be good. You can move faster than me—go to her, quickly."

Yuri ran to her with vampire speed, arriving at her side within seconds. I followed, pleased to note that the pain in my leg had almost disappeared.

Yuri pulled a long, pointy object out of the woman's hood before throwing it into the field. There was a loud bang and huge yellow sparks shot out into the darkness.

A firework! I couldn't believe it. These people had no conscience. No good in them whatsoever. The woman was screaming, and Yuri had to hold her tightly for a moment to calm her down.

Yuri used mind control to erase the woman's memory of what had just happened, as well as our presence here, and with cold fury coursing through every inch of me, I made my way over to the three men. They were laughing while taking more fireworks out of a box, and I could see evidence of drug use in the shape of crack pipes and foil wraps. Fuck! They would be less susceptible to mind control if they were high.

I recognised the driver immediately.

"Darren Crossley!" I stated.

"And who the fuck are you?" he shouted.

"The man who is going to kill you," I said calmly before grabbing him and breaking his neck.

I dropped him on the hard, frosty ground before turning my attention to the other two men, who were quickly backing away. Yuri came up behind the man to the left of me, and before he knew what was happening, the man was dead, his neck also broken. I stepped towards the third man, who was crying and begging for his life.

"No, Sergei, this one is also mine. He's the one who put the firework in that poor woman's hood. He could have killed her if I hadn't got to her in time, so he deserves a similar fate. Do you agree?"

I nodded and watched as the man fell to the ground, trying desperately to get away. I picked up one of the fireworks and handed it to Yuri.

"We have a slight problem, Yuri. This man has no hood. Where do you propose we put it?"

"Here," said Yuri as he grabbed the man's hair and yanked his head back. When he cried out in pain, Yuri rammed the firework down his throat, then grabbed his hands to stop him from pulling it out.

After about twenty seconds of watching the man struggle, Yuri broke his neck.

"You do not have the stomach for torture, my friend," I remarked.

"I thought he would shit himself if I left him any longer, and I didn't want to carry him all the way to their car like that."

As it was, all three had pissed themselves when their necks were broken. So, to avoid the mess, we opened the gates and drove their car into the field before placing their bodies inside it as planned. After putting what was left of the fireworks in the car, we opened all the windows and poured the majority of the petrol inside, then tipped the rest over the outside and set it alight.

Yuri drove us back to the Red Lion at a normal speed, so as not to draw attention to ourselves. I took a shower and changed into some of his clothes before heading back to the flat, noting that the fire engines were responding to the blaze.

Chapter Thirty-Five

Holly

Sergei walked into the flat wearing different clothes. I'd heard the sound of sirens before he arrived, so I didn't need to ask if he and Yuri had carried out their plans. The evidence was right there in front of me.

"Do you do this a lot? Kill humans, I mean?" I stared him in the eyes when I asked this question; I wanted to see something there when he replied. Remorse, guilt, shame—something that led me to believe that deep down, he knew this was wrong.

"Only when necessary," he answered, with not a flicker of any.

"How many, Sergei? How many lives have you ended?"

"Do you mean me personally? Or should I also include the ones I have sanctioned?"

It's a good job I was sitting on the sofa because that reply would have floored me.

"The others… Why did you sanction them?"

"To keep the children safe, of course. If I do not do this, who will? With the law, often those that hurt them get away because the police lack the funds and resources to act quickly. My company has that. We've been able to wipe out gangs of child traffickers, paedophiles and other worthless scum that seek to harm the innocent. The stories that come to me from the staff at the orphanages… Let's just say they don't make for pleasant reading. I cannot let that rest."

I could understand his reasons. How often had I watched the news and wished that not only would these people die, but they'd suffer beforehand?

"Have you killed anyone for other reasons—apart from hurting children, I mean?"

"Yes. As you find in humans, immortals can be both good and bad. The difference is, immortals have superior speed and strength, making them ideal killing machines. Some countries have a council or hierarchy. The US has several that control various states. They manage the activities of vampires who reside there, and those who visit. It exists both to protect humans and to keep our secrets hidden.

"In Russia, there is no official council; it's more like a few words spoken to the right powerful vampire at the right time. It's the same in Britain. I have often been called upon to eliminate vampires for harming humans. Earlier this year, Yuri and I killed a vampire who'd hurt Keeley."

"So once again, it's Sergei to the rescue," I said with a sigh.

"Something like that," he conceded.

"I hope the people you protect appreciate the lengths you go to in order to keep them safe," I remarked.

"Holly, I do not want, nor need their appreciation. Just

knowing I have eliminated something or someone that could harm them gives me what I need."

"And what is that?"

"Peace. Enough that I can rest easy."

I suddenly thought of that little boy in the orphanage all those years ago, protecting his cousin and the others, taking it upon himself to keep everyone safe. If you looked close enough, that boy was still there, deeply rooted in Sergei the man.

The trauma he'd experienced as a child had shaped his very long life. Sergei wasn't bad. I'm not saying I believed that killing people was a good thing, but his reasons for doing so were for the good of many. Even though I knew this, I still needed time to come to terms with everything I'd learned today.

"I think I need some time alone, Sergei, so I'd like you to give me some space."

"What about us, Holly? What about our future?"

I didn't know what to say right then, so I didn't answer. Yes, I loved him, despite what I knew. But all this information about Bonding was something I needed to be sure about. I wanted to stay with him, but did I want to look like someone who was about to turn nineteen forever? What would happen when Matty was my age? Or when we had our own children?

I kept my head down as I passed him and made my way to the bathroom. I needed to get my thoughts together, but I couldn't do that in his presence.

Chapter Thirty-Six

Holly

After washing my hair and scrubbing every inch of my skin, I stayed under the spray of the shower for a while. My skin tingled from the severity of the scrubbing. It felt like I'd washed away the old me to reveal a new, more resilient me underneath. It's what I'd need to be if I chose to spend the rest of my life with Sergei. And I *had* made that choice.

Cool air hit my back and I turned to find Sergei stepping inside the shower. Watching the water rain down on his face and body, I imagined it was washing his sins away.

Drops of water clung to those long, dark lashes, and for a moment I was transfixed by those beautiful brown eyes. But the words he spoke brought me back to the here and now.

"I'll make sure you and Matty are financially secure for the rest of your lives. You can stay in the flat until my cottage is finished, then you can either live there or buy somewhere else. Nik, Yuri and Gregor will check in with you regularly, and if you ever need me, I will be with you as soon as I can. All I ask is that for our last night together, you allow me to make love to you and give me a happy memory to look back on."

"What? Are you leaving me? You said you'd never leave me, Sergei. You promised," I cried, my voice cracking along with my heart.

"I thought you did not want me anymore. I thought you could not accept the things I have done. I…I thought you wanted me to leave."

I shook my head, tears rolling down my face. Sergei took hold of me and held me tightly.

"Holly, I never want to be away from you, but if my presence were to make you unhappy, I would leave. Even though doing so would destroy me."

"I don't want you to leave, Sergei. I might not agree with everything you've done, but I love you all the same."

"God, Holly, you do not know how happy I am to hear you say that. To know that you want me—all of me—is something I have hoped for since the day we met."

His kiss was full of love, hope, and eventually lust. He touched me wherever he could, taking in every inch of me —as if he was learning the shape of my body all over again. When his hand wandered to the apex of my thighs, I caught it in mine and stopped him.

"Sergei, we can't. I'm still on my period."

"I don't care. I want you, Holly. Are you wearing a tampon?"

"No."

"Good."

His hand breached my folds, his fingers pressing against my clit, circling it continually. He kissed me forcefully, his other hand at the back of my head so I didn't bump it when he pressed me against the cool tiled wall.

I came in no time at all, clawing at his back as the ferocity of my release overtook my body. Needing to feel him inside me, I wrapped my arms around his neck and jumped up, hooking my legs around the top of his taut backside. I felt him positioning his cock at my entrance, and seconds later, he thrust inside me, his pace quick but measured, the length of him going deeper each time until I had taken all of him.

"I need to taste you, Holly. I need your blood running through my veins. But I have to warn you, your body's response will be sudden. It will send you into a powerful orgasm almost immediately."

How was I supposed to say no to that?

"Okay, go ahead," I told him.

He smiled that beautiful smile that seemed to liquefy my insides, then began kissing me again. He rocked into me in a steady rhythm, picking up speed every couple of thrusts until he was slamming his body against mine.

So many sensations hit me all at once—the lukewarm spray of the shower, my nipples being teased by his hard chest, the base of his cock against my throbbing clit, and the hot, hard length of him hitting that special place inside me with every thrust.

I screamed when the orgasm hit me, the most powerful one I'd experienced so far. Before I came down from the incredible high it left, Sergei's sharp fangs slid into my neck.

The pain was sharp but fleeting. He sucked my blood into his mouth, and I felt every nerve ending in my body tingle. Within seconds, the tingling had centred at my core, resulting in an orgasm that took over me completely—mind, body, and soul.

Epilogue

Holly

We'd been in the air for over an hour, and Matty was loving his first-ever flight. He wasn't the only one. I was loving it, too.

The plane was stunning. It had comfortable cream leather seats for take-off and landing, and beautiful pale oak furniture and panelling. Even the carpet felt thick and luxurious. At the back of the plane was a TV and sofa, where Matty sat with Sergei on one side and Nik on the other.

I couldn't believe there was only a week to go until Christmas Eve and my birthday. The last few weeks seemed to go so fast.

We were flying out to Romania to visit the orphanage where Sergei and Nik grew up, then we'd fly to St Petersburg to spend Christmas at Sergei's palace. I was looking forward to doing both—not for the holidays, but because I felt it would help me learn more about Sergei's life and how he became the man I love. The man I Blood Bonded with two weeks ago.

I was going to wait, take the well-thought-out sensible route and weigh up all the pros and cons. But in the end, I gave in to what my heart told me. Sergei was thrilled that I'd consented to be his forever. I told him I hadn't needed the Bond to make that vow—I was his long before that. From the first time I said I loved him, in fact.

I remember him showing me his cottage, telling me what would go where and about things we could get for the garden for Matty to play on. I knew then that a man with a heart as big as Sergei's was the type of man you fought to keep.

I looked up and found him watching me. He gave me that beautiful, sexy smile. The one he reserves only for me. I wanted to go over there and wrap myself around him, breathe him in and kiss him and…

"Is it the Bond?" asked Gina as she put down her magazine.

"It's not just the Bond, Gina. It's never been about the Bond for me. I've always felt like this when he gives me that smile."

"Yeah, I know what you mean. Nik does it for me with just a look."

"It must be a family thing," I said as I took them both in.

Physically, Nik was a little broader than Sergei, and maybe an inch taller, but you could see the resemblance in their facial features. In their eyes, especially.

"Has Sergei talked to you about their time at the orphanage? Nik says very little about it and doesn't visit as much as Sergei. I know he gives financially, but lately, he's avoided anything to do with the day-to-day running and care side of things."

"Sergei's talked a lot about his time there, and he likes to be involved in the running of it. Less so with the ones in Russia," I told her.

"I know Nik thought a lot about his uncle: the one who ran the orphanage."

"Petre," I confirmed with a nod. "Sergei only ever has good things to say about him. He said he missed being part of a proper family when they were growing up, but he also knows that the staff there did their best. I think that's why he wants to do so much for the children and staff now; he wants it to be as good as it can be for them without being part of a family. But it's a tremendous responsibility, Gina, and one I think takes its toll on him more than he cares to mention."

"I doubt you could get him to give it up, though, Holly."

"I wouldn't want to. It's a part of who he is. Sergei calls me his angel—he has from the very start. But to all those children who've passed through the orphanages over the years, Sergei is the angel."

He's my and Matty's angel, too. The angel I'll continue to love for the rest of my very long life.

The Runaway and the
Russian: Chapter One

TESS

Hungry. Scared. Alone. Same feelings, different day, but once again, I had very little choice.

This had been my life on repeat for many more years than I care to remember, though I knew I'd brought this particular situation on myself. After all, it was my idea to run away to London, yet it didn't feel like I had a safer option at the time.

I thought back to that last day at the children's home where I'd lived for eighteen months. Nearly a week had gone by since I made my escape from The Willows, right under the noses of three residential social workers and two police officers.

Digging deep in my pockets, I found the last few pounds I had left. Even the emergency stash in my backpack had been long since spent. The money I now held in my hand came from begging at the side of a homeless guy whom I befriended my first night of sleeping rough.

I'd sneaked onto the train at Doncaster, staying hidden from the conductor until we reached King's Cross. It was getting late by the time I walked into central London, and the chaos of rush hour was almost at an end. I looked around for a hostel to stay in but couldn't get a place that night, so I carried on walking, stopping at a McDonald's for a burger and a hot drink to keep warm.

There were so many homeless people sleeping rough. Most looked tired and dirty, maybe even high, and a few just downright scared me. You shouldn't judge a person when you don't know their circumstances—I know that more than most, but being homeless was new to me, even if being scared wasn't, so you can forgive me for being frightened, and a little judgemental.

By the time I came across Danny, I was mentally and physically exhausted, and I'd stumbled over his legs as he slid them into his sleeping bag. He'd immediately jumped up to help me, apologising profusely, and from out of nowhere, I felt a wet lick on my ear as his little dog, Bess, fussed over me.

Danny had been sleeping rough for over four weeks since being evicted from his flat. He was an ex-soldier who'd come back from Afghanistan with PTSD, along with injuries sustained from a roadside IED that left him with a permanent limp.

He told me how lucky he was to survive the blast because three of his colleagues hadn't. They'd given him a flat and financial help, along with counselling. But Danny failed to go to some of the sessions when anxiety got the better of him, so he lost his counselling and eventually the benefits he was claiming.

At that time, his PTSD had been more severe, and he'd not been well enough to hold down a job. Consequently, he couldn't pay his rent or claim any housing benefits, so he lost his home, too. There were places at a couple of hostels, but they wouldn't allow him to take Bess. That's why Danny, an ex-soldier, someone who'd served his country, was sleeping out on the streets.

Even though I was wearing a winter coat and knitted sweater, I'd been so cold that first night: a typically cool one for late April in the UK. Danny offered to share his sleeping bag with me, and even though I'd declined his offer at first, by the early hours of the following day, I was so bitterly cold I finally gave in and cuddled up next to him. And I'd done so every night since.

I spent my days trying to keep out of the rain, begging with Danny in the mornings and through the busy lunchtime hours, then settling down somewhere safe with him and Bess at night.

I told him about some of my past, and he could empathise with me a little. Danny's background hadn't been all that great either, and he had no family to speak of. That's why he'd joined the army. Something positive in his life. Somewhere he'd belong and where he'd make a difference. Pity it hadn't worked out for him. Danny's a good man and deserves so much better.

I also told him about Jean's heart attack and my arrival at the children's home—shuddering at the memories that day evoked. Even as I sipped the remnants of my last hot drink of the day, thinking about my time at The Willows, and the problems Sarah and I had during our stay, brought out the same reaction.

My mother had been a drug addict who used prostitution to fund her habit. She'd often brought the men she picked up to the two-up two-down council house we had in central Doncaster, and for more years than I remember, I'd stayed hidden while they were with her.

It had been my fourteenth birthday when I went into

her bedroom to stop a man from beating her. When she brought him home, I'd locked my bedroom door as usual, staying quiet in my room so that I didn't alert him to my presence. I'd heard them having sex, and I prayed he'd be one of those quick finishers who paid well, so I wouldn't have to listen to his grunting and groaning for too long. But then I'd heard a fist hitting flesh and my mother crying out in pain, followed by another blow and a scream.

I ran to my door and listened as more and more punches rained down on her, and I knew I had to stop him. So, after quietly unlocking the door, I took the cricket bat I kept by the side of it and made my way down to my mother's bedroom. I could hear the guy calling her a fucking bitch and a dirty whore while he hit her harder.

She was screaming for him to stop, and though she'd always told me I should never go to her room and interfere —no matter what I heard—when the guy said the world would be a better place if she were dead, I opened the bedroom door and ran towards him, swinging the cricket bat as hard as I could at his head.

Unfortunately for me, the man beating my mother had quick reflexes and ducked down before the bat made contact, which caused me to fall forward. That's when he turned his fists onto *my* face and body before picking up the cricket bat and using that. I tried to shield myself with my arms and hands, but I couldn't stop the bat from connecting with what felt like every inch of my body. It seemed to go on forever, but in reality, it was only seconds before I stopped feeling the pain and hearing the noises that accompanied the violence. And just before my world turned black, I saw my mother diving towards the man's bare back with a knife in her hands.

I woke up a week later in hospital after being put in a

medically induced coma. Once the swelling on my brain from the savage beating had reduced, they'd gradually brought me back to a conscious state, but they couldn't be sure if I'd have any long-term effects.

Thankfully, I hadn't suffered any brain damage, but I was still black and blue all over, with four broken ribs, a fractured cheekbone and collarbone, and three broken fingers. I had various cuts about my face that were already healing by the time they brought me out of the coma, yet they were still sore, and the cut above my eyebrow needed stitches.

The police tried to interview me, but they weren't allowed in until the social worker arrived. Her name was Andrea, and she explained what had happened after I became unconscious. My mother had stabbed the man, Philip Casey, several times, and he'd died twenty-four hours later. She'd used his phone to call the ambulance, then injected herself with a lethal dose of heroin. She died in the ambulance outside our home after several failed attempts at resuscitation.

When I heard my mother had killed herself, I felt my eyes tingle and thought I was going to cry, but due to the extreme swelling and bruising around them, no tears could form. The doctors explained the mechanics of that to me, but they couldn't explain why I didn't cry for her when I'd healed. Maybe it was because I'd expected it to happen one day anyway? She'd been a junkie for most of my life, and I'd found her near death a few times over the years. Still, you'd have thought I'd have cried for her, and the fact that I hadn't had the social workers wanting to send me to counselling. But I refused to go. I'd stopped trusting anyone in authority before the appointment came through.

I was placed in temporary foster care until they checked

to see if I had any family who might come forward and take me in. I told the social worker not to hold her breath on that ever happening. I didn't know who my father was, and the only one left on my mother's side was my grandmother, who was serving time in prison for dealing Class A drugs. The look the social worker gave me when I told her was one I'd been familiar with for years... *Poor Tess, bound to end up the same way as her mother or grandmother. There's no hope for this one.*

I'd seen that look so often from my teachers, Mum's last rehab counsellor, and even Mrs Henshall in the local shop. They all expected me to follow in my family's footsteps, but I was determined that wouldn't happen. I won't ever be like them. I'll never put myself in a position where my life choices are ruled by drugs or alcohol.

The police were more abrupt when speaking to me than I'd expected them to be. They had to be reminded by the social worker that they were speaking to a minor who'd gone through a traumatic experience and was still recovering. They'd even asked if I'd been selling my body alongside my mother.

I'd been examined while I was unconscious, so they knew I hadn't been raped and was still a virgin. I told them I'd never been involved in my mother's profession, but I could tell they didn't believe me. One of them even suggested I performed other services for men while my mother stole from them, and that's why Philip Casey had "*lashed out.*"

I became angry and upset, so they made the police leave, but I knew it wouldn't be the last time I'd be accused of doing something I hadn't done.

I found ways to turn my mind blank and my expression neutral when faced with those questions because I hated the satisfied smirk they wore when they knew they'd gotten a reaction from me.

It was reported in the newspapers that Mr Philip Casey had been a hard-working man who raised money for cancer charities in his spare time. He'd been a loyal husband and doting father before that fateful night he'd been *"lured"* back to our home by my mother.

Despite my telling the police what happened, the full events of that night weren't made public until nearly eleven months later, and by that time, I was staying with my foster mother, Jean Brent.

Jean was there with me throughout the inquest and helped shield me from the reporters outside the court, as well as Philip Casey's family. They'd spat at me a few times, calling me a murdering, junkie slut, even though I was a victim and had never even held the knife.

Jean had been my rock. She was the same with the other two girls who'd been in her care: Sarah and Christine. Sarah was two years younger than me but came from a similar background, and we became friends instantly. I wasn't as keen on Christine, the older girl. She was a bit stuck-up and believed herself better than us. She'd been in foster care because her mum had a nervous breakdown and was in the hospital. Christine had no other family who could take her in, only her grandparents. But they were elderly and in poor health, so she ended up in short-term foster care until her mum was better.

Even though Sarah and I were supposed to be staying with Jean short term, we were with her for over two years. Christine stayed less than eight weeks.

Apart from the police interviews and the inquest, the time I spent living at Jean's home was the happiest I've ever been in my life. I'd felt safe, well cared for, and loved. When

Jean had her heart attack and we were taken to the children's home, all that safety and love went out of the window, and the nightmare that was my life began all over again.

Sarah and I ended up at The Willows an hour or so after they'd taken Jean away in the ambulance. She had a triple heart bypass and wasn't allowed to foster us again after her surgery and subsequent recovery, but I know she tried. She even came to visit us at The Willows until Lisa—a bitchy residential social worker—decided to put a stop to it.

The Runaway and the
Russian: Chapter Two

TESS

Sarah had always been wild and reckless. Being older, I instinctively looked out for her, trying to keep her from getting into trouble. Never an easy task where Sarah was concerned.

Almost a year after we'd found ourselves at The Willows, Sarah and I began attending a youth centre about a mile away. We played basketball and other sports there after school, and on Thursdays, they had a disco.

The DJ was a tall, good-looking Asian guy of Pakistani origin called Tariq. He was fun to be around and always gave us his full attention when he spoke to us. He seemed particularly interested in Sarah and Beth, another teenage girl from The Willows.

At first, I thought he was looking out for Sarah and Beth; his influence seemed to be helping on the behavioural front. Sarah rarely got into any more fights at school and, as far as I was aware, her shoplifting habit had declined. Then one day, when we sat in the bedroom we shared, Sarah pulled an iPhone out of her pocket and began texting someone.

I asked her how she got it, knowing we would never usually get anything as good as that given through social services or The Willows, and my first thought was that she'd stolen it. Sarah laughed at my worried expression and told me it was a gift from Tariq's friend, Farid. She said he was in Tariq's car when he'd given her and Beth a lift back to The Willows. She told me he was really friendly and had asked for their mobile numbers so he could call them and take them to the travelling fair, which was coming to the next town.

When Sarah and Beth told him they didn't have mobile phones, he said he felt sorry for them, but because he liked them and wanted to be friends, he gave them both a phone from a bag he had in the boot of Tariq's car. He said he fixed and sold mobile phones, so he happened to have them going spare. Sarah and Beth were thrilled and listened eagerly while he explained how to use them.

Farid programmed a few numbers into the phones so they could contact him and Tariq, crediting each of them with ten pounds. I remember Sarah sighing and saying how sweet and kind he was, and while not as good-looking as Tariq, his kindness and generosity more than made up for it.

I'd exhausted myself telling Sarah it was a bad idea to meet up with this Farid guy, but both she and Beth were adamant they wanted to see him again, even if it was only to thank him for the phones.

As promised, he picked them up and took them to a travelling fair in Conisborough.

Sarah returned late that night, happier than I'd seen her since we lived at Jean's house. Farid and two of his friends treated her and Beth to a go on every ride at the fair, and each had an armful of soft toys the men had won for them.

Sarah told them how much she hated being at The Willows and how she'd loved living with Jean. She'd also mentioned I was worried about her meeting them. They'd told her to bring me with her next time, so I could see they were only trying to be friends. I declined that invitation and every other one they offered over the next few weeks.

Farid and another guy named Hassan spoiled Sarah and Beth with gifts of clothing and CDs. I watched helplessly while my only friend drifted away from me as she fell in love with both Farid and the new lifestyle she was living.

Nine weeks after she first met Farid, Sarah came to me, heartbroken. She'd cried for an hour before she told me what had happened. She'd been having sex with Farid at least twice a week for the last couple of weeks, but now he said that because he loved her—and was proud of how sexy she was—he wanted to show her off to his friends.

She went with him to a house about an hour's drive away in the Nottingham area—from what she could gather by the road signs. When they got inside, there were at least seven other men waiting for them. Beth and Hassan were already there, and Hassan asked if Beth would kiss some of the other men—which she did. But when Farid asked Sarah, she refused.

Farid hadn't expected her refusal. He told her if she loved him, she would do it.

Sarah refused again.

Farid became angry. He'd said if she wasn't willing to do it, it would mean she didn't love him, so he'd have to dump her. Sarah had cried and begged him not to, but he hadn't backed down. He told Sarah that if she didn't show him how much she wanted to be with him by kissing those men, then that would be the end, and he'd have to take back the phone and all the other things he'd bought her.

So, to make Farid happy, Sarah kissed all the other men in that room. They didn't only kiss her, though; they touched her while they masturbated over her too. When they were done, she told me Farid came to her and held her tightly, telling her how much he loved her and how thrilled he was that she was his girlfriend. He said it made him happy that his friends found her so sexy. But Sarah felt disgusted by what they'd done. She was upset and confused about Farid allowing his friends to *do that* to her.

We talked well into the night, and Sarah came to a decision: she was going to tell Farid it was over.

But Sarah didn't give Farid his marching orders, and she confided in me less and less as time went on. I also began noticing certain changes in her. Sarah's thick and glossy hair became lank and greasy, and her deep-blue eyes looked glazed and lifeless.

I suspected drugs. My mother had been an addict for most of my life, so I knew the signs. When I asked Sarah if she was using drugs, she started screaming at me, saying I knew nothing about her and should keep my nose out of her business. She said I was jealous because she had a boyfriend who loved her. I pointed out that boyfriends shouldn't want their girlfriends kissing other men.

Sarah began yelling all kinds of nonsense, which ended with—by having sex with her boyfriend's friends, she was showing him she loved him. Then she'd stormed off in a rage, but I knew if I didn't report the matter, Sarah could be in real danger.

I didn't trust any of the staff at The Willows; I hated nearly every one of them for their uncaring attitude and complete indifference to our welfare. So, without further delay, I told one of the teachers at school instead.

There'd already been concerns about Sarah's continuing truancy and lack of effort whilst in lessons, which I was aware of from overhearing a telephone conversation with a social worker. But as Sarah was younger than me, she wasn't in the same school year, so I wasn't aware of how bad it had become.

The female teacher I'd told of my concerns was Mrs Keating, who immediately rang the police and social services. They pulled Sarah out of her lessons and brought her to the head's office. That was the last I saw of her for a few days. She was taken away and temporarily placed elsewhere.

Five days later, Sarah was brought back to The Willows. She looked much cleaner and healthier, and I hoped the change would continue.

That night, when it was time for bed, I expected some soul searching or anger from her. What I heard instead was something far worse.

I entered our room and found an anxious-looking Sarah sitting on the end of my bed, wringing her hands together, so I instantly went to sit beside her. She took a deep, hesitant breath before saying, "I've told the police you were telling lies, Tess. I said you were jealous of me, and because I'm best friends with Beth, you hate it. I said you made up that stuff because you didn't want me to be friends with anyone but you."

I asked her why she'd lied, and what she told me made my blood run cold. Farid and Hassan had stated if she ever told the authorities what happened at the houses they took her to, they would hurt me and Jean.

From their phones, they'd shown her photos of Jean as

she got into the car outside her house, so they knew where she lived. They then showed her photographs of me waiting for the school bus and walking out of the library. Farid had remarked it'd be such a shame to see Jean's house burning down during the night while she slept, and he told her it would be easy to kidnap me and take me to one of their houses, strip me naked and tie me to a bed.

She insisted everything would work out okay, anyway, because, although the other men used condoms with her, Farid hadn't because she was on the pill. But Sarah hadn't been taking it. She'd been trying to get pregnant so that Farid wouldn't share her anymore.

I shook my head, knowing how wrong she was, but Sarah insisted she knew what she was doing. By getting pregnant, she said it would keep Jean and me safe, and Farid would probably want to marry her. I tried everything I could to reason with Sarah, but it came to nothing as usual. A determined Sarah could not be stopped, so I let it go, cuddled up close to her, and tried my best to sleep that night.

We caught the bus together in a rush the next morning after oversleeping, and the last I saw of her was when she went the opposite direction down the school corridor towards her classroom.

When Sarah didn't come home with me from school, I wasn't worried. Detention was a regular occurrence, and she often missed the bus. But when she didn't come home at all that night, I became concerned.

In the months since Sarah first met Farid, she'd regularly rolled in around 2 a.m. after sneaking out—although rarely unnoticed—down the fire escape. So, as per usual, I waited up for her. But Sarah didn't return. At 3 a.m., one of the social workers came into the room and asked if I knew where she was, but there was nothing I could tell them. I was as clueless as they were. At 4 a.m. I heard a warning beep alerting me that her iPhone battery was running low, so I got up and found the charger, plugging it in as quietly as possible. I thought it was odd that she'd gone without her phone; Sarah always carried it with her in case Farid got in touch. Then I remembered we'd overslept and had left in a hurry.

I scrolled through her messages, and the last one received was from Farid. It read, *"will pick u up @ 11 a.m. next 2 school bus stop and take u 2 McDs."*

There were other messages on there with various pickup places, and one that said, *"don't b sad, u no I luv u."*

I flicked through her photos and saw numerous pics of Farid and her together, of Beth and who I assumed to be Hassan, along with one or two of Tariq. If she didn't come home, I knew what I would do. I'd take the phone to Jean, and we'd go to the police together. I didn't want either of their threats against us to happen, but I wanted my foster sister safe and sound.

The next day, I took the phone and charger with me to school and kept it in the bottom of my blazer where the lining had ripped, and that's where it stayed all day.

Leaving school, I'd walked amongst a crowd of rowdy sixth-formers and noticed a silver car parked where the bus normally pulled in. Being seventeen, I only had a few months left to finish my A levels, and on that particular day, my schoolbag had been heavy with files and books. My slender five-foot-four frame had struggled with the weight of them as I sank further into the crowd.

Some of the lads in my sixth form class were almost six feet in height, and when they noticed the car, they began banging on the windows and roof. It wasn't until one of them shouted *"PAKIS,"* before banging even harder, that I glanced inside, wanting to apologise for their racist, ethnic slur.

But there, in the passenger seat, sat Hassan, and driving the car was Farid.

I froze, staring right at them until Hassan made his hand and fingers into a gun shape that he pointed straight at me. He made it as if he pulled an imaginary trigger, then laughed as Farid drove the car away.

My breath caught in my throat, and I felt the hairs bristle on the back of my neck as fear took over me. Luckily the bus came, so I got on it as quickly as I could. As it was a double-decker, I ran to the upstairs level. From there, I knew I'd have a better vantage point to see if the car was following the bus.

I didn't spot the car again, so I got off at the stop across from The Willows and ran as quickly as I could over the road, narrowly escaping being run over by a guy on a moped.

I made it inside without further incident, but before I could do or say anything, Beth grabbed my shoulder and pushed me against the door.

"Where's Sarah's phone?" she spat as she pulled my schoolbag from my shoulder, tipping the contents onto the floor in the hallway.

I told her I didn't have it, so she slapped my face, then thrust her hands inside my school blazer, searching the internal pockets for the phone. I grabbed her hair and pulled her to the floor before I punched her in the nose and screamed, "Where is she?"

I carried on punching her until I was pulled away by Lisa and Ben, two of the residential social workers. Beth leapt to her feet, but before she ran out of the door, she made a gun shape with her hand and said, "Hassan says he's coming for you."

Lisa and Ben tried questioning me about the fight, and about Sarah's whereabouts, but I screamed at them to let me go. They'd already been told about Sarah's problems before she went missing, and that had gone nowhere.

Lisa shouted up the stairs as I ran to my room, informing me that the police were coming to speak to me about Sarah, so I wasn't to go anywhere. I knew after Beth's threat that telling them anything would be a risk to Jean—if I couldn't get her to leave the area first—and I was torn about what I should do.

I changed out of my school uniform, dressing hurriedly in jeans and a long-sleeved top. Because I couldn't seem to get warm, I put on my thickest sweater—one that Jean had bought me when I lived with her. Then I ran to the window and looked outside, immediately spotting a silver car parked on the side street next to The Willows. I didn't need to see its occupants to know who they were.

I was hungry, but I didn't want to chance going downstairs in case Beth had come back. If she accused me of stealing Sarah's phone in front of anyone, I'd get into even more trouble.

Because the phone held photographs of Sarah and Farid together, if Sarah didn't return soon, I knew the police would need to see it. And I couldn't risk Beth getting her hands on it.

After about thirty minutes, the silver car drove away; when I saw the police car pull into the driveway, I knew why. But it was the vehicle following the police car that captured my attention. I watched as the occupants got out and looked up towards The Willows' front door. One of them was that bloody detective who'd accused me of being involved in my mother's profession and the death of Philip Casey.

I realised then I couldn't stay and speak to them. They wouldn't believe what I had to say, anyway. So I quickly threw some clothes and underwear into my backpack—along with the iPhone charger—then I lifted the carpet underneath my bedside drawers and took out the money I'd been saving. It was only sixty-five pounds, but it was better than nothing. I'd earned it by doing the odd bit of gardening and other errands for Jean's neighbours.

Stuffing the money in one pocket and the iPhone in the other, I took one more look out of the window.

The silver car hadn't come back.

There was a knock on the bedroom door, and Ben shouted, "Tess, the police are here!" I shouted back, telling him I needed a few minutes to get dressed as I'd just got out of the shower. Ben told me to come straight down to the office when I was done, so I said I would.

I waited until I heard his footsteps descending the stairs before glancing outside again. Other than an old man walking his dog, the street was empty.

The windows were alarmed but not locked because of fire regulations. Sarah had cut through the wires weeks ago so she could come up the fire escape and through the bedroom window when she'd been out late with Farid.

I gently opened the window and placed my backpack on the fire escape steps. Then I made my way out the window as quietly as possible—which was hard to do while wearing my heavy winter coat. Still trying to make as little noise as possible, I hurried down the metal fire escape.

Keeping the hood up on my padded green parka to disguise my distinctive copper-coloured curly hair, I ran swiftly across the garden, clambering over the boundary wall and onto the street.

As luck would have it, a bus was just pulling up to the stop, so I got on it, not even caring where it went. The bus took me all the way to Doncaster's bus and rail interchange, then I made my way from the bus station over to the train station.

I wasn't sure where I was headed, but I knew I had to get as far away as possible. There was a train due to leave the station for London's King's Cross, so I made a split-second decision that was where I should go.

I couldn't afford a ticket, but I jumped on the train anyway, managing to avoid the conductor by spending nearly all the journey in the surprisingly clean toilet cubicle, slipping out just moments after we entered King's Cross Station.

So that's how I found myself sleeping rough in London. Rather that than fall into the hands of Hassan and Farid.

Grab your copy…
vinci-books.com/therunaway

About the Author

Helen Bright was born and raised in Yorkshire, UK, and often bases her novels in and around the county.

Whether she's writing paranormal or contemporary romance, her novels often have darker elements hidden inside a deep and meaningful love story.

www.ingramcontent.com/pod-product-compliance
Ingram Content Group UK Ltd.
Pitfield, Milton Keynes, MK11 3LW, UK
UKHW041603100326
468839UK00005B/1295